ALSO BY SOPHIE LARK

Brutal Birthright

Brutal Prince

Stolen Heir

Savage Lover

Bloody Heart

Broken Vow

Heavy Crown

Sinners Duet

There Are No Saints

There Is No Devil

HEAVY CROWN

SOPHIE LARK

Bloom *books*

Published by Bloom Books, an imprint of Sourcebooks
P.O. Box 4410, Naperville, Illinois 60567-4410
(630) 961-3900
sourcebooks.com

Originally self-published in 2022 by Sophie Lark.

Cataloging-in-Publication data is on file with the Library of Congress.

Printed and bound in Canada.
MBP 10 9 8 7 6 5 4 3 2

For all my Love Larks who made Brutal Birthright such a smashing success! I hope this series brought you as much happiness as it did me; 2020 was a crazy year, but we made it through together. ♥

XOXO

Sophie Lark

SOUNDTRACK

1. "Blood // Water"—grandson
2. "Bubblegum Bitch"—MARINA
3. "Deep End"—Fousheé
4. "Naval"—Yann Tiersen
5. "Once Upon a December"—Emile Pandolfi
6. "City of Stars"—Gavin James
7. Hate the Way—G-Eazy, blackbear
8. "Where Is My Mind?"—Pixies
9. "Riptide"—Vance Joy
10. "Prisoner"—Miley Cyrus, Dua Lipa
11. "But I Like It"—Lauren Sanderson
12. "I See Red"—Everybody Loves an Outlaw
13. "Fetish"—Selena Gomez, Gucci Mane
14. "Sucker for Pain"—Lil Wayne, Wiz Khalifa, Imagine Dragons, Logic, Ty Dolla $ign, X Ambassadors
15. "Play with Fire"—Sam Tinnesz, Yacht Money
16. "River"—Bishop Briggs
17. "Saints"—Echos
18. "O Death"—Kate Mann
19. "Bulletproof"—La Roux
20. "willow"—Taylor Swift

Music is a big part of my writing process. If you start a song when you see a 🎵 while reading, the song matches the scene like a movie score.

Spotify   Apple Music

THE GALLOS

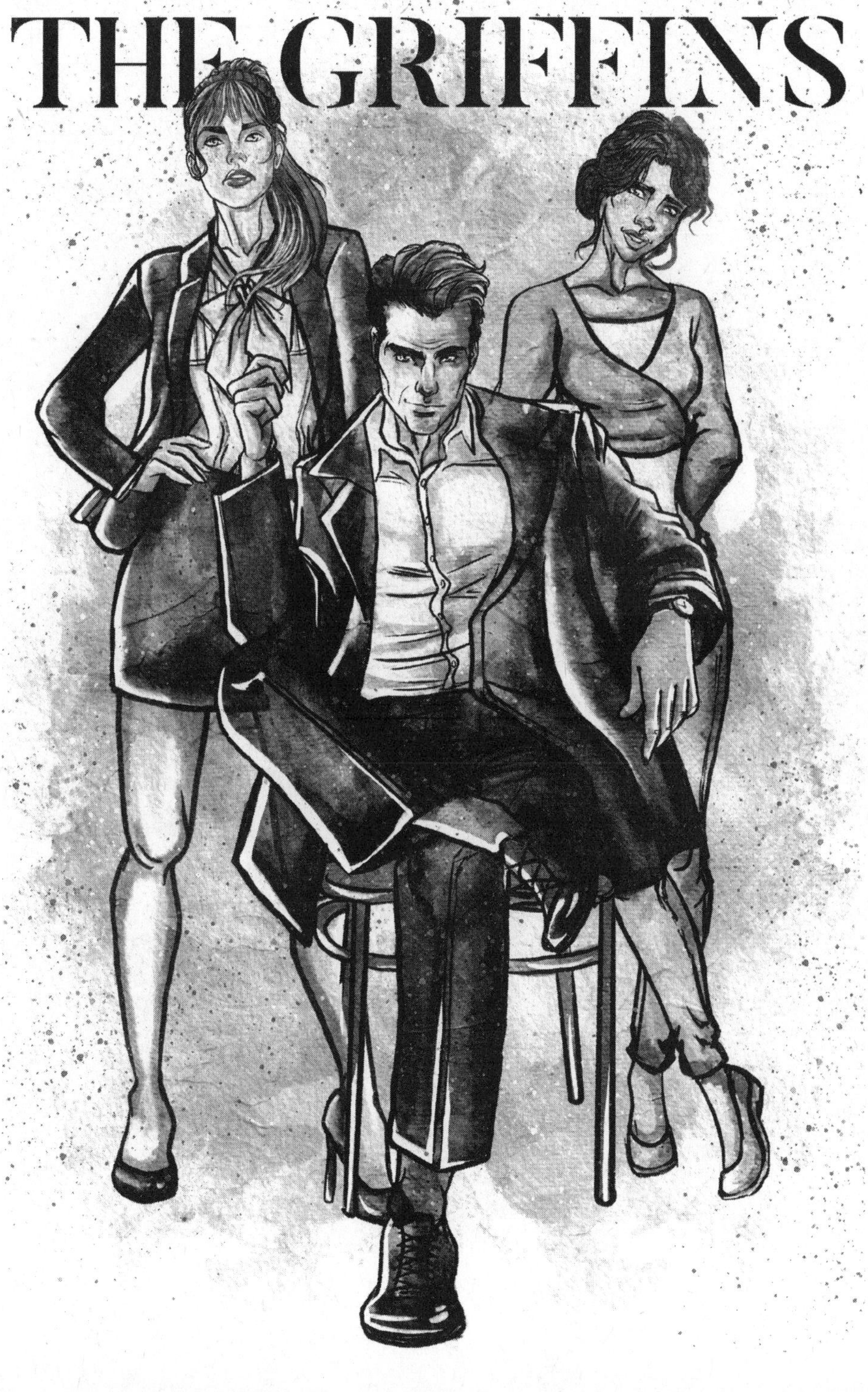
THE GRIFFINS

CHAPTER 1
SEBASTIAN

I'M SITTING IN THE CORNER BOOTH OF LA MER WITH MY TWO brothers and my little sister, Aida. It's an hour past closing time, so the servers have already taken the linen and glassware off the tables, and the cooks are just finishing their deep clean of the stove tops and fridges.

The bartender is still doing his nightly inventory check, probably lingering longer than usual in case any of us wants one last drink. That's the perk of owning the restaurant—nobody can kick you out.

La Mer is known for its high-end seafood—halibut and salmon flown in from the East Coast every morning and king crab legs longer than your arm. We all feasted on butter-drenched lobster earlier in the evening. For the past several hours, we've simply been sipping our drinks and talking. This might be our last night all together for a while.

Dante leaves for Paris tomorrow morning. He's taking his wife, his son, and his brand-new baby girl across the Atlantic for what he's calling an extended honeymoon. But I've got a feeling that he's not coming back.

Dante never wanted to become the *capocrimine*. He's been the de facto leader of our family for years only because he's the eldest—not because it was his ambition.

Of course, my father is still the real Don, but his health is getting worse every year. He's been delegating more and more of the running of our family business. It used to be that he personally handled every meeting with the other Mafia families, no matter how small the issue. Now he only puts on his suit and goes out for the direst of situations.

He's become a hermit in our old mansion on Meyer Avenue. If our housekeeper Greta didn't also live there full-time, eating lunch with him and listening to him complain about how Steinbeck should be ranked higher than Hemingway in the pantheon of authors, then I might be seriously worried about him.

I guess I feel guilty because I could be living there with him, too. All the rest of my siblings have moved out—Dante and Aida to get married, Nero to live with his girlfriend, Camille, in the apartment over her brand-new custom car mod shop. Once I finished school, I could have come back home. But I didn't. I've been living with my lieutenant Jace in Hyde Park.

I tell myself that I need a little more privacy for bringing girls home or staying out as late as I want. But the truth is I feel a strange kind of wedge between me and the rest of my family. I feel like I'm drifting—in sight of them, but not on the same boat.

They're all changing so rapidly, and I am, too. But I don't think we're changing in the same way.

It's been three years since we had our last run-in with the Griffin family.

That night changed my life.

It started with a dinner, very much like this one, except it was on the rooftop of our family home while we were all still living there. We saw fireworks breaking over the lake, and we knew the Griffins were holding a birthday party for their youngest daughter.

How different our lives would be if we hadn't seen those fireworks. If Aida hadn't perceived them as a sort of challenge or a call.

I remember the bursts of colored light reflecting in her eyes as she turned to me and whispered, "We should crash the party."

We snuck onto the Griffins' estate. Aida stole their great-grandfather's watch and accidentally lit a fire in their library. Which made Callum Griffin come hunting for us later that night. He trapped Aida and me on the pier. Then his bodyguard smashed my knee.

That was the fracture in time that sent my life shooting off in a completely different direction.

Before that moment, all I cared about was basketball. I played for hours and hours every day. It's hard to even remember how much it consumed me. Everywhere I went, I had a ball with me. I'd practice dribbling and crossovers in every spare moment. I'd watch old games every night before bed. I read that Kobe Bryant never stopped practicing until he'd made at least four hundred baskets a day. I decided I'd sink five hundred daily, and I stayed for hours after our regular practices, until the janitors turned off the lights in the gym.

The rhythm and feel of the ball in my hands was burned into my brain. Its pebbled texture was the most familiar thing in the world, and the most familiar sound was sneakers squeaking on hardwood.

It was the one true love of my life. The way I felt about that game was stronger than my interest in girls, or food, or entertainment, or anything else.

When the bodyguard's boot came down on my knee and I felt that blinding, sickening burst of pain, I knew my dream was over. Pros come back from injuries, but injured players don't make pro.

For over a year, I was in denial. I did rehab every single day. I endured surgery, heat packs, cold packs, ultrasound therapy on the scar tissue, electrostimulation of the surrounding muscles, and countless hours of tedious physiotherapy.

I went to the gym daily, making the rest of my body as strong as possible, packing thirty pounds of muscle onto a formerly lean frame.

But it was all for nothing. I got rid of the limp, but the speed never came back. During the time I should have been getting faster and more accurate, I couldn't even get back to where I used to be. I was swimming against the current while slowly drifting downstream.

And now I live in this strange alternate reality where the Griffins are our closest allies. My sister, Aida, is married to the man who ordered his bodyguard to smash my knee.

The funny thing is I don't hate Callum. He's been good to my sister. They're wildly in love, and they have a little boy together—the heir to both our families—Miles Griffin. The Griffins have upheld their end of the marriage pact. They've been loyal partners.

But I'm still so fucking angry.

It's this churning, boiling fury inside me, every single day.

I've always known what my family did for a living. It's as much a part of the Gallos as our blood and our bones. We're mafiosos.

I never questioned it.

But I thought I had a choice.

I thought I could skirt around the edges of the business while still unfettered, able to pursue anything else I wanted in life.

I didn't realize how much that life had already wrapped its chains around me. There was never any choice. I was bound to be pulled into it one way or another.

Sure enough, after my knee was fucked and I lost my place on the team, my brothers started calling me more and more often for jobs.

When Nessa Griffin was kidnapped, we joined the Griffins in their vendetta against the Polish Mafia. That night, I shot a man for the very first time.

I don't know how to describe that moment. I had a gun in my hand, but I didn't expect to actually use it. I thought I was there for backup. As a lookout at most. Then I saw one of the Polish soldiers pull his gun on my brother, and instinct took over. My hand floated up; the gun pointed right between the man's eyes. I pulled the trigger without a thought.

He went tumbling backward. I expected to feel something: shock, horror, guilt.

Instead I felt...absolutely nothing. It seemed inevitable. Like I'd always been destined to kill someone. Like it had always been in my nature.

That's when I realized that I'm not actually a good person.

I always assumed I was. I think everyone does.

I thought, *I'm warmer than my brother Dante. Less psychopathic than Nero. More responsible than Aida.* I considered myself kind, hardworking—a good man.

In that moment I realized I have violence inside me. And selfishness, too. I wasn't going to sacrifice my brother for somebody else. And I certainly wouldn't sacrifice myself. I was willing to hurt or to kill. Or a whole lot worse.

It's a strange thing to learn about yourself.

I look around the table at my siblings. They all have blood on their hands, one way or another. Looking at them, you'd never guess it. Well, maybe you'd guess it with Dante—his hands look like scarred baseball mitts. They were made for tearing people apart. If he were a gladiator, the Romans would have to pair him up against a lion to make it a fair fight.

But they all look happier than I've seen them in years.

Aida's eyes are bright and cheerful, and she's flushed from the wine. She wasn't able to drink the whole time she was nursing, so she's thrilled to be able to get just a little bit tipsy again.

Dante has this look of contentment like he's already sitting at some outdoor café in Paris. Like he's already starting the rest of his life.

Even Nero has changed. And he's the one I never thought would find happiness.

He's always been so vicious and full of rage. I honestly thought he was sociopathic when we were teenagers—he didn't seem to care about anyone, not even our family. Not really.

Then he met Camille, and all of a sudden, he's completely different. I wouldn't say he's a nice guy—he's still ruthless and rude as hell. But that sense of nihilism is gone. He's more focused than ever, more deliberate. He has something to lose now.

Aida says to Dante, "Are you gonna learn French?"

"Yes." He grunts.

"I can't picture that," Nero says.

"I can learn French," Dante says defensively. "I'm not an idiot."

"It's not your intelligence," Aida says. "It's your accent."

"What do you mean?"

She and Nero exchange an amused glance.

"Even your accent in Italian...isn't great," Aida says.

"What are you talking about?" Dante demands.

"Say something in Italian," Aida goads him.

"All right," Dante says stubbornly. "*Voi due siete degli stronzi.*" *You two are assholes.*

The sentence is accurate. The problem is that Dante keeps his same flat Chicago accent, so it sounds like, *Voy doo-way see-etay deg-lee strawn-zee.* He sounds like a Midwestern farmer trying to order off a menu in a fancy Italian restaurant.

Aida and Nero burst into laughter, and I can't help letting out a little snort myself. Dante scowls at us all, still not hearing it.

"What?" he demands. "What's so damn funny?"

"You better let Simone do the talking," Aida says between giggles.

"Well, it's not like I actually lived in Italy!" Dante growls. "You know, I speak some Arabic, too, which is more than you two chuckleheads." When they won't stop laughing, he adds, "Fuck you guys! I'm cultured."

"As cultured as yogurt," Nero says, which only makes them laugh harder.

I think Dante would have knocked their heads together in the old days, but he's above their nonsense now that he's a husband and father. He just shakes his head at them and signals the bartender for one more drink.

Becoming a mother hasn't made Aida above anything. Seeing that Dante isn't going to respond to her teasing anymore, she looks across the table and fixes her keen gray eyes on me.

"Seb has a gift for languages," she says. "Do you remember when we were coming back from Sardinia and you thought you were supposed to talk to the customs officers in Italian? And they kept asking you questions to make sure you were actually an American citizen, and you wouldn't say anything except '*il mio nome è Sebastian.*'"

That's true. I was seven years old, and I got flustered with all those adults staring at me, barking at me. I was so deeply tanned from my summer in Italy that I'm sure it looked like my father had snatched some little island boy out of Costa Rei and was trying to bring him back across the Atlantic.

The customs officers kept demanding, "Is this your family? Are you American?" And I, for some reason, had decided that I had to respond in their native language even though they were speaking English. In the moment, all I could think to say was "my name is Sebastian," over and over.

Damn Aida for even remembering that—she was only five herself. But she never forgets something embarrassing she can bring up later at the most inopportune time.

"I wanted to stay on vacation a little longer," I tell Aida coolly.

"Good strategy," she says. "You almost got to stay forever."

I am going to miss Dante. I miss all my siblings, the more they branch out into their own lives.

They can be infuriating and inconvenient, but they love me. They know all my faults and all my mistakes, and they accept me anyway. I know I can count on them if I really need them. And I would show up for them, anytime, anyplace. That's a powerful bond.

"We'll come visit you," I say to Dante.

He smiles just a little. "Not all at the same time, please. I don't want to scare Simone away right after we finally got married."

"Simone loves me," Aida says. "And I'm already bribing my way into your children's hearts. You know that's the path to becoming the favorite aunt—giving them loud and dangerous gifts that their parents wouldn't allow."

"That must be why you liked Uncle Francesco," I say. "He gave you a bow and arrows."

Aida smiles fondly. "And I always adored him."

So did I. But we lost Uncle Francesco two years after that particular gift. The *Bratva* cut his fingers off and set him on fire while he was still alive. That sparked a two-year bloodbath with the Russians. My father was in a rage like I've never seen before. He drove them out of their territory on the west side of the city, killing eight of their men in revenge. I don't know what he did to the *bratok* who threw the match on Uncle Francesco, but I remember him coming home that night with his dress shirt drenched in blood to the point where you couldn't see a single square inch of white cotton anymore.

I still have my favorite gift from my uncle: a small gold medallion of Saint Eustachius. I wear it every day.

Uncle Francesco was a good man: Funny and charming. Passionate about everything. He loved to cook and to play tennis. He'd take Nero and me to the courts and play two against one, smoking us every time. He wasn't tall, but he was compact and wiry, and he could fire a shot into the very back corner of the court so the ball touched the lines while still remaining inside. It was impossible to return. Nero and I would be sweating and panting, swearing this would be the time we finally beat him.

I sometimes wish we could have him back for a day so he could see what we all look like as adults. So we could talk to him as peers.

I wish the same thing about my mother.

She never saw who we turned out to be.

I wonder if she'd be happy.

She never liked the Mafia life. She ignored it, pretended to be ignorant of what her husband was doing. She was a concert pianist when my father first spotted her playing onstage. He pursued her relentlessly. He was much older than she was. I'm sure she was impressed that he spoke three languages, that he was well-read and well-spoken. And I'm sure his aura of authority was impressive to her. My father was already the head don of Chicago, one of the most powerful men in the city. She loved who he was but not what he did.

What would she think of us? Of what we've done?

We just completed a massive real estate development on the South Shore. Would she look at that in awe, or would she think that every one of those buildings was built with blood money? Would she marvel at the structures we brought into being or cringe at the skeletons buried in their foundations?

The bartender brings Dante's drink.

"Can I get another for anyone else?" he asks.

"Yes!" Aida says at once.

"Sure," Nero agrees.

"Not for me," I say. "I'm gonna head out."

"What's your rush?" Nero says.

"Nothing." I shrug.

I don't know how to express that I feel impatient and uneasy. Maybe I'm jealous of Dante leaving for Paris with his wife. Maybe I'm jealous of Aida and Nero, too. They seem sure of their paths, happy in their lives.

I'm not. I don't know what the fuck I'm doing.

Dante stands to let me out of the booth. Before I leave, he hugs me. His heavy arms almost crack my ribs.

"Thanks for coming out tonight," he says.

"Of course. Send us postcards."

"Fuck postcards. Send me chocolate!" Aida pipes up.

I give her a little wave, and Nero, too.

"She hasn't had wine in a while," I say to Nero. "You better drive her home."

"I will," Nero says, "but if you puke in my car, I will fucking cut you, Aida."

"I would never," Aida says.

"You have before," Nero snarls.

I leave them in the booth, heading out into the warm Chicago evening. It's summertime—even at ten o'clock at night, the heat is barely beginning to fade.

We're close to the river. I could walk home along Randolph Street, but I take the river walkway instead, passing all the restaurants with their strings of lights reflecting on the dark water. I cross over into River North, where the streets are quieter and less brightly lit. I stroll along with my hands in my pockets. It's a nice area, and I'm six-seven. I'm not worried about getting mugged.

Still, when I hear a shriek, I tense up and look around for the source of the noise.

About fifty yards down the sidewalk, I see a blond girl struggling with a man in dark clothing. He's burly, with a tattoo of an arrow on the side of his shaved head. He appears to be trying to shove her in the open trunk of his car.

The girl looks like she was headed out to a party—she's wearing a short dress and sky-high heels. The heels aren't helping her keep her balance while the man bodily lifts her off her feet and tries to throw her backward into the trunk. She gets a hand free and slaps him hard across the face—hard enough that I can hear the blow all the way down the street. He retaliates by slapping her back even harder.

That really pisses me off. Before I even think about what I'm doing, I'm sprinting down the sidewalk, charging right at him.

Just as he manages to shove her into the trunk but before he can close the lid, I barrel into him from the side. I hit him hard with my shoulder, sending him flying into a wrought iron fence.

He slams into it, but he's back up on his feet again a moment later, coming at me with both fists swinging.

I don't actually have all that much experience with fighting—I've only been in three or four fights, while Nero's probably been in a hundred. But I'm a big fucking dude with a long reach. And with two older brothers, you learn some things.

The guy comes at me in a blitzkrieg, both fists flying. I keep my own arms up, blocking most of his punches at my face. He hits me a couple of times in the body, which doesn't feel great. I watch for an opening. When he sends another wild right cross at my face, I step aside and hit him in the eye with a left. That rocks his head back. He's still coming at me but not quite as steadily.

He's got a broad, ugly face. Discolored teeth. His skin is the color of uncooked bread dough. He's in a rage, snarling at me, sweating and panting while he keeps throwing haymakers at me that can't quite reach my face.

I'm not raging. Actually, I feel colder and more calculated by the moment. I find myself analyzing him like a character in a video game. Looking for the quickest way to annihilate him.

I start hitting him again and again in the face and the gut. Each blow feels solid and satisfying, like punching a heavy bag. Every grunt of pain from this asshole gives me a glow of pleasure.

He gets me with a jab to the lip, and I taste blood in my mouth. That just pisses me off more. I grab him by the face like I'm palming a basketball, and I slam his head back into the fence. I do that three or four times, until the light goes out of his eyes and he slumps on the sidewalk. I don't even bother to break his fall.

The blond girl has pulled herself out of the trunk. Seeing her assailant out cold on the pavement, she runs up and kicks him in the gut.

"*Chtob u tebya hui vo lbu vyros!*" she shouts, pulling back her high-heeled foot and kicking him again.

To be honest, I kinda forgot about the girl for a minute while

I was beating the shit out of this guy. Now I turn around and really look at her for the first time.

She's tall, and that's saying something from my perspective. She's got to be over six feet in those heels. With her face aflame with fury, she looks like a vengeful Valkyrie. She's got white-blond hair pulled up in a high ponytail on her head. Her features are sharp and exotic—high cheekbones, almond-shaped eyes, full lips, fierce white teeth. And her body...

I feel bad thinking about that when some dude just tried to abduct her. But it's pretty impossible to miss the Amazonian figure stuffed into that skintight dress. Full breasts, tiny waist, mile-long legs... It's hard to snap my eyes back up to her face.

"Are you okay?" I ask her.

Her left cheek is red and swollen where the man slapped her. I can see his individual finger marks on the side of her face.

"I'm fine!" she says angrily. She has a hint of an accent. I'm pretty sure she was shouting in Russian a minute ago.

"What did you say to that guy?"

"What?"

"When you kicked him—what were you saying?"

"Oh." She shakes her head impatiently. "It means...something like, 'May a dick grow on your forehead.'"

I let out a snort. "Really?"

"Yes." She frowns at me. "This is a very common insult in Russia. Very rude, trust me. He would not like it if he could hear what I said."

"Well, he can't hear shit. But he deserved it anyway."

"He deserves to be castrated!" the girl says, spitting on the sidewalk next to her fallen assailant. It's funny—spitting is the furthest thing from ladylike, but I find it oddly attractive. It seems wild and foreign, like she's a warrior princess.

Speaking of which...

"Do you know him? Why was he grabbing you?"

The girl makes a sharp dismissive sound. "You wouldn't understand."

That just makes me curious. "Why don't you try me?"

She looks me up and down like she's trying to figure me out. At last, she shrugs, maybe thinking she owes me an explanation.

"My father is a powerful man. He has a lot of enemies. I suppose this one here thought it would be easier to attack me instead."

"Who's your father?"

"Alexei Yenin," she says, not expecting me to recognize the name.

I do, though. He's the head of the *Bratva* in Chicago. Or, I should say, he's the new boss—after the Griffins killed the old one.

"What's *your* name?" I ask her.

"Yelena Yenina," she says with a proud upward tilt of her chin.

"Sebastian Gallo," I tell her.

I don't see any flicker of recognition in her eyes. She doesn't seem familiar with my family.

Instead, she looks me up and down again with a mistrustful expression.

"Why are you so huge?" she demands, as if it's suspicious to be this tall.

"Genetics," I say blandly.

"No." She shakes her head. "You know how to fight. What do you do?"

"As a job?"

"Yes, of course as a job," she snaps.

It amuses me that this girl barely seems grateful that I helped save her. Instead she's haughty and imperious.

I don't know how to answer her question.

I've been doing a lot of jobs lately. All family business: Running our underground gambling ring. Handling the various issues that arise at our restaurants and clubs. Doing some work on the South Shore project, too, though Nero has mostly taken that over.

"My family owns a few businesses," I say vaguely. "Restaurants and whatnot."

"Hm," the girl says, still suspicious.

"Where are you going? You want me to walk with you?" I offer.

"Why not," she says, as if she's doing me a favor. "It isn't far."

"Just a second…" I grab her assailant by the front of his shirt and heave him up, his head flopping limply. I toss him in the trunk of his own car and slam the lid. "He can enjoy kicking his way out of there when he wakes up."

The girl gives a short laugh. "Well, well… Here I thought you were a good boy with that face."

"This face?" I grin.

"Yes. Smooth cheeks. Big eyes. Soft curls. Like a little baby."

I can tell she's trying to wind me up, but I don't give a fuck. "I think you look like a Viking," I tell her.

She doesn't want to smile, but I think she likes that.

Her eyes are an unusual color—more violet than blue, striking against her fair hair and pale skin. I've never met a woman like this. She's not like anybody I've seen around here.

"So where are we going?"

"What's this 'we'?" she says.

"Is it a party?" I persist. "I like parties."

"You weren't invited," she says, a hint of a smile playing on her full lips.

"I bet you could get me in."

"Maybe. If you were my date."

I look down at her, grinning all the way now. "What do I have to do to be your date?"

CHAPTER 2
YELENA

Sebastian walks me the three blocks to the party. He is very handsome, I'll admit, though I was never raised to have my head turned by a pretty boy. In Russia, beauty is for women. Power is for men.

What impresses me is his height. I've never seen a man who made me feel small. Even in my heels, Sebastian towers over me. I have to tilt up my chin to look in his face.

I've always loved and hated my own height. I like feeling strong. But I hate the way everyone wants to comment on it as if they're the first person to notice. Their jokes are unoriginal, and the way their eyes comb over me is even worse. They want to collect me like I'm a trading card that will complete their set.

But, of course, I'm not available for collection.

I'm the daughter of Alexei Yenin, *pakhan* of the Chicago *Bratva*. My father will find the appropriate match for me when the time is right.

I'm not excited for that. Marriage does not appear to be a happy institution from what I've seen. Too many men beating their wives, controlling every moment of their day, and taking mistresses whenever they please.

In Russia, it's not a crime to beat your wife. It's only a criminal offense if she requires hospitalization. You may have to pay a small fine—but that is paid to the government, not the woman.

I watched my own father hit my mother many times. And she was a good wife.

I don't think I'll be a very good wife.

I'm not a very good daughter. Or at least that's what my father tells me.

I think it's better to be smart than to be good.

We arrive at the house on Madison Street where Grisha is throwing his party. Grisha is my second cousin. He likes pretty girls, fast cars, and expensive drugs. I wouldn't say we're close friends, but I'm allowed to come to his house because he's family.

Tonight he's celebrating his twenty-sixth birthday. I turned twenty-five last week. There was no party—my father just looked at me coldly and told me I'm getting old. He used to say that to my mother: *Men age like wine; women age like milk.*

Well, she ages like ivory now because she's bones in a box.

Lucky you, Father. You won't have to be offended by the lines on her face.

That's what I'm thinking as I climb the steps to Grisha's house. It makes me scowl, so when his friend Andrei opens the door, he startles and says, "You look like you're about to murder someone, Yelena."

"I might," I say, pushing past him into the house.

Sebastian follows along after me. He doesn't seem uncomfortable coming into this house where he knows no one. I guess a man that big doesn't get intimidated easily.

It's dark in the house, the rooms lit only by blue track lights that give everyone an alien look. The music is throbbing. The air is humid with body heat.

♫ *"Deep End"—Fousheé*

I find Grisha. He's already half-drunk. His usually slicked-back hair is flopping over his eyes, and his shirt is half-unbuttoned to show his bare chest and his collection of gold chains.

He throws an arm around my shoulder and kisses me hard on the cheek.

"There she is," he says in Russian. "My little Elsa."

"Don't call me that," I snap in English.

"I thought you said your name was Yelena?" Sebastian asks.

"He means Elsa from *Frozen*," I say, rolling my eyes.

"You gonna turn me to ice?" Sebastian says lightly.

"She might." Grisha laughs. "She doesn't like men. Just like Elsa."

"I like you," I say sweetly to Grisha. "But then, you're not much of a man."

Grisha snorts, taking another swig of his drink. He's drinking directly out of a bottle of Stolichnaya Elit.

"Want some?" he says to me.

"Sure."

There are plenty of people here who will rat me out for drinking, but at this moment, I really don't give a fuck. I take a long pull, enjoying the bright citrus flavor of Grisha's expensive vodka. I could take a bath in that.

Grisha squints at Sebastian. "You look familiar."

Sebastian nods like he gets that a lot. "I played point guard for Chicago State."

Grisha shakes his head. "No, no." He snaps his fingers. "Ah! I know your brother Nero. We raced each other once."

Sebastian grins. "Did you win?"

Grisha scowls. "No! He's a tricky fucker. Took twenty K from me."

"That sounds like Nero," Sebastian agrees.

Bored of my cousin, I pull Sebastian away from Grisha. If I let him, Grisha will go on about drag racing all night long. And I've heard more than enough on that particular topic.

I'd rather hear more about the other thing Sebastian mentioned.

"You're an athlete?" I ask.

He shakes his head. "Not anymore." This is the first time I've seen the smile fall off his face.

"You played basketball?"

"Yeah."

"Were you any good?"

"Yes," he says without arrogance. "Pretty good."

"Why did you quit?"

He hesitates a fraction of a second. "I got bored of it."

Hmm. I think this good boy Sebastian just lied to me.

That heavy pull of vodka is starting to take effect on me. I can feel pleasant warmth spreading through my chest. My mood lightens ever so slightly.

"You want a drink, too?" I ask Sebastian in an almost-friendly tone.

We head into the kitchen, where Grisha has a veritable cornucopia of alcohol laid out: liquor, mixers, beer of all types, and a horrific-looking punch that I wouldn't drink to save my life.

"What do you like?"

"You ever drink tequila?" Sebastian asks me.

I wrinkle my nose. "Does this look like Tijuana?"

Sebastian just chuckles. "It's not so bad. You just have to take it right."

He grabs my hand, his large warm fingers closing around mine. This is presumptuous, but I allow it out of curiosity. He pulls me over to the countertop, where I see several bottles of Patrón.

Sebastian pours us each a shot. I go to pick it up, and he says, "Hold on."

He takes my hand and turns it over, exposing my wrist. Then he brings his lips to the delicate flesh where my veins show blue beneath the skin. He kisses me there. It's only a brief kiss, but I feel the fullness of his lips and the surprising heat of his mouth. It sends a shiver all the way up my arm. He looks at me with eyes that are dark and deep beneath heavy brows.

"Now the salt," he says.

He picks up a shaker and sprinkles my wrist with salt. It clings to the spot where his lips touched.

"Like this," Sebastian says.

He licks the salt off my wrist. His tongue is rough and hot. He takes the shot in one gulp, then bites a wedge of lime. Then he sets down his shot glass with a flourish. "Try that."

We're standing very close to each other in the hot kitchen. His method of taking a shot is ridiculous. But I can't deny that my heart is thumping, and I feel a strange compulsion to do exactly as he said. There's a kind of elegance to his movements—I want to see if I can imitate it.

I take his hand, which is almost twice the size of mine. His fingers are outrageously long. I bet he could span two octaves on a piano.

I turn his hand over and see a smooth wrist, lean and brown, with tendons running up the forearm. I raise his wrist to my mouth and press my lips against his skin. I sprinkle salt on the damp patch. Then, looking Sebastian dead in the eyes, I run my tongue up his arm. I feel his shiver, and I see the twitch of his jaw. I taste the burst of salt.

I take the shot, chasing it with lime. It still tastes awful, though admittedly not as bad as usual.

I wonder if I'd taste tequila on his mouth if I kissed Sebastian.

Of course, I'm not going to kiss him.

But I find my eyes lingering on his lips, which are full and finely shaped. I've never seen a man with a face like this. With his thick dark curls all around his face, he reminds me of a saint in an oil painting.

He's so unlike the *boyeviks* I usually see. At first that made me disdainful. But now I find myself…intrigued.

"Do you want to dance?" Sebastian asks.

There are plenty of people grinding against each other in the

living room. Grisha's house is five stories stacked on top of each other. It's in awful condition because he's always throwing parties and always pissing off his housekeepers, so they quit and he has to hire another.

I know all Grisha's friends. I don't want to dance with Sebastian under their watchful eyes.

If we went upstairs, we'd find people fucking in every available room or playing blackjack on the level above. On the rooftop Grisha installed a cedar barrel sauna, big enough to fit eight, and a large hot tub next to it. He won't let any girls in the hot tub unless they're topless.

None of that sounds appealing to me. Instead, I say, "Come on," and I pull Sebastian in the direction of the basement.

The basement is unfinished, so not many people want to come down here. Bare light bulbs dangle from the ceiling. The floor is cement. It's much cooler than upstairs. It smells damp, and the ceiling thuds alarmingly overhead as if it might collapse from the weight of everything above.

Sebastian has to duck his head to go down the stairs.

I find the light switch, surrounded by bare metal without any proper cover, and I flip it up. The bulbs crackle on, casting light in swinging circles.

"You play pool?" I ask Sebastian casually.

"Sometimes."

I take two cues down off the wall, handing the longer one to Sebastian. I take my favorite.

"What about a friendly wager?"

"Sure," Sebastian says. "How much is friendly?"

"How about a hundred to start?"

He lets out a low whistle. "Let me see what I've got."

He takes out a billfold that looks plenty thick. He slips out a hundred-dollar bill without flashing the rest of the cash. If Grisha were doing that, he'd be sure to let me see exactly how much he was carrying.

Sebastian lays the bill on the polished wooden rail of the pool table.

"What about you?" he says teasingly. "How do I know you're good for it?"

"You won't be seeing my money," I inform him. "Not now or after."

Sebastian laughs. "I like the confidence."

He racks the balls, and I take position to break. I split the stack cleanly, sending balls ricocheting in every direction across the smooth green felt. I already sank the nine, so I take stripes. I line up my cue behind the eleven ball. I can feel Sebastian's eyes on my body as I bend over the table. I've got to bend over a long way because of my heels. I feel my skirt pulling up.

I give the cue ball a smart tap, sending it hard into the eleven, just left of center. The eleven cuts to the right, spinning directly into the side pocket, landing with a satisfying thump. Without pausing, I sink the thirteen and fourteen as well.

"Uh-oh," Sebastian says softly. "I think I'm in trouble."

I miss my next shot by an inch. Sebastian takes his cue and surveys the table. Quickly and smoothly, he sinks the two and the four. His large hands are steady as he spreads his fingers across the felt, stabilizing his cue. He only has to give the ball a glance to calculate his angle.

He's incredibly precise and incredibly sure of himself. He sinks the one and the five as well, before missing the three.

I hadn't realized I was holding my breath. I know that if I miss any more shots, I probably won't get another chance.

Scowling, I approach the table like it's a battleground. I picture where the cue ball will land after each shot, making sure I'm not going to strand myself. Once I'm certain of my strategy, I sink the ten, the twelve, and the fifteen in rapid succession.

Now only the eight ball is left. It's pressed against Sebastian's three. They're both rather close to the left corner pocket. I'm afraid that I'll knock them in together if I'm not careful.

Cautiously, I take aim. I split the balls apart, knocking the eight ball into the pocket and nudging the three aside. The cue ball rolls a little too far, trembling at the edge. If it falls in, too, I lose the game. But it stays put.

I pluck up Sebastian's hundred-dollar bill and tuck it into my bra. "I win."

"I think I just got sharked," Sebastian says.

"It wouldn't be the first time." Men always overestimate their skills. And underestimate mine.

"Should we go one more?" Sebastian says.

"Double or nothing?"

"I'm not sure you have any money," Sebastian says with a cheeky smile. "Other than what you took from me. What about…for every ball I sink, you take off a piece of clothing. And I'll do the same."

I scoff, shaking my head at him. It's a transparent ruse.

On the other hand…I can't resist the temptation of humiliating him further. I'd love to win the game while he stands there in his boxer shorts.

"Sure," I say. "But I break."

"You broke last time," Sebastian points out.

"Take it or leave it."

"I'll take it," he says, his voice low and intent.

Sebastian racks the balls again, and I take my position on the other end of the table. I break, though not as cleanly as last time. Only one ball drops into the side pocket—the three—and only just barely. I throw a look at Sebastian.

"That's one."

"We're counting the break?" he says.

"Of course we are."

"Fair enough." Sebastian shrugs.

Crossing his arms in front of himself, he grabs the bottom of his black T-shirt with both hands and pulls it over his head. I can't help staring as he bares his long lean torso, deeply tanned and rippling with muscle. He's even fitter than I expected. His shoulders and chest are thick and full, his abdominal muscles cut all the way down. A trail of dark hair leads from his belly button into the waistband of his jeans. My eyes follow.

When I snap them back up again, he's grinning at me. "Like what you see?"

I toss my ponytail back over my shoulder contemptuously, facing the pool table once more.

I don't know if it was the sight of Sebastian or my own haste to keep playing, but I miss my next shot. Worse still, the cue ball rolls into the pocket, so Sebastian can position it wherever he likes behind the line.

"*B`lyad!*" I swear in annoyance.

I'm even more annoyed by Sebastian's smug expression as he takes his spot at the top of the table. Without even aiming, he sinks the ten.

"Your turn," he says.

He means my turn to strip, not to play. Irritated, I slip off my left shoe. It's a Manolo Blahnik, and I don't fancy putting my foot back into it if I get my soles dirty on the dusty concrete.

Sebastian sinks the twelve as well.

"Can't have you standing lopsided." He grins.

I take off the right shoe. Now my heart is beating fast. I planned to run the table, not put myself on the receiving end of a streak. I can't believe I missed.

Sebastian puts the fifteen in the corner pocket.

Frowning, I pull the elastic out of my ponytail so my hair falls loose around my shoulders.

"I'm not sure that counts as clothing," Sebastian says.

"Yes it does," I hiss.

"Whatever you say." He sinks the fourteen easily.

Fuck.

I should have worn many more layers before I agreed to this game.

Slowly, I reach behind me and unzip the back of my dress. It's an electric-blue minidress, which didn't cover much to begin with. It's about to cover a whole lot less.

I pull down the shoulder straps, letting the dress fall to my feet in a puddle. Now it's Sebastian's turn to let his jaw drop.

His reaction is, at least, satisfying. He looks mildly stunned, like he just received a blow to the head. He doesn't even pretend not to let his eyes roam over my body in my black silk bra and panty set.

Hopefully my figure will have a similar effect on him, and he'll miss his next shot.

Instead, the opposite occurs. Sebastian faces the pool table with a new level of focus. Before he was playing around—now he's dead serious. He wants to win this game.

His next shot is tricky. With my solids in the way, he doesn't have a clean shot. He has to bank the nine off the wall to sink it in the side pocket.

He hits the ball slightly off-center, and for a second, I think he's going to miss. But it hits the edge of the pocket and falls in.

Silently, Sebastian turns to face me.

I don't know why I'm so nervous.

I didn't mean for the game to go this far.

I'm suddenly conscious of how tall he is, especially now that I'm not wearing heels. I'm aware that we're alone down here in this dimly lit space, with the music thumping so loudly overhead that no one would hear us. Sebastian's eyes look dark and deeply shadowed.

A bet is a bet.

My hands are trembling as I reach behind me to unclasp my bra.

"Wait," Sebastian says.

He crosses the space between us in two long strides. He looks down into my face. He hasn't touched me yet, but I feel the heat coming off his bare chest. I'm pinned against the pool table, no more room to back up.

"You don't have to strip," he says.

I lick my lips. "We made a deal."

"I don't care. I want something else…"

I look up into his eyes, seeing the flecks of gold in the brown irises, seeing how thick and dark his lashes are.

"What?" I whisper.

He brings his lips down to mine.

He kisses me with a mouth that is warm and tastes slightly of salt and lime. His lips are even softer than they seemed against my wrist, but the kiss isn't soft. It's deep and hungry.

His right hand finds my hip, and his left hand slips under my hair to cradle the back of my neck, pulling me closer against him.

The whole world seems to drop away with that kiss. I can't feel the cold concrete beneath my feet, and I can't hear the music pounding overhead. All I can hear is my heartbeat thundering in my ears while I seem to float in space.

Then we break apart, and I'm in a basement again.

"Should we finish the game?" Sebastian asks.

"No." I shake my head. "I have to get home."

He looks disappointed but not sulky. He helps me gather my dress and shoes so I can make myself decent again.

"Don't forget your shirt," I tell him.

"Oh." He laughs. "Right."

Once we're dressed, Sebastian follows me back upstairs. He waits while I call an Uber and even offers to ride back to my house with me.

"Just for company," he says.

I shake my head. "My father wouldn't like that."

"You'll give me your number, though, won't you?"

I hesitate for a long moment. I know what I'm supposed to do, but suddenly I don't want to do it.

"Yes," I say. "I will."

Sebastian copies the number into his phone, looking pleased. "Talk to you soon," he says.

I ride back to my house, my stomach churning.

My father bought this massive stone mansion two years ago

when he came here to replace Kolya Kristoff as head of the *Bratva*. He never asked my brother or me if we wanted to move from Moscow to Chicago. He didn't give a damn what we thought.

I can see the lights on all across the main floor.

He's waiting for me.

The security gates part automatically, and I tell the driver to go all the way up to the front door. He looks slightly awed at this house. "You live here?"

"Unfortunately."

I climb out of the car. Iov opens the door before I can even touch the handle. His face is bruised, and he's hunched slightly like he might have broken a rib.

"You didn't have to kick me," he says sourly.

"You slapped me too hard!"

I push past him, impatient to get in the house. I'm exhausted, and I want to go to bed.

But first I have to speak to my father.

He comes padding silently into the entryway wearing his velvet slippers, his silk pajamas, and his long belted robe. His iron-gray beard is neatly combed, as is the thick gray hair reaching down to his shoulders. He looks like a medieval king. The kind who would invade a nation without hesitation.

"How did it go?"

"Exactly as you said," I reply.

The tiniest of smiles pulls at the corners of his lips. "Did you engage his interest?"

"Of course."

Now he does smile, showing his straight teeth the color of bone. "Well done, *moya doch.*"

CHAPTER 3
SEBASTIAN

I CAN'T STOP THINKING ABOUT YELENA.

I've never seen a woman so ferocious, so haughty, or so utterly gorgeous.

I have no problem getting girls. When I was the star of the U of C team, they quite literally threw themselves at me after every game. I had a cheerleader do a backflip onto my lap at one of the after-parties. She was a little bit drunk, and she clocked me with her heel, but I still let her give me a BJ to make up for it.

Even now, it's not hard to pick a girl up at a club or a party.

But that's all it is—a quick encounter. A few dates, plenty of sex, and then I move on to the next one as soon as my head turns in a different direction.

I've never actually had a girlfriend. Never wanted one. At first because I was too focused on sports, and later because I was stewing in frustration, feeling like I hated everyone and everything.

This…this is different.

I want this girl.

I want her badly.

I should have let her take her bra off. Trust me, I wanted to see those tits bare and close enough to touch. I only stopped her because I felt the tiniest bit guilty about running the table on her. Also, now that I know who her father is, I have to be careful.

We're not on the best footing with the Russians at the moment.

The Chicago *Bratva* has been going through a decade-long rough patch. And a lot of their problems can be directly or indirectly traced to my family.

Our territories overlap. Sometimes we've been able to cooperate and keep the peace. Other times we've had skirmishes that resulted in some of their men dead, or some of ours. Warehouses blown up, product stolen, soldiers arrested.

All that could be forgiven.

But they've lost two of their bosses now, and I can't think that's gone unnoticed in Moscow.

The first wasn't our fault. Ajo Arsenyev got himself thrown in federal prison when he got sloppy with his weapons shipments. But his replacement, Kolya Kristoff—that's a different story.

When my family allied with the Irish Mafia, the *Bratva* and the Polish Mafia made their own alliance in return. They tried to attack us. But their pact didn't last. Mikolaj Wilk, the head of the Polish Mafia, fell in love with Nessa Griffin, the youngest daughter of our Irish allies. He turned on the *Bratva*. Kolya Kristoff tried to gun her down in the Harris Theater—Fergus Griffin riddled him with bullets instead.

Without a leader, the *Bratva* went rabid for a while. We had to beat them back, driving them underground, smashing their businesses, seizing their assets.

Alexei Yenin was dispatched from Moscow to clean up the mess. He took over as the new *pakhan*. We came to a shaky kind of truce. Without making a formal agreement, it seemed mutually determined that our skirmish was over. We would each stay within our newly defined borders.

But my family hasn't exactly kept to that.

It's Nero's fault.

He saw a temptation he couldn't resist.

He found out that Kolya Kristoff was storing the Winter

Diamond in a vault on LaSalle Street. After Kristoff died, nobody came to collect the stone…so Nero decided nobody knew about it.

That's where I got roped in.

Nero and I broke into the vault. We stole the diamond. We sold it. And we used the money to fund the South Shore development.

That was over a year ago. We haven't heard a peep about it. So I'm assuming that we got away with it. Nero is an evil genius, after all… He doesn't usually make mistakes.

But there's always the chance fate will intervene in even the best-laid plans.

So with all that in mind, I'm wary to kick this particular hornet's nest. The *Bratva* are some nasty fucking hornets. They're not going to appreciate me fucking around with one of their queens.

From what I've heard, Yenin is an old-school gangster. I can only imagine how he protects his one and only daughter.

The smart move is to walk away right now. I saved her from her would-be kidnapper. Probably earned myself a little goodwill with the Russians if she told her dad about it. I can chalk that up as a win and let the rest of it go.

The face of a warrior princess…the body of an Amazon…the spirit of a wild wolf…surely I can find that again in a girl whose father doesn't crush skulls and break spines for entertainment.

I tell myself that. But the other part of my brain scoffs at the idea that there's more than one Valkyrie walking around on the earth.

All week long, I throw myself into activities to try to distract myself. I go to the gym every day with my roommate, Jace, lifting harder than ever until I'm grunting like an animal and sweat is running down my body.

"What's your deal?" Jace laughs. "You training for Mr. Olympia?"

"Yeah." I grin. "Gonna make Arnold look puny."

Jace isn't the largest of my lieutenants, but he's the most loyal. We've been friends since we were kids, and I'd trust him with my life.

He's not even Italian—he's a redheaded European mutt. His parents are schoolteachers. Still, he wants to be a made man.

He's helping me pick up the slack left by Dante's departure. With a couple of my favorite soldiers, including Jace, I take a shipment of guns from Micah Zimmer, exchange them for what we call in the business *a metric fuck ton* of cocaine out of Florida, and then I split that up among the Marino and Bianchi families because they handle distribution. I supervise the underground poker ring, including the monthly high roller game in the Drake Hotel, and I deal with a petty squabble between the Carmine and Ricci families.

I handle it all to the point that even my father seems surprised nobody had to bother him all week long.

I meet him for dinner on Friday night. Nero was supposed to come as well, but he's tied up down on the South Shore, closing a deal for an entertainment complex on one of the last available patches of land.

I had planned to take my father out to the Anchor, which used to be his favorite restaurant. At the last minute, he said he'd rather eat at home instead.

I'm concerned how little he leaves the house these days.

I drive over to see him, dressed nicely in a button-up shirt and slacks to show respect to him. In return, my father is wearing one of his custom-made Italian suits, straight from the Zegna mill in the Alps, with a short stop in Savile Row for the actual tailoring.

My mother designed every one of his suits. She selected the silk lining, the thread for the pick stitching, the cut of the jacket, the positioning of the pockets, even the color and material of the buttons. My father hasn't bought a single suit since she died. He just retailors the ones she chose to fit his shrinking frame.

Today he's wearing the navy notch lapel with the horn buttons. His dark hair, with its stark streaks of white, has grown long enough that you can see it's not really straight—more wavy like mine. His heavy brows hang so low that they half cover his eyes, like an old basset hound. His beetle-black eyes glimmer underneath, still bright and fierce, no matter how tired the rest of him looks.

I can smell his aftershave, the same Acqua di Parma he's been wearing all my life. Made of cypress and sage from the sunny slopes of Tuscany, it's a scent that makes me feel like a child again—awed by my father and feeling like I'll trip over my own feet if he looks at me.

All boys are frightened of their fathers to some degree. To me, he was a god-king. Every man I saw paid homage to him. You could tell by the way they bowed to him, the way they barely dared to meet his eye, that he was feared and respected.

He was a large man and a stern one. He spoke slowly and carefully. The only person he deferred to was my mother. And even then, we still knew he was the boss.

It's strange to look down on him now that I'm taller. Strange to see his hand tremble when he picks up his glass of wine.

Greta is eating with us. She eats most meals with my father these days. She's been his housekeeper for as long as I can remember. I wouldn't say she's like a mother to me—no one can replace your actual mom. But I love her like family, and she certainly helped raise me.

Greta is one of those people who looks almost the same at sixty as she did at thirty. She was a mature young woman and a youthful older woman. Her hair is more gray than red now, but her cheeks are still ruddy and her eyes are as bright a blue as ever.

She used to make feasts of all the traditional Italian foods my father loves, but under the repeated nagging of Dr. Bloom, she's tried to cut down the fat and salt in his food so he won't die of a heart attack too soon.

Tonight she's made a poached-salmon salad with raspberry vinaigrette. She's poured a small glass of wine for each of us, and I see her watching the bottle, ready to scold Papa if he tries to take more.

"You handled the Carmines and the Riccis very well," my father says in his low, gravelly voice.

I shrug, taking a bite of my salmon. "I just did what you always said."

"What's that?"

"You said a don has to be like King Solomon—if either of the parties leave happy, then the compromise wasn't fair."

Papa chuckles. "I said that, did I?"

"Yup."

"I'm glad you listened, *mio figlio*. I meant to instruct Dante. I always thought he'd take my place."

"He will," I say, shifting uncomfortably in my chair.

"Perhaps," Papa says. "His love is taking him in another direction."

"He'll come back," I say. "Like he came back from the army."

Papa lets out a long sigh. He hasn't touched his food. "When he enlisted, I knew he would never be don."

"Nero will, then."

"Nero is brilliant. And ruthless," Papa agrees. "But he was born on an island. He's always been that way."

I would have agreed with that before—that Nero was meant to be a lone wolf. Until he surprised me by falling in love.

"He seems pretty wrapped up in Camille," I point out.

"Camille is an extension of himself," Papa says. "*Anime gemelle.*" *Soul mates.*

I eat more of my salad so I don't have to look directly at my father.

I'm afraid of what he's trying to say.

We're sitting up on the rooftop under the fragrant fox grapes that hang in heavy bunches. Their thick leaves keep the table beneath shaded and cool, even at the height of summer.

We're eating off the heavy pewter plates my great-grandmother brought from the old country. Poor Greta has had to haul them up and down the stairs for countless meals on the roof. But she never complains. She just rolls her eyes at us when we try to help. She says sloth is the only sin and work keeps you young.

Maybe that's why my father is getting so old.

"I built this empire," Papa says quietly. "As did my father and his father. Each generation has added to it. Increased our wealth and power. We own this city now, along with the Griffins. Miles is the link between our families, the assurance that our futures will be entwined."

He pauses to catch his breath. Speaking for too long makes him winded.

"But never think we are secure, Sebastian. All dynasties seem invincible until they fall. There is always a challenger digging at the foundations. Clawing at the walls. You don't know how much your fortress has eroded. Until it comes tumbling down around you."

"We've beaten back plenty of challengers."

My father reaches across the table to lay his hand over mine. His fingers are still thick and strong, but his palm is cool, without any warmth radiating from within.

"There is no going back," he says, his glittering eyes burning into mine. "There is no retrenchment and no retirement. We keep our power. Or we'll be destroyed by our enemies. If the fortress tumbles…there is nothing to protect us anymore. The jackals will come to pick us off, one by one. Every old enemy. Every old grudge. They will return to find us."

"You're in a mood tonight!" Greta says, trying to break the tension. "Nobody is coming to get us."

"We're moving toward legitimacy all the time," I say to Papa. "Someday soon we'll be like the Kennedys or the Rockefellers—all our criminal history swept under the rug of our licit wealth."

Papa isn't placated. His fingers clench around my hand, squeezing hard. Harder than I thought he could.

"Legitimate, maybe, but never soft," he tells me. "Promise me, Sebastian."

"I promise," I say, not entirely sure what I'm agreeing to.

"What do we do when we're hit?" he demands.

"For every blow, return three more," I recite. "Our fury overwhelms their greed."

"That's right." Papa nods.

Greta presses her lips together. She doesn't like this kind of talk. Especially not at the dinner table.

"Is there dessert?" I say to change the subject.

"I have sorbet downstairs," Greta says.

She starts to gather the plates, and I help her, even though I know it will annoy her. She *tsks* at me and says, "Stay here!"

I help her carry the dishes down anyway, noticing my father never touched his food.

"Has he been like that all week?" I ask her once we're out of earshot down the stairs.

"Gloomy?" she says. "Paranoid? Yes."

"What's the problem?"

Greta shakes her head, not wanting to talk about my father behind his back. She's been unwaveringly loyal to him all my life.

"It's hard having you all gone," she says. And then, after a moment, she admits, "He's forgetting things."

My father is only seventy-one. Not so very old. Time is cutting away at him faster and faster, but he could live twenty years longer. Maybe more. He's always been so sharp. Even if he's forgetful compared to his old self, I can't help but think that's still better than most people.

"Does he need to see Dr. Bloom again?" I ask Greta.

"I give him the supplements the doctor says to give him. I follow the diet. I try to make him walk on the treadmill downstairs, but he says he's not a hamster on a wheel."

"You could go for a walk outside together."

"Well..." Greta sighs. "That's the paranoia. He thinks people are trying to kill him. He brings up old rivals who aren't alive anymore. Bruno Salvatore. Viktor Adamski. Kolya Kristoff."

I cast a quick glance over at her. We never talk to Greta about our business—or at least I thought we never did. The fact she knows those names means my father has been telling her things. Maybe a lot of things.

I study her face, wondering if she'd rather not know. Of course, she's always been aware of who my father is and what he does. But that's different from hearing details. If Papa is losing his inhibitions, he might be spilling all kinds of secrets.

Seeing my concern, Greta says, "It's all right, Seb. You know that anything your father says will die with me."

"Of course. I just don't want you to be…upset."

Greta snorts, stacking the dishes in the sink and running hot soapy water over them. "Don't be ridiculous. I'm no wide-eyed girl. I've seen things that would make your hair curl." She reaches up to touch my cheek, smiling a little. "More than it already does."

I relax a little. Greta is family. She'll take care of Papa no matter what happens. No matter what he says.

She dishes lemon sorbet into three small bowls, and I help her carry it back up to the roof. In our absence, Papa has gotten out the chessboard. I'm no match for him at chess—only Nero can beat him. Still, I take my place opposite, playing black.

Papa taught us all how to play, from Dante down to Aida. Dante is a competent player; Nero is near unbeatable. Aida has flashes of brilliance undermined by her impatience. She either wins or loses spectacularly.

I was always too fidgety to want to play much. I'd rather be doing something physical versus sitting and thinking. But I learned the rules and the basic strategies, just like my siblings.

Papa starts with the King's Gambit, one of his favorite opening moves. It's a risky opening move for white, but it was fashionable in the romantic era of chess, which my father believes was the best era—full of dramatic and aggressive forays, before the time of computer analysis, which favors a more defensive technique.

I accept the gambit, and Papa develops his bishop to an active square.

I put him in check, forcing him to move his king so he won't be able to castle later.

Papa nods, glad to see I haven't entirely forgotten what I'm doing. "Chess makes men wiser and clear-sighted," he says. "Do you know who said that?"

"Some grand master?" I guess.

"No." Papa chuckles. "Vladimir Putin."

Papa moves his king, menacing mine in turn. I try to drive away his bishop so he can't attack me diagonally.

We each take several pawns from each other as we skirmish, but no major pieces yet.

Papa sets up a tricky offensive where he simultaneously traps my queen and tries to attack my knight. I defend by moving my knight back to a square that protects my queen, but I've lost positioning on the board, and Papa is advancing.

I manage to take one of his rooks and then his bishop. For a moment I think Papa was only sacrificing his pieces—I must have missed a threat coming from another direction. But then I see Papa is flustered, and I realize he made a mistake.

I don't usually last this long against my father. I'm struck by the uncomfortable thought that I might actually beat him. I don't want that to happen. It would be embarrassing for us both. It would mean something that I don't want to admit.

On the other hand, if I let him win, he'll know. And that would be even more insulting.

Papa has to scramble to recover. He attacks hard, taking a knight and a bishop in return. In the end he wins, but only at the expense of his queen. It was close—much closer than usual.

"Got me again," I say.

I think we're both relieved.

It's a beautiful evening. The stars are coming out in a pale violet sky. The air is warm with a hint of breeze up here on the rooftop. The scent of the fox grapes is rich and sweet.

I ought to be happy. But my stomach twists as I think that some night like this, I'll play my last game of chess with my father. And I won't know at the time that it's the last game.

"I would like to play like Rudolf Spielmann," Papa says. "He always said, 'Play the opening like a book, the middle game like a magician, and the endgame like a machine.'"

I puzzle that over in my head, thinking about what it means.

"That's true of any strategy," Papa says, his dark eyes fixed on mine. "Remember that, Seb. Follow the rules at first. Confound your opponent in the middle. And in the end, finish him without hesitation, without mercy, and without thought."

"Sure, Papa."

My father's face looks drawn, shadows carving deep lines across his skin. Papa has always been like this, teaching and training us at any opportunity. But tonight it seems particularly intense. There's something almost spooky about his glittering eyes in the fading light.

Whatever prompted this, I tell myself that it's a good reminder that I shouldn't call Yelena. She may be gorgeous, but she's also the epitome of forbidden fruit. I couldn't pick a more dangerous target if I searched the whole city. I should leave things exactly as they are—with me doing the Russians a favor and nothing more.

The thought of never seeing her again leaves me dull and disappointed.

But that's how it will have to be. I'll have to find something else to fill this black pit in the center of my chest.

CHAPTER 4
YELENA

SEBASTIAN DOESN'T CALL.

My father is intolerable about it.

"I thought you said you secured his interest?" he sneers at me.

"I did," I say, my lips thin with irritation.

"Then why hasn't he called?"

"I don't know. Maybe he's smarter than he looks."

While it's hardly flattering to be ignored, a tiny part of me is relieved. I never liked this plan. I never wanted to be a part of it.

"Maybe he's gay," my brother says.

He's lounging by our pool, wearing a pair of his ridiculously short European briefs. Adrian loves to show off his body. He has the physique of a gymnast—lean, powerful, broad in the shoulders, and narrow in the hips. Despite all his time in the sun, he has only a hint of a tan. He's fair like me—ash-blond hair and skin that goes paler than milk in the winter and only slightly gold in the summer.

I always find it amusing to look at Adrian because he is the walking, talking embodiment of what my life would be like if I had been born a man. Instead, he came out two minutes before me, the firstborn son and heir, and I followed afterward—the unexpected twin. The unwanted girl.

"He's not gay," I tell Adrian. "I would know."

"He has to be," Adrian insists. "Or else how could he resist my beautiful baby sister?"

He grabs my wrist and pulls me down on his lap, tickling my ribs right where I'm most sensitive. I shriek and slap him away, jumping up again.

I love Adrian, and I love his playfulness. He's been my best friend since birth. But I wish he wouldn't behave this way in front of our father. I can feel Papa's cold eyes boring into me. I feel them combing over my bare flesh.

I'm not dressed nearly as revealingly as my brother is—I've got on a modest one-piece swimsuit, a cover-up, and sandals. Still, I see my father's lip curl at the sight of my bare thighs where the loose smock pulled up.

My hatred for him is like a blue gas pilot light, continually burning deep down in my guts. It never goes out, and it's always waiting to flare up with the addition of any sort of fuel.

He expects me to dress like a nun around the house so all his men keep their eyes to themselves. But then, when it's time to use me for something—like his little errand the other night—then he's happy to tart me up like a street whore.

Pulling my cover-up down over my legs, I try to scrub my voice of resentment as I ask my father, "What would you like me to do?"

He considers for a moment, his top lip still curled up, like it's my fault Sebastian hasn't called. Like he can't trust me to complete the simplest of tasks.

He knows as well as I do that I can't be too obvious. The Gallos are clever. If the lure is too apparent, they'll know. Besides, men don't want something that's offered to them freely. They're predators. They need the hunt.

"We'll find a way for you to bump into him again," Papa says with a dissatisfied frown.

He goes back into the house, leaving Adrian and me alone on the deck.

The relief I feel at his departure is immense.

The only time I'm comfortable at home is when it's just Adrian and me. Even then, I know someone could be watching us. One of the *bratoks*, one of the many cameras all over the house, or Papa himself, standing at a window.

Or his *avtoritet* Rodion Abdulov. A shiver runs across my skin as I look around the yard, scanning for him. He's my father's top lieutenant. I hate him almost as much as I hate Papa. I think of him as Papa's attack dog: ruthless, vicious, and just a little bit mad.

He's always lurking around, watching me even more closely than Papa does, eager to report anything he sees. I can always feel his piggy little eyes crawling over my skin.

But not at the moment, thank god.

Adrian doesn't have to worry about any of that. He can lounge on that chair, perfectly comfortable in the summer sun, wearing whatever he pleases.

He's not scrutinized like I am. He has so much more freedom. As long as he follows the rules, he can do whatever he likes in his spare time.

I don't have a moment to myself. Anything I do, anything I say, is picked apart later.

"What's wrong?" Adrian asks.

"Nothing," I say irritably. I shuck off the cover-up and my sandals and dive into the water.

It's an Olympic-size pool, set in a gorgeous oasis of flowering trees and privacy hedges. Our yard is like something you'd find behind the Palace of Versailles. Our house is a temple of marble and glass, full of luxuries beyond anything I'd ever seen in Moscow: heated floors and towel racks, a refrigerator the size of a walk-in closet, closets the size of entire apartments.

Yet I despise it all. What's the good of being in America if I'm just as constrained as I was back home?

Nothing has changed for me here. If anything, it's worse. Because

Papa knows that we might be corrupted by the individualism and hedonism of America. So he's only cracked down harder on me.

I hoped I might be allowed to take music composition classes at one of the many colleges in the city, but he's strictly forbidden it. My only option is to practice on my own like I used to do. I'm not sure when or where I'll be able to manage that—Papa has refused to get a piano for our new house yet. He keeps putting me off, acting as if he'll do it as a reward for some unspecified behavior. I think he enjoys denying me this thing that I need, one of the only things that makes me happy.

Adrian jumps into the water, too, though I know he prefers sunbathing over swimming. He strokes the length of the pool back and forth, in tandem with me. When I push off the wall and do a front crawl, he does the same. When I flip over to backstroke, he imitates me. He's the faster swimmer, even though he barely practices. He keeps perfect pace with me, trying to goad me into attempting a race.

After a few laps, I do start swimming faster. Sure enough, he stays right next to me. Even though I know how this will end, I speed up even more until I'm pushing off the wall with all my strength, swimming half the length of the pool underwater, then stroking madly for the wall, trying to beat him.

Adrian's fingers touch the tile a moment before mine, and he pops up, grinning.

"Ohhh..." he says. "You almost got me that time."

"The hell I did." I scoff. "You weren't even trying."

"I was trying a little."

We're both holding on to the edge of the pool, breathing hard.

Looking into my brother's face is like looking into a fun house mirror. He doesn't look like a separate person. He looks like me, just slightly different.

I think if I didn't have Adrian, I would have killed myself a long time ago. Since our mother died, he's the only person who's loved me, the only person who's brought me any happiness.

"I hate it here," I tell him.

"Why? The weather's better. The food is better. The shopping, too! You can get anything here. And you know it's real—not some knockoff. Which is why it's all so goddamned expensive." He laughs.

"I just thought..." I sigh.

"You thought it would be different," Adrian says. He always knows.

"Yes."

"It will be, Yelena. Give it more time."

"I don't like this thing with the Gallos. I feel like a lamb tied to a stake, set out in the snow to entice a wolf. Even if you shoot the wolf, he doesn't always fall before his jaws close around the lamb."

"I'll help keep you safe," Adrian promises me. "And besides... you're no lamb, Yelena."

Grinning, my brother wraps his arms around me and pulls me under the water. We sink to the bottom of the pool, hugging each other tight. This is how we spent the first nine months of our lives— floating in each other's arms.

Now it's the only way to show affection without anybody watching.

Two days later, Papa throws a garment bag down on my bed.

"Get dressed. It's time to do some charity work."

I have no idea what that's supposed to mean, but I know better than to question him. I put on the dress, which is skintight and flame red, with a halter top and a slit almost up to the hip.

I put on a pair of gold sandals and a single bangle, plus a pair of gold earrings. I pull my hair up into a sleek ponytail because I like the way it makes my face look sharp and ferocious, the high pony adding to my height.

I paint my lips, fingers, and toes the same shade of crimson as the dress. I don't know where we're going, but I know my father will expect me to look flawless.

The armored car is already waiting out front, with Timur driving. He knows better than to look at me as he jumps out to open the back door. Still, I catch the involuntary flick of his eyes that lets me know I've done well with my preparations.

Timur and I are distantly related on my mother's side. He's fiercely loyal to my father because Papa got him out of a fourteen-year sentence in Taganka Prison. Papa always starts his business relationships with a favor. He wants you to be in his debt.

I'm surprised to see Adrian climbing into the back seat beside me, dressed in a neat black tux with his blond hair combed back from his brow.

"You're coming along?"

"Of course!" He grins. "I want to see the show."

"What show?" I demand.

He gives me a look of maddening mystery. "You'll see soon enough."

I scowl at him, debating whether it's worth trying to wring the information out of him or if that will only result in more teasing. I love my brother, but he's spoiled and not always considerate of the difference between his situation and mine. What amuses him often drives me to absolute fury. He and I live parallel lives with entirely different stakes. He always knows things will work out for him in the end. I have no such assurance.

We have to wait almost an hour for my father to come out of the house. He could be handling some other business, locked up in his office. Or he could be keeping us waiting for the hell of it.

He, too, is dressed formally in a smoke-gray tux, his beard and hair freshly washed and fragrant with Moroccan oil. He smells of cigar smoke and liquor, so maybe he was taking some kind of meeting with one of his brigadiers.

"Go ahead, Timur," he says as soon as he's in the car.

Adrian and I are crunched over in the corner to give him more space. He glances over at us and gives a grunt of approval at our appearances.

"No drinking tonight," he says to Adrian.

"It will look odd if I don't at least have a glass of champagne," Adrian says.

"*Only* champagne," Papa growls. "If I see you with anything harder, I'll have Rodion tie you down and waterboard you with a bottle of Stoli."

"That doesn't sound half bad," Adrian murmurs in my ear. He says it so quietly that a mouse could hardly hear him. He's not foolish enough to talk back to our father.

The car pulls up in front of Park West, a long flat building with almost no windows and dark painted sides. I suppose it must be an event center of some type—I can see a stream of high-society types heading inside, so clearly, we're here for some kind of gala or dinner. I look around until I spot a navy-and-gold banner that reads CHICAGO GREEN SPACES CHARITY AUCTION.

Fantastic. Maybe Papa will bid on a yacht.

Papa gets out of the car first, and Adrian and I follow. Adrian gives me his arm to help me scale the steps in my heels. As soon as we're out of the car, camera flashes explode in our faces. I doubt any of the Chicago press knows who we are, but my brother and I always make an irresistible pairing. On our own each of us is beautiful—as a matched set, we're stunning. I see even the fanciest guests turning to stare at us, and I hear a murmur from those who want to know who we are.

Papa walks just ahead of us, looking smug. He views us as assets, and as such, our beauty is a credit to him. He's not a handsome man himself, though he is striking. To ensure good looks in his children, he married the most beautiful woman in Moscow. Our mother wasn't wealthy or accomplished. Her father was a sanitation worker, and her mother ran a small daycare out of their house.

My mother's best friend convinced her to enroll in a national modeling contest, *Svezhiye Litsa*. It was a televised event where viewers could vote for their favorite contestants. Out of the twenty-five thousand girls who entered, my mother received a landslide of votes. She had more than double the first runner-up.

She was called the Jewel of Moscow, the Princess of the North. My father watched the contest and bet on her from the start. When she won, he received $3 million rubles, more than the entire contest prize. Actually, all my mother won was the equivalent of five hundred American dollars, plus a fur coat and a packet of coupons for Natura Siberica cosmetics, who had sponsored the event.

Papa became fixated on her, watching the show. He used his contacts to find out her name, where she lived, and where she worked (the shoe department at Tateossian).

He came to her workplace the following week. He actually wasn't the first man to do so—an elderly mechanic and a lovestruck student already had the same idea. But my mother had been able to turn them away. There was no getting rid of my father. He ordered her to join him for dinner, and he waited outside the shop until she complied.

They married two weeks later. She was nineteen years old at the time. She gave birth to me and my brother within the year.

Carrying twins was hard on her body. I don't think my father found her quite as beautiful afterward. He used to sneer at the loose skin on her stomach and the stretch marks across her sides. This was years later, when—to most people's eyes—she had regained her figure. I certainly thought she was lovely still.

She had the same violet eyes as my brother and me—though hers were large and round, like a doll's. She had a heart-shaped face with a pointed chin, delicate little features, and a rosebud mouth. Her hair was so pale and fine that it floated around her head, soft as a rabbit's fur.

She was quiet. She wouldn't speak to us unless Adrian and I were alone in a room with her. Otherwise she communicated with us through little signs and gestures. My father didn't realize that at first—when he discovered it, it enraged him. He accused us of spreading secrets behind his back. Really, she was just trying to avoid his attention. She'd do anything to stay small and hidden.

When we were alone, she'd read to us. Always fairy tales or fantasies. Stories that took you away to another world, completely different from the one we actually lived in.

She died in a car accident four years ago. Or at least that's what I was told by my father.

But he's a fucking liar. The possibility that it might have been something else, that she might have died by his hand, will always haunt me.

"We're sitting at table eight," Papa says to Adrian and me.

Adrian has already snatched his second glass of champagne off a waiter's tray without Papa noticing the first. I'm not sure whether I should drink or not. I'd like to, to ease the knot of tension in my stomach. But I don't want to get tipsy if I'm expected to perform some task for my father later.

Papa wanders over to the tables where they're displaying the various items for bid in the silent auction. It looks like the usual shit: vacation packages, golfing trips, spa days, signed memorabilia, concert tickets, celebrity encounters, gourmet food items, jewelry, paintings, and so forth.

It's all a circle jerk of wealth—the rich people buy the luxury items at a steep discount, the companies that donated write it off as a charitable expense and enjoy the free advertising, and the charity itself pockets the funds, to be disbursed to their CEOs and executive directors who scrape high six-figure salaries. If anything is left over, maybe it will be used to help someone.

I'm in a sour mood tonight. It annoys me to see that an event like this is just the same in America as it was in Moscow. Corruption everywhere. Kindness in short supply.

I decide I would like some champagne after all, and I snatch a bubbling flute off the nearest tray, gulping it down.

Adrian has charmed an entire tray of Kobe beef skewers away from some hapless waitress, and he's gobbling them down.

"Want some?" he says, his mouth full.

Before I can try a bite, Papa grabs me by the arm and hauls me out of my chair again.

"Come on," he says. "Time to get to work."

"What am I supposed to be—"

"Here." He thrusts me into the arms of a rather flustered-looking redheaded woman with a headset and a clipboard.

"Oh, hello!" the woman says. "You must be Yelena! Thank you *so* much for volunteering. We wanted to have an even dozen girls, and we had three cancellations last minute! I think a few of the girls got nervous, which is perfectly understandable, but it did leave me in a bit of a pinch."

She's talking a mile a minute. While my English is excellent, I struggle when people talk too fast. Mistaking my look of confusion, she says, "I'm Margaret, by the way!"

"Nice to meet you," I say, without meaning it.

"Come along this way! We're just about to get started. I'll show you where the other girls are waiting, and then I'll give you a quick breakdown of how this is going to go."

Before I can cast so much as a look back at my father, she's hustling me behind a large empty stage on which I see no sign of musicians or any other sort of performer.

She thrusts me into a small dressing room full of what looks like eleven other girls. They're all between the ages of twenty and thirty, all pretty, well dressed, and looking mildly nervous.

"You'll wait here until your name is called," Margaret tells me. "Then you'll walk out to the middle of the stage—you'll see a little X on the floor. The MC's name is Michael Cross. Hahaha, so he really is an 'MC,' isn't that fitting?" She giggles. "Michael will read your bio. And then the bidding will start!"

"Bidding?" I say stupidly.

"Yes! But don't concern yourself about that—the amount doesn't matter at all. Remember that it all goes to charity! The dates are always our most popular items every year! And nobody has ever failed to get a bid. Especially not a girl as pretty as you."

She hurries away, leaving me standing there with my mouth hanging open.

I'm about to be sold in a date auction.

I assume—though I can never be sure with all my father's twisted machinations—that Sebastian Gallo is going to be here tonight. My father must have seen his name on the guest list and decided that the best way to remind him I exist is to literally offer me to him on the auction block.

This plan seems insane for a number of reasons. First, I didn't see Sebastian when I walked in. And second, he already has my phone number. If he wanted to call me, he could have done that for free anytime this week.

I think my father might actually be unhinged. His hatred of the Gallos is driving him to ridiculous measures.

"Don't you believe her," a sulky-looking brunette says to me.

"What?" I say, lost in my own thoughts.

"Don't believe Margaret," the girl says. "Everybody gets bids, but not everybody gets the same amount. You damned well better believe these prissy little bitches are going to remind you till the end of time if they sell for five hundred more than you do."

She casts a resentful eye at the other women in the room.

"Why are you even doing it, then, Gemma?" a haughty-looking blond sneers at her.

"Because my father's on the board of the charity," Gemma says, as if she's explaining addition to a toddler. "And when the Twitterverse was calling the date auction 'sexist' and 'outdated' and 'akin to human trafficking,' he decided the best way to quash those concerns was to sell his own daughter to the highest bidder."

"I'm just doing it because I heard Ian Happ is coming tonight," the blond says carelessly. "If he's going to buy a date, I want it to be with me."

"Who roped you in?" Gemma asks, turning back to me.

"Uh…my father."

"So you know exactly what I'm talking about." Gemma sniffs. "It *is* sexist, and it *is* medieval."

"You don't have to marry the guy." The blond rolls her eyes. "You don't even have to fuck him. If you get bought by a dud, you just go out to dinner with him, drink a gallon of wine, then ignore his calls thereafter."

A slim Asian girl pipes up. "Last year my date took me to Tiffany's and bought me a necklace. It was really pretty. I still have it."

"Did you keep seeing him?" Gemma asks.

"Oh, no." The girl shakes her head. "He was like ninety years old. Actually, he might be dead by now. I never followed up."

"There you go," Gemma says to me with a small smile. "You might get a date with a baseball player, or you might get a gift from a geriatric. The options are endless."

"I'm Yelena, by the way," I tell her.

"Gemma. But you already heard that."

"I did."

We're smiling at each other, feeling more relaxed now that we at least have someone to complain with.

That feeling evaporates as Margaret pops into the room again, clapping her hands to get our attention and crying, "All right, ladies, we're about to begin! Make sure you've got your number pinned to your dress so you know what order to go out in. Oh—you don't have one yet, Yelena. Here you go."

She pins the number twelve to my dress, right above my left breast. This makes me feel more than ever like a piece of livestock being forced down a chute.

I'm not thrilled about going last. That means I have to sit back here watching everyone else take their turn while my discomfort grows.

"Oh! Here's Mr. Cross!" Margaret says.

"Hello, ladies! Excited for the auction?" Michael Cross says.

He's a short trim man with a full grin of bleached-white teeth. His hair is almost the exact same shade of bronze as his overly tanned skin, which makes him look—to my eyes—a bit like Lisa Simpson.

There's an unenthusiastic murmur from a few of the girls and a chipper "oh yes!" from those who apparently entered this voluntarily. Gemma just scowls at him.

"Looks like you're up first, Aubrey," Cross says to the blond girl who was hoping for a date with the apparently famous athlete. "Wait for me to call your name, then walk out to center stage. You can stand and pose while I read your bio, and then the bidding will start. Feel free to smile or wave to the crowd, or even blow a cheeky kiss!"

The idea of blowing a "cheeky kiss" makes me want to vomit, but Aubrey nods like she's taking mental notes.

"All right, ladies! Good luck—and happy hunting!" Cross winks at us.

Gemma looks at me and rolls her eyes so hard, I think they might never come back. I give her a look in return that I think conveys, *It's not too late for a mutual suicide pact.*

Cross strides out onto the stage. I hear his voice echoing through the speaker system: "All right, gentlemen—and also ladies. We don't discriminate, all are welcome to bid! I know you've all been waiting for everyone's favorite part of the night! The Green Space date auction has a long and storied history—I'm proud to inform you that over the twenty-two years we've been holding this event, our philanthropic matchmaking has resulted in no less than *seven* actual marriages!"

Gemma leans over to mutter, "How many of them *stayed* married is a different question."

"Even better," Cross continues, "we've raised hundreds of

thousands of dollars for Chicago's green spaces, a cause near and dear to my heart since I myself grew up in a green-impoverished neighborhood, without access to a park close by."

He pauses for a moment to allow everyone to feel the weight of this tragedy.

"Not to mention they pay him a hefty fee to run the fundraiser every year," Gemma interjects. This time she says it a little too loudly, and Margaret throws her a warning glare.

"The best way to help beautify Chicago is to bid on all the wonderful items we have for you tonight—most especially the crème de la crème of our young ladies, the shining stars of Chicago high society! Let me introduce the first of our available bachelorettes: Aubrey Lane!"

Aubrey goes strutting out across the stage to applause from the crowd. Peeking out from the dressing room, I can see that she has no compunction about posing and turning like a *Price Is Right* model, with the item on offer being herself. When she pauses in the middle of the stage, Cross informs the crowd, "Aubrey has her master of fine arts from Cornell, and she is currently working as an art buyer for the Fourteenth Street Gallery. She enjoys horseback riding, scuba diving, wine tastings, and international travel. Her favorite movie is *Love Actually*."

The reading of her bio is interrupted by several whoops and hollers from the crowd. Aubrey winks at her admirers and, as instructed, blows them kisses.

"As you can see," Cross says, "Aubrey is a stunning young woman whom any of you would be privileged to take on a date. Shall we start the bidding at two thousand?"

With that, Cross breaks into his auctioneer patter. The bidding swiftly increases from two thousand dollars to five thousand dollars.

"How much do we usually sell for?" I ask Gemma drily.

"Anything over five grand is good. Over ten is impressive."

Great. Not only do I have to hope Sebastian bids on me, but I have to hope the price is high enough to please my father's vanity. He'll never let me hear the end of it if I sell for a measly two thousand dollars.

I'm not worried about my looks per se—I know I'm pretty. But I'm basically a stranger. The rest of these girls probably have friends and family and boyfriends in the crowd. They're already well-known in Chicago high society. I'm a nobody as far as these people know. Or worse, they might be aware that my father's a Russian gangster. Which is hardly going to entice them.

The bidding slows down. Aubrey is finally sold for $8,700. Not the ten thousand Gemma deems "impressive," but not far off. Aubrey looks pleased as she exits the opposite side of the stage, despite the fact she wasn't purchased by the famous Ian Happ.

I can't see the crowd from the dressing room. But I can hear that they seem to be getting rowdier by the minute. A curvy redhead goes out next, with Cross announcing her hobbies as "baking" and "reading." This is apparently less enticing to the horny bachelors, as the redhead sells for only $4,400.

They're much more interested in the Asian girl who apparently loves "skydiving, NASCAR, and Cubs games." She sells for twelve thousand dollars after a ferocious bidding war between two brothers—Caleb and Walker Littenhouse.

"Sorry, Caleb," Cross says in his smarmy tone. "Looks like big brother takes home the girl. But don't you worry—we've got plenty more lovely ladies waiting in the wings. Let's bring out our next bachelorette! You may know her father, Ransom Rothwell, the head of our very own charity board. He's offering up his lovely daughter for a date with one of you lucky men as proof of his commitment to our cause! So don't let him down—give a warm welcome to the beautiful and sultry Gemma!"

Gemma stalks across the stage looking anything but "sultry." She barely offers a strained smile to the crowd. No kisses or twirls from her—she faces the audience with her arms crossed over her chest.

The bidding starts, and immediately I can see Gemma grow

even tenser. She keeps glaring at one particular person in the crowd and even shakes her head at him when he continues to bid.

"What's going on?" I ask the tall black-haired girl standing next to me.

She cranes her head around the corner to get a better look. "Oh," she says. "Gemma's ex is bidding on her, and she's pissed."

"Who's her ex-boyfriend?"

"Carson Woodward. He's good-looking, but *god*, he's a douche. My sister used to date him—she said he can't come unless he's fucking in front of a mirror."

I snort at that mental image.

I have my fingers crossed that Carson won't win the bid, but I can tell from the look of fury on Gemma's face that he does, even before Cross announces it. Gemma stomps off the stage, face flaming.

The black-haired girl is up next.

"Good luck," I say to her.

"Oh, don't worry about me." She laughs. "My boyfriend will pay whatever it takes. He's sitting right in the front row."

She strolls out without a hint of concern. Meanwhile, my stomach is churning because we've gone through almost half the girls and my turn is coming up.

I don't even know if Sebastian is here. Even if he attended the event, he doesn't strike me as someone who has to pay for dates.

I wait until Margaret's back is turned, and then I sneak over to the edge of the stage to peek around the curtain.

It's difficult to scan the crowd, with the floodlights trained on the stage and the overhead lights dimmed in the rest of the room. I can only pick out Sebastian because, even sitting, his head of dark curls pokes up taller than anybody else's.

My heart gives a lurch at the sight of him. I don't know if it's relief, because at least there's a chance that I can do what my father's demanding, or if it's just that Sebastian looks even handsomer than I remembered.

Even in this room full of wealthy and attractive people, he stands out. It's not just his height—his features are incredibly striking. The dim light casts shadows in the hollows beneath his high cheekbones, and his lips look simultaneously stern and sensual.

He's scrolling on his phone, mildly bored. I see that he's sitting next to a pretty woman with dark curly hair and a well-groomed man in an expensive-looking suit. Neither of them is watching the auction either—the man has his arm around the woman's shoulders, and he's whispering in her ear. Her shoulders shake as she tries to hold back laughter.

I let the curtain fall back in place.

Sebastian is here.

Now I just have to hope he bids on me.

I'd like to stay and see if he bids on anyone else, but Margaret catches sight of me and motions for me to come back in the dressing room.

"Don't worry," she says. "There's no need to be nervous! We've never had a girl fail to get a bid."

"I'm not nervous," I say, but that's not really true. Two more girls have gone out, and my turn is drawing closer and closer.

"Here," Margaret says. "Have a little champagne! That helps *me* calm down."

It looks like she's already taken advantage of that particular cure. Her cheeks are flushed, and her red hair is starting to come down from its updo.

She grabs me a drink while taking another for herself.

"So far so good!" She holds up her glass in a kind of cheer.

I clink her glass and take a sip of the bubbling champagne. It does help a little, even if it's just a placebo effect.

The next girl up is an absolutely stunning brunette with hair down to her bottom. Cross announces that she owns the Tremont Fitness Center, which I could have guessed from the triceps popping on the back of her arms and her ass that looks sculpted out of marble.

This obviously appeals to the men in the crowd because she goes for the highest bid yet: seventeen thousand dollars.

"I can't believe people pay that much for one date," I say to Margaret.

"Well, it's for a good cause." And then, with surprising honesty, she adds, "Plus it's sort of an ego thing. They're showing off how much they can spend. There's this unspoken cachet if you can take home the hottest girl of the night."

Realizing she's said too much, she amends, "I mean, you're all gorgeous of course! But you know how men are."

"Better than most."

I'm starting to get impatient. Instead of being nervous, I just want this whole thing to be over.

Two more girls take their turn.

Margaret grabs another glass of champagne, probably feeling that her job is almost done and she can start celebrating. She whispers to me that between the date auction and the silent auction, they've taken in a record amount of donations this year.

"Thank god! After all that snafu about political correctness..." She hiccups loudly, interrupting herself. "We were worried...it's damn hard to get a job in the nonprofit sector. But I'm sure the board will be pleased!"

Now it's the last auction before mine. This girl isn't quite as flashy as the others—she's wearing a modest prairie-style dress and glasses. She looks a bit shy and awkward, so I'm worried she won't get many bids. She seems like the type to take that to heart.

Instead, the bids fly fast and furious from the moment she steps onstage. She ends up selling for $15,500, one of the highest numbers of the night.

"What's that about?" I ask Margaret.

"That's Cecily Cole," she says as if I should know what that means. "Her father owns Western Energy. I would think one meeting with him would be worth fifteen grand. Not to mention a shot at her trust fund, if by chance she hits it off with whoever buys her."

Margaret is leaning on my shoulder, tipsy and friendly.

"I hear your father's a powerful man, too… But he's a little bit terrifying, isn't he? Maybe it's the accent…"

"It's not the accent," I say. "It's his personality and morals."

Margaret stares at me wide-eyed, not sure if I'm joking.

Cecily exits the stage, and I realize it's finally my turn.

"I think we just might have saved the best for last," Cross croons into his microphone. "Our final bachelorette is a new face on the Chicago social scene. She recently moved here from Moscow! So you can be sure there's plenty of places you can take her on a date that she hasn't visited yet. Please welcome Yelena Yenina!"

I walk across the stage, my legs feeling stiff beneath me like my knees suddenly forgot how to bend. The lights are far more blinding from this angle, and I have to resist the urge to shield my eyes with my hand. The little X mark that we're supposed to find has completely disappeared on the shining wooden floor. I have to guess where I'm supposed to stop.

I face the crowd. I wouldn't say I have stage fright exactly, but I don't love being stared at by strangers. I feel like the crowd is quieter than it was with the other girls—fewer catcalls, maybe because I don't have any friends out there, or maybe just because I look fierce and angry under the harsh light.

I see my father first. He's sitting next to Adrian, his eyes boring into mine. He's looking me over like an architect examining a building in progress—with calculation and judgment. Not with love.

Then, slowly, I turn so my eyes meet Sebastian's. He's not looking at his phone anymore. He's staring at me, his lips slightly parted. He looks surprised. And—I hope—interested. I wonder if his heart is beating as fast as mine.

"Yelena speaks three languages: English, Russian, and French. She's an accomplished pianist and an excellent skier," Cross recites. "And no, your eyes aren't fooling you—I'm told she's five foot eleven and three-quarters." Cross laughs.

I don't know if that's actually true. I haven't measured myself in ages; I could be over six feet tall. But that's not ladylike, so my father gave the tallest permissible height. He's always torn between convention and his desire to boast.

"Shall we start the bidding at the standard two thousand?" Cross says.

I'm almost afraid to look at the crowd to see if anyone raises their bidding paddle. To my immense relief, five or six paddles immediately shoot into the air. Not Sebastian's, however.

"Three thousand?" Cross says. "Four thousand?"

There's no reduction in the number of bidders. In fact, the obvious eagerness of a few men seems spur others into action. Now there are seven or eight people bidding as Cross says, "How about an even five thousand? Six?"

I'm not really paying attention to the other men. My eyes are flitting over to Sebastian, to see if he'll raise his paddle. It lies stubbornly flat on the table in front of him. I doubt he's touched it all night.

The dark-haired girl sitting next to Sebastian leans over and murmurs something to him. He gives one quick shake of his head. I don't know if they're talking about me, but it makes my heart race all the faster.

"Seven thousand? Eight? What about nine?" Cross says.

The bidding hasn't slowed at all. As it crosses ten thousand, a couple of the men drop out, but those remaining raise their paddles faster and faster to secure their bids.

"Twelve," Cross says. "What about thirteen? That's to you, Mr. Englewood. Fourteen now? And fifteen."

The bidding is mostly concentrated between the man apparently called Englewood, who looks to be about forty years old, with thick black hair and beard, and a handsome younger man in a flashy suit, who looks like a finance type. He's sitting at a whole table of men who look just like him, and they're egging him on. The third bidder is a much older man who might be Persian or Arabic.

"Sixteen?" Cross says. "Seventeen?"

Suddenly, impulsively, Sebastian snatches up his paddle. He calls out, "Twenty thousand!"

Even the woman and man sitting at his own table look startled. The dark-haired girl mouths something that looks like, "What the fuck?" She peers up at me, grinning.

My eyes meet Sebastian's for one swift moment. I have to look down again because my face is burning.

I don't have to look over at my father. I can feel the triumph radiating off him.

The Persian man drops out of the bidding, but the other two are still in.

"Twenty-one!" Englewood calls, raising his paddle.

"How about twenty-two?" Cross says.

After a moment's hesitation—with his friends nudging him on—the finance guy bids again.

I look at Sebastian. My face is still—no smile. Definitely no blowing kisses. Just my eyes looking into his, asking him…what exactly? I'm supposed to lure him to bid on me. But do I actually want him to?

I like Sebastian. I can admit it to myself now. I was disappointed when he didn't call me. A secret tiny part of myself wanted to see him again.

But that's all the more reason to tell him not to bid. I could frown or shake my head at him. I could warn him off. Maybe my father would see it, but probably not.

That's what I should do. I should warn him away.

Instead, I just stare at him. I'm afraid my eyes are showing the anxiousness and longing in my chest.

"Twenty-five thousand," Sebastian calls out.

Quiet falls over the room. That's the highest bid of the night so far.

"We've got tough competition for the new girl in town, our

beautiful blond Russian," Cross says, barely able to contain his glee. "How about it, gentlemen? Can anyone beat the youngest Gallo brother? Does anyone want to bid twenty-six?"

He glances over at the table of financiers. The young guy in the flashy suit looks like he wants to raise his paddle. Instead, he tosses it on the table in irritation. I guess we've come to the end of his bankroll.

Englewood hasn't given up. He raises his paddle once more. "Thirty," he says coolly.

He looks over at Sebastian, his dark eyes glowering beneath thick brows. I don't know if these two know each other or I'm just witnessing a territorial display between two powerful men. Either way, the tension is palpable.

Sebastian ignores Englewood and gazes up at me instead. I'm illuminated by the burning-hot stage lights, my red dress aflame all around me.

Staring right at me, Sebastian says, "Fifty thousand."

Cross tries to quiet the roar that erupts from every table. "We've got a bid of fifty thousand!" he says. "That's a new record, ladies and gentlemen, and remember it's all for a great cause! Mr. Englewood… do you care to match it?"

Englewood's lips tighten beneath his dark mustache. He gives one jerking shake of his head, and Cross says, "Sold! Ms. Yenina will be going on a date with Sebastian Gallo."

I don't know if it's fear or relief that floods me. All I know is that I'm suddenly cold, even under the hot lights. Cross has to take me by the arm and point me to the stairs leading down off the stage.

I stumble over to my father's table. He lays a heavy hand on my shoulder and mutters in my ear, "Well done. He's invested now."

Yes, Sebastian is invested. To the tune of fifty thousand dollars.

CHAPTER 5
SEBASTIAN

I THINK AIDA DRAGGED ME ALONG TO THE CHARITY AUCTION because she's under the impression that I'm depressed. Her efforts to engage me in social and family events have been ramping up by the week, including several unsolicited blind dates. I didn't agree to take any of the girls out. I told Aida I was enjoying being single.

I only went to the auction because Cal, Aida, and I had some business to discuss. Specifically, Cal's upcoming mayoral campaign. The Griffins intend to go 100 percent legitimate. That means divesting themselves of any remaining illegal business operations and making sure that any bodies they've buried stay buried. And that's not a euphemism—the most recent body was Cal's own uncle, Oran Griffin, who currently lies beneath the foundation of one of the South Shore office towers.

While the Gallo family is turning our attention to large-scale real estate, I don't think we're ready to wash our hands clean just yet. The Griffins exiting the Mafia sphere leaves a huge power vacuum. Somebody needs to fill it. The question is, who?

I suppose Mikolaj Wilk and the Polish Mafia will step up. We're on reasonably good terms with Mikolaj, but I can't say we're best friends. There's a certain uneasiness that occurs when someone kidnaps the youngest daughter of your ally and then frames your brother for murder.

Mikolaj did marry the captive Nessa Griffin, and Riona Griffin sprang Dante out of jail. But let's just say Mikolaj and I aren't exactly exchanging Christmas cards.

It's a prickly situation, especially with the Russians beaten back but not subdued. Whenever you shift the pillars of a power structure, there's a chance the whole thing could come crashing down.

Maybe that's why Papa has been so paranoid lately. He can feel the uncertainty in the air.

With all that in mind, I agreed to come to the charity event even though I hate these things. I hate the glad-handing and the phoniness. It disturbs me to see how good Aida's gotten at it. It used to be that you couldn't take her anywhere without her stealing something or offending somebody—usually multiple somebodies. Now she's all dolled up in a gown and heels, remembering everybody's name, charming the pants off the hoity-toity society types.

Callum is the same, but even more so. He's the alderman of the Forty-Third Ward, which is the wealthiest and most influential district, incorporating Lincoln Park, Old Town, and the Gold Coast. I can see that he's known to almost everyone in the room. There's hardly a person here not eager to bend his ear on some personal objective.

Meanwhile, I'm bored out of my skin. I steal a couple of canapés off passing waiters' trays, and then I take a look at the long list of silent auction items on offer, including a football signed by the entire Bears' offensive line.

There's some pretty cool shit to be sold. But honestly…I can't seem to rouse up interest in any of it. I just don't care. The past two years have been a dark and blank expanse of time, punctuated by only a few jolts of excitement. I haven't felt truly interested in something for a long fucking time…

Other than last week.

Yelena interested me.

There was an energy between us that actually made me feel something, ever so briefly.

After all this time, when I finally see something worth chasing…
I'm supposed to ignore her. I'm supposed to let her go. Because of
my family.

My goddamned family.

Somehow they always manage to take away the only things I
care about.

I look over at Aida, who's talking to some short balding man
with a hideous purple bow tie. He's laughing at something she said,
his head thrown back and all his crooked, crowded teeth on display.
Aida has that look I know so well, that sly grin that shows she's
thinking of something even more outrageous and trying to keep
herself from saying it out loud. That's a battle she used to lose every
time, but she's finally learned a little self-restraint.

My sister is lovely. Dark curly hair, bright gray eyes that look like
a coin flashing in cloudy water, a perpetual expression of mischie-
vousness that makes you equal parts curious and anxious whenever
you look at her.

How can you love someone so much and also resent them?

That's how I feel about all my family these days.

I fucking love them, down to my bones. But I don't like where I
am because of them.

I know it's partly my fault. I'm drifting without purpose. But
whenever they pull me in some new direction, I never like where I
end up.

Like this fucking auction.

I sigh and head back to our assigned table, over at the edge of
the stage. I don't know what sort of performance they have planned
for tonight. Probably something tedious like a classical quartet or,
worse, a cover band. If it sucks, I'm leaving. Actually, I'll probably
leave either way.

As I'm sitting, a blond waitress comes by with a tray of
champagne.

"Drink?" she offers.

"You have any real liquor?"

"No, sorry," she says with a pretty little pout. "We only have prosecco and champagne."

"I'll take two prosecco."

She passes me the flutes, saying with a pretend air of casualness, "Is one of those for your date?"

"No," I say shortly. I plan to slug them both down to take the edge off my boredom.

"Bachelor?" the waitress says. "You'll probably need one of these, then." She passes me a cream-colored paddle with a number on it.

"What's this for?"

"The date auction, of course!"

Jesus Christ. I can hardly keep my eyes from rolling out of my skull. "I don't think I'm going to need that."

"Why?" she says, with a coy little smile. "See something else you like?"

Under other circumstances, I might take her up on the hints she's laying down so thickly. Unfortunately, the fact she's tall and fair-haired just reminds me of Yelena, who shares the same features but with ten times the intensity. This girl is like a daisy in a field, while Yelena is a ghost orchid: exotic, rare, and impossible to reach.

"No," I tell her. "There's nothing here for me."

The girl leaves, and Aida and Callum immediately take her place.

"This is a date auction?" I say to Aida.

"Yeah!" she says. "It's your birthday present. I'm gonna buy you a wife."

"I thought the best wives were free," I say. "And forced on you against your will."

"Can't argue with that," Callum says, swinging his arm around Aida's shoulders.

Aida and Callum had what could essentially be termed an arranged marriage, but it seems to have worked out surprisingly well for them. We were all just hoping they'd make it through the first year without murdering each other.

"You used to be such a romantic, Seb," Aida says.

"Oh yeah? When was that?"

"Remember when you had that picture of Margot Robbie in your locker at school?"

I flush, wondering how in the fuck Aida even knows that. And how does she always manage to bring up the one thing you tried to scrub out of your own memory?

"I don't think that was me," I mumble.

"You don't remember watching *The Wolf of Wall Street* like eight hundred times and fast-forwarding to that one part where she's standing naked in the doorway so you could jer—"

"If you finish that sentence, I will strangle you," I hiss at Aida.

"Cal, you wouldn't let him strangle me, would you?" Aida says to her husband.

"Not to death," he replies.

"Thank you, love," she says, kissing him on the cheek. "I knew I could count on you."

Before Aida can resume her friendly harassment, an overly tanned MC comes marching out on the stage to start the evening's cattle auction. I have zero interest in the proceedings, especially once he starts listing off the women's accomplishments like they're Midwestern geishas.

It doesn't help that half the men in the room are hooting and hollering or leaning forward on the tables to leer at the girls. The whole thing feels icky. I'm embarrassed to be here.

The idea of paying for a date is ridiculous, especially at these astronomical prices. Five grand to take out some high-society hussy? No thank you. And that's before you include the price of whatever fancy dinner you have to feed her.

I'm bored out of my mind.

"How many of these do we have to sit through?" I whisper to Aida.

"I don't know." She shrugs. "How many pretty girls can there be in this city? We can leave right after."

I'd leave now, but Aida, Cal, and I all drove together, and the lights have been dimmed to the point that I probably couldn't weave my way through the tables without tripping and landing in somebody's lap.

Besides, it is mildly amusing to see these horndog men practically coming to blows over some of the girls. There are a couple of brothers bidding for the same chick. When the older one wins, the younger brother looks ready to pluck up a rock and reenact the fourth chapter of Genesis right here and now.

By the time we get to the tenth or eleventh girl, I'm starting to yawn. I stayed up too late last night. Too late every night this week, actually. The champagne is getting to me.

That is, until I hear the name "Yelena Yenina."

My head jerks up. I watch my Valkyrie stride across the stage.

Fucking hell. I already forgot how gorgeous she is. She's wearing a red dress that clings to her every curve. From this angle her legs look about ten miles long. She's so stunning that an actual hush falls over the crowd. All the girls were pretty, but Yelena isn't pretty. She's a fucking enchantress.

I can't believe she's here. That's twice in just over a week. If I believed in signs, I'd think this was an obvious miracle.

I'm staring at her with my mouth hanging open when she turns and looks right at me. She goes still, an electric jolt passing between us.

This doesn't go unnoticed by my sister, of course. Nothing does.

Aida leans over to whisper, "Do you know her?"

I give a quick shake of my head.

"It looks like you know her," Aida mutters.

The bidding already started.

Every man present wants her. The price is increasing by the second. I look around at the men bidding, wanting to rip the head off every last one of them. How dare those fucking sleazeballs try to buy a night with her, like they have a chance with a goddess like that?

I don't like the look of any of them. Actually, I fucking hate them. Especially Carl Englewood. He's an arrogant shithead my brothers butted heads with a few years back when he tried to block our permits for the Oak Street Tower. He's a real estate developer and just as cutthroat as any mafioso. Plus, he collects cars, watches, and women. I bet he'd fucking love to get his hands on Yelena.

Why is she even up there? I glance around the tables, searching for her father.

I know what Alexei Yenin looks like. I haven't actually met him, but Nero showed me a grainy photograph when he first replaced Kristoff as the head of the Chicago *Bratva*. It was an old photo from his days in the KGB—when he was young and slim, with a carefully trimmed mustache.

I spot him on the opposite side of the room. He looks much the same as the photograph, only dressed in a tux instead of a military uniform—a little thicker in the chest and shoulders, with a full beard now. He's smirking up at Yelena, pleased that she's stirring up this kind of interest.

I hate him, too. I don't know what his purpose is in putting his daughter up for sale, but I don't like it.

I watch the bidding war bounce back and forth between a man who's way too old to even consider putting his wrinkly hands on Yelena, a cocky frat boy type who's practically drooling on the table, and that covetous fuck Englewood.

I don't want any of them to take her out.

If anyone's going to take her on a date, it should be me.

Without thinking, without even considering what I'm about to say, I snatch up my paddle and shout, "Twenty thousand!"

Callum looks at me like I've just grown a second head. Aida is equally shocked, then gleeful.

"What the fuck are you doing?" She chortles.

The frat boy can't keep pace with that—he has to drop out. But Englewood fixes me with a stubborn glare. We've had words before. Now he's thrilled to have a chance to stick it to me in a public setting where I can't knock his fucking teeth in afterward.

The bidding goes back and forth between us, jumping from twenty to twenty-six thousand.

Englewood looks pissed, partly because I'm sure he thought he was taking Yelena home for certain, and also because I've aroused his competitive fire. His pride is on the line, and he doesn't want to back down.

I guess you could say the same about me. But I don't give a fuck what these other people think. I'm bidding for one reason only: because I want to see Yelena again. If her father agreed to put her up onstage for this date auction, he's obviously all right with somebody winning a night with her. Why shouldn't it be me?

This could be my one and only chance to take her out with his blessing, my chance to see her without sparking a war between our families.

"Thirty thousand," Englewood says, throwing me a triumphant look, like there's no way I'm gonna top that.

It's a ludicrous amount to pay for a date.

I don't care. How the fuck else should I spend my money?

I look up at Yelena. I'm trying to read her face. Does she want me to keep going? Does she want to see me again?

It's so hard to read her. I don't expect her to do anything as commonplace as actually smile at me. She's Russian—they don't do "friendly."

But I look at those brilliant violet-colored eyes, big and wide and shining like stars, and I'm almost certain that she wants this, too.

"Fifty thousand," I say.

That's it for Englewood. With a sneer of frustration, he tosses down his paddle.

Yelena is mine. If only for a night.

I feel a swoop of elation stronger than anything I've felt in months. Finally, a win.

"You're out of your mind." Callum chuckles.

"If you're going to blow all your money on a girl, at least you picked the hottest one." Aida grins. "Oh my god, think how tall your kids would be...you could make an entire NBA team!"

She winces as Callum steps on her foot under the table.

"Ow! Why did you—? Oh, sorry, Seb. Didn't mean to bring up...you know."

"You can talk about basketball. It's not Voldemort."

"I know," she says. "Just trying to be sensitive."

"Well, don't. It's weird, and you suck at it."

I'm giving Aida a hard time, but I really don't care. For once, the mention of my former dream hardly stings at all. I'm too distracted with thoughts of what I should do with Yelena on the world's most expensive date. Now that I've already spent fifty thousand dollars, I might as well go all out.

"You paid fifty thousand dollars. You can make her do anything you want..." Aida says in an awed tone. "You could make her play *Call of Duty* with you. Or listen to John Mayer. Or go to that shitty diner on Broadway that you love so much..."

"Don't take suggestions from Aida," Cal tells me. "She thinks raiding the Wrigleyville merch shop is the ultimate date."

"Uh, *it is*," Aida says with absolute conviction. "I got us matching Cubbies pajamas. And fuzzy slippers! You love those slippers—don't try to act cool in front of Seb."

"They're so soft," Cal admits.

I shake my head at the pair of them, my chest feeling strangely light.

I think my luck is finally changing.

———

I didn't get a chance to speak to Yelena in person after the auction—she went over to her father's table on the opposite side of the room, and they left almost immediately.

I'm hoping that wasn't an indication that Alexei was pissed I bought the date with his daughter. After all, he allowed her to participate, knowing the outcome was up in the air.

My hefty donation to the charity almost clears out my checking account, but it doesn't matter—I've got a fuck of a lot more cash stashed elsewhere. Each of us Gallo siblings takes a yearly "allowance" from the family funds, and we can get more if we need it. I've been living cheap, sharing that apartment with Jace. Fifty thousand isn't exactly pocket change, but I'm happy to pay it.

In return, the event organizers provide me with Yelena's contact information to set up the date. Of course, I already have that—it's the permission to call that I was lacking. I text her immediately, saying:

I hope you don't mind that I stole that bid.

After a few minutes, she responds:

That was the point of the auction.

I type:

Is your father alright with me taking you out?

She responds:

Do you need his permission?

I can picture her expression of disdain. I don't know if she's annoyed because she's being treated like cattle or because she prefers a bad boy to a rule follower. But, of course, her father isn't your average overprotective parent. There's a lot more at stake here.

I'm just gauging the chances that I'll be shot walking up to your front door.

A moment's pause, then she replies:

No Kevlar required. But I hope you'd come either way.

I grin.

Absolutely I would.

We set our date for the following Saturday. All week long, I'm walking on air. I haven't looked forward to anything in a very long time.

I'm lucky that Dante's in Paris. If he were here, he'd definitely try to put a stop to it. I can imagine his gravelly voice and his thousand-yard stare: *You think that's smart, Seb? Taking out the only daughter of the Bratva boss? You know they'll feed you to their fuckin' dogs if you put a hand on her.*

Dante would try to get me to cancel. But he's not here, and Nero would be the biggest hypocrite in the world if he tried to lecture me on inappropriate romantic entanglements. Before he met Camille, the main thing that attracted him to a woman was that she was off-limits and likely to get him in a whole lot of trouble.

Aida can't take the moral high ground either. I've had to bail her out of countless scrapes. She doesn't seem inclined to dissuade me—probably because she saw Yelena with her own eyes, so she knows how pointless it would be. All Cal says, bidding me good night when I drop them off at their apartment, is, "Good luck."

It seems to take forever for Saturday to roll around. I try to distract myself with more work, more exercise, and plans to make this a date that Yelena won't soon forget.

I pick her up at her father's mansion on Astor Street. It's at the very end of a shady, tree-lined lane, set back on a sprawling property surrounded by high stone walls.

The gate stands open like they're expecting me. I take my truck down the long driveway, which leads directly up to the forbidding stone facade.

The house looks a bit like a castle, with several levels of walls and towers and tall narrow windows topped by Gothic arches. But it's not particularly beautiful. It's heavy and hulking, with security cameras perched at every vantage point. The manicured hedges likewise have an oppressive look—too orderly and uniform and not actually providing any privacy on the grounds.

I feel almost certain that Alexei Yenin will be there. As I park my truck and walk up to the front doors, I steel myself to meet him face-to-face. Instead, one of his soldiers opens the door—a brutal-looking man with a Cro-Magnon brow, squinting eyes, and a close-cropped beard. He's a big boy. Not quite as big as Dante, but pretty damned close.

"*Dobryy den*," I say politely in Russian. That's one of only four phrases I know.

The guard looks me up and down silently. I almost expect him to search me for weapons. Instead he opens the door a little wider and steps aside so I can enter the house.

Now Alexei comes striding forward, dressed in a cashmere sweater and slacks with velvet slippers on his feet.

"Sebastian Gallo," he says in his booming voice.

He holds out his hand for me to shake. His hand is large and stiff, the fingers swollen so that the gold ring on his right hand cuts into the flesh.

I feel a kind of atavistic hesitation to touch him, but, of course, you have to quash those impulses when dealing with gangsters. You have to shake their hand, clap them on the shoulder, and sit down with them to eat, even when every instinct in your body screams for you to get away from such a clearly dangerous person.

Alexei's features are broad and rough, without any of the striking beauty his daughter possesses. But he does resemble her in one way: with his lank gray hair down around his shoulders, he has that same look of a barbarian—wild and foreign.

A second man comes to join us. He's much younger, probably twenty-five, the same age as me. He looks exactly like Yelena. So much like her that it startles me. He's white blond, with the same violet-colored eyes and the same sharp features. He's wearing a sober dark suit with a high collar like a cleric. But his expression is anything but sober—he grins and holds out his hand for me to shake.

"Adrian," he says. "I'm Yelena's brother."

"*Priyatnoh poznahkohmeetzah*," I say, exhausting another 25 percent of my repertoire.

"Ho! Very good," Adrian says, nodding his head with approval. "You've done your homework, my friend."

Like Yelena, Adrian has a Russian accent, but his English is also flawless.

I can feel Alexei watching our interaction. His expression is much harder to read than his son's. He doesn't seem displeased, but he doesn't seem friendly either.

"Let me clear the air," I say at once. "There's been some conflict between my family and the *Bratva*. I hope we can put all that behind us. Now that you're at the head of the Chicago chapter, I hope we can coexist peacefully. Perhaps even profitably."

"Do you speak for your family?" Alexei asks, narrowing his pale blue eyes at me.

I hesitate a moment. That's the crucial question these days. But if not me, then who? My father won't be meeting with the *Bratva* any time soon, and neither will Dante.

"I speak for the Gallos," I say. "Not the Griffins. But I believe they would say the same. Peace benefits us all."

"Does it benefit us all equally, I wonder?" Alexei asks in his low voice.

"Come on, Father," Adrian says. "Sebastian isn't here for business. He's here to get what he paid for."

Adrian's tone is light. Still, I want to clarify that point as well.

"I bid on a date with Yelena," I say. "Only a date. I intend to treat her with respect."

"Of course," Alexei says. "I know the honor of Italians."

I can't tell if he's being sarcastic or not.

I feel tense and uneasy, as if I have to track Alexei's every movement. It reminds me of guarding an opponent on the court—you have to be their shadow, moving and shifting in tandem with them, watching for the moment when they'll try to trick you into stumbling in the wrong direction or when they'll drive hard to push past you.

I don't know exactly what Alexei intends. But I do feel that we're opponents.

"Rodion!" Alexei calls sharply, summoning the soldier who opened the door for me. "Get Yelena."

Yelena comes down the stairs so quickly that I think she must have been waiting at the top. She's dressed in high-waisted shorts and a pretty floral top that ties in the front. I want to compliment her, but I feel awkward with her father and brother standing by.

"Let's go," she says without quite looking at me.

"Nice to meet you," I say to Adrian and Alexei again, this time in English.

Yelena follows me out to my car. She seems surprised to see that I drive a beat-up F-150.

"What's this?"

"A truck," I reply, opening her door for her. My truck is lifted, so I give her my hand to help her step up inside, though that's not as necessary for Yelena as for more petite girls.

"I thought mafiosos drove BMWs and Cadillacs."

"I don't fit in a sedan very well," I say, going around to the driver's side. "And honestly, neither would you."

The corner of her full lips pulls up just a little.

"This truck looks old."

"It is old."

"You don't like to draw attention?"

"Depends what for."

She raises an eyebrow, waiting for me to continue.

I start the engine, saying, "For example…I wouldn't mind every man I meet staring at the girl on my arm."

Her smile widens just a little, showing a dimple on the right side of her lips. "You wouldn't be jealous? Most men hate anyone looking at their woman."

"With a girl as gorgeous as you, I could hardly blame them."

Yelena examines me, her lips pursed. "You're free with compliments."

"Compliments, by nature, are free."

"A Russian man would point out my flaws to keep me humble."

"I'm not sure how he'd manage that."

"Keeping me humble?"

"Finding a flaw on you."

Yelena scoffs and shakes her head. "I don't trust your flattery."

I shrug. "I'm just being honest. That's what I liked about you as soon as we met. You said what you thought. No bullshit."

A shadow falls over her eyes, turning them from violet to navy. "If only that were true."

I think she's talking about her father, who's falling away behind us as we drive, but not fast enough.

I say, "I guess you can't always say what you think in that house."

"Not if you want to keep all your fingernails."

I glance over at her, wondering if she's joking. He wouldn't actually hurt her, would he? She's his only daughter…

"What about your brother?" I ask.

The tension fades from her face as we switch to this topic. Yelena smiles fully for the first time, showing the lovely white teeth between those soft lips. "Adrian is my best friend," she says simply. "We're twins."

I don't know any other twins. A dozen questions spring to my mind, most of them stupid and things that Yelena's probably been asked a hundred times before.

I settle for asking, "Is that different from normal siblings? I know everyone thinks it is, but I'm assuming you can't actually read each other's minds…"

Yelena laughs softly. "Well, I don't know for sure because I don't have any other siblings. But yes, I think it's different. We understand each other. I do know what he's thinking or feeling. Not because I can read his mind—only because he's so familiar to me."

I can understand that. I know Dante, Nero, and Aida pretty damn well. But my bond is split between four siblings. Yelena's is focused on one person.

"What about your mother?"

"She's dead," Yelena says in a tone that forbids further inquiry.

"So's mine."

"She is?" Yelena turns to face me, her voice softening.

"Yeah. She died when I was eight. She was a concert pianist. You play piano, don't you?"

I'm remembering Yelena's bio from the date auction.

"Yes," Yelena says quietly, twisting her hands in her lap. Her fingers are long and slim and beautifully shaped. It doesn't surprise me that she's a musician. "I'm sure I'm not as good as your mother was. I never played professionally."

"Did you want to?"

She presses her lips together, still looking down at her hands. "Maybe."

"I'd like to hear you play."

She clenches her hands into fists and shakes her head. "I haven't practiced in a long time."

I'm driving us over to Grand Avenue, where a street fair is in full swing. It's the Summer Food Festival, held every year during the first week of June. Long before we arrive, we can smell the tantalizing scents of sizzling meat and fresh-baked pastry and hear the cacophony of music, laughter, and the patter of street performers.

Yelena perks up at the sight of all the color and bustle. "Is it a holiday today?"

"No," I say. "There are all kinds of street fairs in the summer. This one's my favorite."

I have to park the car a few blocks away since the street is roped off. Yelena doesn't seem to mind the walk—she hurries along, eager to immerse herself in the throng of people.

Buskers are performing on both sides of the street—magic tricks, acrobatics, sword-swallowing, and slapstick comedy shows. Yelena seems particularly intrigued by two girls who are bending and balancing themselves in intricate positions, stacked on top of each other.

"They're strong," she says approvingly.

"You think you could do that?"

She considers. "Not without a lot of practice."

"Are you hungry?" I ask her.

"Yes." She nods.

If she wasn't before, she would be as soon as she smelled the enticing aroma of the food trucks lined up almost a mile down Grand Avenue. I try to explain the various offerings she hasn't seen before, including funnel cakes, Navajo tacos, lobster rolls, street corn, pulled-pork sandwiches, wine slushies, and whoopie pies.

In the end, I buy a dozen different things for us to sample even though Yelena wrinkles her nose at a few of them.

"Come on," I tease her. "I know you've eaten weirder things than this in Russia."

"What do you mean?" she demands. "Our food is perfectly normal. Not all fried and skewered on a stick!"

"If you can eat fish eggs and herring, you're going to like deep-fried cheesecake a fuck of a lot better."

"I don't like herring," Yelena admits.

She takes at least one bite of everything, even the bacon-wrapped jalapeño poppers, which she had eyed with particular suspicion.

She likes the street corn but not the brisket nachos, which she deems "messy" and "greasy." The desserts are almost universally pleasing, particularly the browned-butter banana and Nutella croissant, which she polishes off in three bites.

"This is very good," she says. "This you could sell in Moscow."

"I think Catherine the Great would have appointed me heir to the throne if I made that for her."

Yelena snorts, licking chocolate from her thumb. "She would have at least given you a *dacha* in Zavidovo."

"I don't know what that is, but it sounds nice."

As we explore the little booths full of jewelry and dried herbs, handmade soap and fresh honey, Yelena explains to me the system of Russian summer houses, originally given by the tsar to his nobles, then seized during the Russian Revolution, and now resurfacing in the form of modern mansions built in the countryside by wealthy oligarchs.

"We have those here, too," I tell her. "We call them 'cabins' even when they're massive. And even when it's nothing like camping."

"I don't understand camping," Yelena says. "Sleeping in bugs and dirt."

"Under the stars," I say. "In the fresh air."

"With bears."

"I don't know why I'm defending it." I laugh. "I've never been camping in my life."

Yelena and I are smiling at each other, enlivened by all the people around us, the chaos of sights and sounds. Even with all that as a backdrop, I only want to look at her face. The more people that surround us, the more she stands out as the most beautiful creature I've ever seen. Every head turns to look at her—none more than mine.

I like arguing with her about camping. I like talking to her about anything. I ask about her favorite books and music, her favorite movies. She tells me that she learned to speak English by watching American movies with her mother.

"She loved movies, any movie. She was obsessed with Yul Brynner. He was Russian, too, you know. Born in Vladivostok. She used to say they were practically neighbors." She pauses, seeing that I don't understand the joke. "Vladivostok is a port city close to Japan. It's the opposite corner of Russia from Moscow," she explains. "Nine thousand kilometers apart."

I'm wondering how to hide the fact that I might not even be able to point out Moscow on a map—not unless it was labeled.

Luckily, Yelena doesn't quiz me. She continues. "We watched all of Brynner's movies. I could probably quote *The King and I* from heart. She used to tell me how he came to New York, how he modeled nude to make money, and then started acting…"

A muscle jumps in her jaw as she adds, "My mother was a model, too."

"I could have guessed that—I didn't think you got your looks from your father."

Yelena gives a short laugh, but her face isn't happy.

"Maybe she had a similar dream," she says. "She never said it exactly, but the way she talked about Brynner…maybe she dreamed of running away and coming here, too…"

"*You* came here," I say to Yelena. "Not to New York, but Chicago's pretty damn close."

Yelena nods slowly. "She might have liked that."

The whole afternoon has gone by while we've been walking around the fair. We've come to the end of it, and we're a long way away from the truck.

"Do you want to take a cab back to the car?" I ask Yelena.

She's looking ahead along the lakeshore. "What's that up there?" She points to the Centennial Wheel at the end of Navy Pier.

"Do you want to ride it?" I ask.

With a slight look of nervousness, Yelena says, "Yes."

"Are your feet sore yet?" I look down at her sandals.

"Not yet." She shakes her head.

We walk down the length of Navy Pier, through the park and the shops, stopping only to buy our tickets. I can see Yelena looking more and more apprehensive the closer we get, as the massive wheel towers overhead. It's not until we're climbing into the car that she admits, "I'm a bit afraid of heights."

"Why do you want to ride it, then?"

"Because it looks beautiful!" she says fiercely.

As our car begins to rise into the air, her face turns paler than ever. But she peers out the window at the view across the lake, encircled along the western rim by high-rises.

The car rocks a little as the wheel stops and starts, letting more people climb on below us. Yelena jumps, grabbing my thigh. Her fingernails dig into my flesh even through my jeans, but I don't mind. I put my hand on top of hers and massage gently until she relaxes.

To distract her, I say, "You know, the first Ferris wheel in the world was built here in Chicago."

"It was?"

"Yeah, for the World Exposition in...I'm gonna say...1893? They were trying to show up the Eiffel Tower."

Yelena raises an eyebrow. "The Eiffel Tower is hard to beat."

"Yeah." I grin. "But it doesn't move."

We're almost at the peak of the wheel now. The motion stops once more, and we look out over the water. The sun is sinking. The whole sky is turning orange, the clouds as gray as smoke and the sun like a burning brand above the water. The waves lapping the shore are deep indigo, tipped with peaks of white. It looks so unearthly that we're both silent, just staring through the glass.

"Look," Yelena says, pointing. "A star."

The star is faint, just glimmering into being in the darkest strip of sky.

I turn to look at Yelena. The sunset glow is burning on her skin, painting it gold. Her eyes look lighter than usual—pale as lavender and gleaming beneath her dark lashes. Her lips are parted.

I lean over and kiss her. Right as our lips meet, the wheel swings into motion, and we plunge down, down the other side of the circle. The motion is slow, but my heart rises in my throat, and I grab her face between both my hands to keep our mouths pressed tightly together.

Yelena does the same, her long slim fingers twined in my hair. She kisses me deeply, her lips tasting of powdered sugar and a hint of chocolate.

The kiss goes on and on. I pull her onto my lap so she's straddling me. The motion makes our little car rock back and forth, but Yelena doesn't seem to mind. My arms are wrapped tightly around her, and hers around me, which makes it seem like nothing could harm us even if we tumbled down a hundred feet.

I've never been so consumed by a kiss. The whole world has disappeared around us. There's nothing but this car full of sunset light and our two bodies wrapped together.

Then the car jolts to a stop, and the attendant pulls the door open.

Yelena and I break apart, surprised. The ride is over. We missed the whole thing, lost in that kiss.

As we climb out of the Ferris wheel, I say, "Sorry about that—I didn't mean to distract you the whole time."

If I didn't know better, I'd think Yelena was blushing.

"I don't mind," she says. "Actually…it was perfect."

Maybe I should wait to ask her this later, via text, so I don't put her on the spot. But I can't help myself.

I say, "Will you go out with me again? For free this time?"

I say it lightly, like I'm joking. But my heart is hammering against my ribs.

Yelena is quiet. I can tell she's running through something in her mind. I hope she's wondering how her father will react to that and not trying to decide if she likes me or not.

At last she says, in her low sober voice, "I'm not sure that's a good idea, Sebastian."

"I know it isn't. Do you want to, though?"

She looks up at me, those beautiful eyes still illuminated in the fading light. "Yes," she says, just as fiercely as she told me that she wanted to ride the Ferris wheel. "I want to."

"Don't worry about your father, then. I'm a big boy. I can take care of myself."

CHAPTER 6
YELENA

WHEN SEBASTIAN DROPS ME OFF AT MY HOUSE, IT'S FULLY DARK outside. Rodion Abdulov opens the door for me. He's silent, as always. Rodion had his tongue cut out by his former *Bratva* boss for reasons unknown. My brother says Abdulov used to be jovial and sarcastic—until he made a joke at the wrong time and his boss punished him so he could never speak again. But my brother can't be trusted when it comes to letting truth get in the way of a good story.

I certainly can't imagine Rodion ever making a joke. I've never seen him smile, and in executing my father's orders, he's not just obedient—he's zealous. I think he enjoys cruelty.

Tonight his silence seems particularly judgmental. I always feel like I'm in trouble when I come home, no matter what I was doing while I was out.

My father is working in his office, a tumbler of whiskey sitting in his right hand. He's puffing on one of those fat cream cigars that smell like vanilla and coffee. It's not an unpleasant scent, but it sets me on edge, as does every familiar element of this office: the heavy leather chairs, the dark ebony desk, and the portrait of Generalissimo Alexander Suvorov on the wall. Suvorov is my father's hero—he never lost a single major battle in the whole of his military career. Even Napoleon admired him.

My father's pale eyes peer at me through a haze of blue smoke. "How was your date?"

"Fine," I say shortly.

"Anything of note?"

"No." I shake my head. "We just went to a street fair."

Just a street fair. Just the most enjoyable afternoon of my life.

I felt so free and happy walking through all that color and noise, seeing all those strange and unusual things I'd never seen before.

I'm used to having big men walk beside me as my guard. But with Sebastian, it was different—he wasn't there next to me. He was there *with* me, showing me any pretty or intriguing thing I missed, explaining anything I didn't understand, entertaining me with jokes and conversation.

I misjudged Sebastian. I assumed he'd be a spoiled American mafioso—arrogant and presumptuous, but ultimately soft. The more time I spend with him, the more I see Sebastian isn't arrogant or presumptuous at all. Actually, he's perceptive and quite respectful.

And I don't think he's soft either. Iov wasn't holding back when they fought—Sebastian beat the shit out of him. Plus, the way he bid for me at the auction…he wasn't doing it to show off. He saw what he wanted, and he went after it.

Of course, I'm not going to say any of this to my father.

I feel him studying me, his eyes drilling into my face as if he can see through my skull to the thoughts swirling around within.

"You will continue to see him," he orders.

That's what I want to do anyway. But not because my father commands it. Not under his observation, as part of his plan.

I don't know what his plan is, exactly. He doesn't share details with me. In fact, he delights in withholding them. I'm not permitted in the room while he has his strategy sessions with his top lieutenants and my brother.

I know more about his business than he thinks, though. I'm

smart, and I'm observant. I don't skulk around spying like Rodion does, but I hear things all the same.

Adrian tells me things, too. Or at least he used to. The closer my father pulls him into the business, the more Adrian drifts away from me. Sometimes things are just as they always were between us. But sometimes they're not.

Whatever Papa has in store for the Gallos, it isn't good.

I've seen his expression when he talks about the Italian and Irish Mafia. He's furious at how they've insulted the *Bratva*. How they've stolen our territory and crushed our businesses. How they've killed our men.

Fergus Griffin shot Kolya Kristoff at the Harris Theater, then used his political connections to walk away without a backward glance. That *might* have been forgiven—after all, Kristoff was an arrogant shit who thought he could take on the two most powerful families in the city without properly securing his alliance with the Polish Mafia.

But then the Gallos stole the Winter Diamond.

That's an insult that can never be forgotten.

That stone has an almost mythic quality for the *Bratva*. All sorts of rumors and legends center around it. It's believed to bring luck to anyone who possesses it. Once lost, however, all that luck turns to ruin.

I don't believe in curses. But it is true that shortly after the stone was stolen from Tsar Nicholas II, his entire family was executed by revolutionaries.

From then on, the diamond passed from owner to owner. From thief to collector, from collector to oligarch. Finally, it was recovered by the Hermitage Museum in Saint Petersburg.

It's a near-flawless blue diamond, fifty carats, almost priceless—though, of course, when people want to sell something, they'll always agree on some price.

The *Bratva* knew Kristoff had the stone. He stole it from the museum. He pretended he didn't, but you can't keep something like that a secret. He used one of his lieutenants in the robbery without telling him what they were stealing. The timing of the theft was obvious, and the lieutenant kept his eyes open constantly, looking for where Kristoff had hidden it in his house. He glimpsed it once in Kristoff's personal safe, as Kristoff was putting away a deposit of cash. Probably Kristoff knew it had been seen because when he died shortly thereafter and his lieutenants cleared out his safe, the diamond was nowhere to be found.

It took several more months to trace where he'd put it. Like a fool, he'd stored it with an outsider: Raymond Page, the man who operated Alliance Bank in Chicago. He'd put it in his vault, which was supposed to be impenetrable. But, of course, every vault has its weakness. In this case, that weakness was Nero Gallo.

It was my father who discovered the truth. He invited Page for an evening cruise on Lake Michigan. He acted as if he wanted to resume the *Bratva*'s business relationship with Alliance Bank now that he was replacing Kristoff as head of the *Bratva*.

I was there that night, along with my brother—maybe to put Page at ease. To make it look like a social event.

Page was not at ease. He'd brought two bodyguards, both selected for size and intimidation, and both armed.

As we all enjoyed a dinner of poached halibut and fine dry Riesling, Raymond Page began to relax. More importantly, his guards relaxed, too.

Rodion offered them cigarettes laced with opium. The drug took effect quickly. It wasn't enough to kill them outright, but it slowed them down to the point that it was easy for Rodion and Iov to put bullets through their foreheads before they could pull their guns.

Their bodies dropped to the deck, and Page dropped his fork on his plate, his béchamel sauce splashing on my bare arm. I was seated right next to him, a position that had thoroughly annoyed me as it allowed him to peer down the front of my dress all night long.

Now he wasn't looking anywhere but at my father, his face frozen in horror.

He started to sputter and beg, trying to explain himself.

"It wasn't my fault! I didn't give them any information! They broke into the vault! They stole the stone! I had nothing to do with it. I didn't—"

My father stayed perfectly calm and even kept eating his halibut in measured bites. "Who stole it?"

"It was Nero Gallo!" Page cried. "I'm sure of it. He came to the vault a week before. He was looking at the layout, the cameras…"

"Where is the stone now?"

"I don't know!" Page moaned. "I've been looking and listening. I have money out in a hundred places, bribes if anyone can tell me where it went…"

My father ignored this, since obviously Page's efforts were yielding nothing. "How did Nero Gallo find out about the stone?"

That was where Raymond Page hesitated. He didn't want to tell that particular piece of information. Maybe that's when my father decided to torture him. Or maybe he planned to do that either way.

We had sailed far out on the lake by that point. Far away from shore or any other boats. If Page had been paying attention, he would have noticed that we weren't following the usual cruise route.

The water was rough that far from shore. It rocked the boat hard, making my wine slosh over the rim of my glass. I hadn't touched the wine or my food. That was another thing Page might have noticed, had he not been so distracted by my chest instead.

Rodion tied Page to a chair. He stripped off his shoes and socks. He got a set of bolt cutters with wicked curved blades, and he opened them around Page's big toe.

"Noooo!" Page howled. "Please! I'll tell you everything!"

"Yes. You will," my father said, taking another bite of his fish.

He nodded to Rodion, and Rodion squeezed the handles of the

bolt cutters with a vicious snap. Page's toe rolled away across the wooden deck.

In the end, Page confessed everything—that he'd told his daughter about the diamond because she had a fascination with gemstones. That he'd even let her hold it once after swearing her to secrecy. That Nero Gallo had seduced said daughter and convinced her to bring him down to the vault. That she had likely told him about the diamond concealed within.

"Please don't hurt her," he mumbled through lips pale with shock and blood loss. He had lost every one of his toes by that point, and some of his fingers. "It wasn't her fault. She didn't know...she didn't know anything..."

I was forced to watch the whole thing—Adrian, too. He sat on the other side of me, holding my hand beneath the linen tablecloth.

I wanted to scream. I wanted to cry. But I couldn't do any of that with my father so close. I kept my eyes fixed on my plate, wishing I could stop my ears from hearing Page's howls of pain.

Certain that he'd learned every piece of information Page knew, my father nodded to Rodion. Rodion put a bullet in the back of the banker's head. Then he finished removing the rest of Page's fingers and pulled his teeth, too, so it would be harder to identify the body if it were ever found. He stripped off Page's clothes, as well as the bodyguards'. Then he weighed down the bodies and dumped them over the railing into the lake.

The deckhands started mopping the blood off the floor. My father had bought the boat and hired the staff himself. That's another thing Page might have noticed—that every one of the staff had *Bratva* tattoos on their arms or necks beneath their crisp white polo shirts.

But most people aren't very observant. Even in our world, where a momentary lapse can get you killed.

As the boat turned around to head back to shore, my stomach lurched. I had to stand and walk to the railing, where I leaned over and vomited into the water.

"What's wrong, *malen'kiy*?" my father asked.

"Nothing," I said. "Just a little seasick."

"Drink your wine. That will help."

I sat again, picking up the slender stem of my glass between shaking fingers. When I lifted the glass to my lips, I saw a tiny droplet of blood suspended in the wine, dark as garnet against the amber-colored Riesling. My father was watching, so I had to drink it.

These are all the things I'm remembering while my father watches me with his ice-chip eyes. Eyes that look very like Suvorov's portrait hanging on the wall.

My father was in the KGB, in the OP Directorate—the division tasked with combating organized crime. After being blocked for promotion by a rival, my father quit the agency and used what he learned to rise through the ranks of the *Bratva* instead. Within three years he was one of the biggest bosses in Moscow. He ordered his former antagonist to be murdered, along with his family.

Papa has a military mind. He's a strategist. He makes plans and he executes them—ruthlessly and flawlessly. He's no flashy gangster like Kristoff, egotistical and easily outwitted.

"You will keep seeing Sebastian Gallo," he repeats. "But don't give yourself to him. You have to keep him hungry. Leave him wanting."

"Yes, Father." I nod.

My virginity is just one more tool in my father's arsenal—something he'll give away at a time of his choosing, to the man of his choice.

I won't have any say in the matter.

CHAPTER 7
SEBASTIAN

I KEEP TAKING YELENA OUT, MORE AND MORE FREQUENTLY.

She asks me to meet her in different places, probably because she doesn't want me getting the third degree from her father any more than necessary. She tells me he knows that we're dating. Which is a relief—this could blow up in my face spectacularly if we were caught sneaking around behind his back.

Actually, it's my family who's in the dark more than hers.

I know Nero will think I'm out of my mind dating the daughter of the newest *Bratva* boss—especially when our past conflicts aren't entirely smoothed over. But he's too busy with the South Shore development to notice.

As long as I keep handling my side of the family business, picking up the slack now that Dante's gone, and taking care of anything my father doesn't feel like doing, nobody pays much attention to what I do in my spare time.

That spare time is increasingly devoted to Yelena.

The more time I spend with her, the more I want.

I take her all over Chicago, showing her the city.

I take her to the Art Institute of Chicago and the Cloud Gate sculpture in Millennium Park. We go shopping on the Magnificent Mile and visit the Lincoln Park Zoo. I offer to take her up to Skydeck, the observation deck, knowing she might decline since she's not a fan of heights. But, buoyed by the success of our Ferris wheel ride, Yelena agrees to go.

We take the elevator up 94 floors. When we step out, we're faced with a wall of glass, the entire city spread out beneath us. We're so high up that it's almost like being in an airplane instead of a building. I point out the parts of the city I recognize: the marinas, the river, the area of Lincoln Park we visited two days ago.

Yelena looks down on the city, her eyes wide. "Everything here is so...grand," she says. "It's all on such a massive scale."

"Does it make you feel tiny?"

"It does...and it doesn't. It makes me feel insignificant...but also like I could accomplish anything here. Like there's no limit."

"What would you do?" I ask her. "If you could do anything?"

"I don't know..." She looks down at the spreading grid of streets and high-rises. "I guess...I'd like to go to school for music. Not as a performer—for composition. I get these melodies playing in my head...I wish I were better at arranging them and setting them down."

"I want to hear you play," I tell her. I've been curious for a while.

Yelena flushes. "I told you I haven't practiced in a long time. There's no piano in our new house."

"There is at mine."

It was my mother's, and it's still upstairs in her music room. Nobody uses it anymore except Aida on rare occasions. But I know my father would never get rid of it.

He's not home today, surprisingly. Aida roped him into some dinner with Fergus and Imogen Griffin and a bunch of people from the Chicago Literary Society. Maybe she thought he'd like it, since he's one of the most well-read people I've ever met. Or maybe she was just desperate to get him out of the house and thought that was a good excuse.

Regardless of the reason, it means I can show Yelena my mother's music room without having to make awkward introductions.

"You want to show me your house?" Yelena says.

"Yes."

"All right. But I want to stand in that glass box first."

The box in question is suspended from the side of the building, about thirteen hundred feet in the air. The floor is completely transparent, as are the walls.

"You want to get in there?" I say in surprise.

"Yes," she says firmly.

As we approach, I can see shivers running up and down her body. Her face is pale, and her lips are white.

I don't want to talk her out of it, so I just take her arm instead, to help steady her steps.

She clings to my bicep, shuffling her feet along like she's scared to even pick them up. Bit by bit, we go into the box until we're entirely outside the tower, floating in the air with only a few inches of plexiglass between us and an endless drop.

Yelena looks like she might pass out. Her expression is equal parts horrified and fascinated.

"I don't know why this scares me so much," she says. "Logically, I know it's safe—hundreds of people stand in here every day without falling. Still, my whole body is screaming at me."

Her muscles are tight with tension. She forces herself to look down even as a soot-gray swift soars by directly beneath our feet.

I can't help but be impressed by her force of will, her desire to push her own limits. I usually do what comes naturally to me. I don't often force myself to do the opposite of what I like.

At last, Yelena lets out a little sigh and says, "All right, we can go now."

She seems calm and relieved as we head back toward the elevator.

"Maybe you're just a masochist," I tease her.

"I could be," Yelena says quietly. "Sometimes when you're denied the usual pleasures…you find other ways to entertain your mind."

She's alluded to the fact her home life hasn't been happy, though she doesn't often give me specifics. She much prefers to talk about her brother, whom she adores, versus her father.

I want to learn everything about her, but she's tricky—like a puzzle box where you have to line up every piece perfectly to get it to open. Often, right when I think we're getting closer to each other, she pulls away again.

I can tell it's going to take a long time for her to truly trust me.

I drive Yelena back to my family's house on Meyer Avenue. It's a massive old Victorian mansion on a heavily wooded lot. The trees grow so thick all around that you can only see bits and pieces of the house as you approach. The parts you can see don't look particularly impressive— the gables are sagging with age, and the wooden trim needs painting. The leaded windows look mysterious and dark even in the daytime.

But to me, it's the most beautiful old house imaginable. Every bit of it is home. I love the creaks and groans, the scent of the dusty drapes and the oiled wood floors.

I park on the street so I can take Yelena inside through the front door instead of via the underground garage. We walk through the front garden, which is full of fragrant lilac bushes, black cherry trees, and box elder maples. A stone birdbath reflects a circle of sky like a mirror.

The wooden steps are sagging, covered in blown lilac blossoms. As we crush them beneath our feet, that sweet scent rises, warm and summery.

"Have you always lived here?" Yelena asks me.

"All my life. Until I moved on campus for school."

"What was it like being at college? Just like in the movies?"

I consider. Before this month, I would have told you that was the happiest time in my life: Surrounded by friends, famous at my school, playing a sport I loved, and barely paying attention to my classes. Parties every weekend and games I treated with the seriousness of an all-out war.

But now…it's all starting to seem a little silly. I was a kid, playing a game, reveling in the attention.

I think about all the high fives and the pats on the back, and they don't seem particularly valuable anymore.

Now I think I'd prefer the approval of just one person…if it were the right person.

"Yeah, it was like in the movies," I tell her. "Only the cafeteria food is even worse than you think."

Yelena smiles. She's already learned how much I love food. "That must have been hard for you."

"It was. I almost wasted away."

I unlock the front door. I still have my key. All the Gallo children have keys. This will always be our home, no matter where we go.

"No guard?" Yelena says in surprise.

"There's an alarm system and cameras," I tell her. "But we don't have live-in security."

She frowns. "Your father lives here alone?"

"With our housekeeper."

I call out for Greta, but she doesn't answer. She's probably grocery shopping—taking the opportunity to dawdle around to all her favorite shops while my father is out.

"Too bad," I say. "I wanted you to meet her."

Yelena still looks uncomfortable at our lack of security—probably because her father's house is so closely guarded at all times. She might be right. When Dante and Nero were living here, it wasn't a concern. But we do have plenty of old enemies who might still hold a grudge.

I take her through the main part of the house—the ancient sitting room with its portraits of ancestors long dead. My father's library, which is stuffed with every book he's ever read.

Then I show her my old room, papered with posters signed by Kobe Bryant and John Stockton.

"What about Michael Jordan?" she says, raising an eyebrow at me. "Isn't he from here?"

"No poster—but I do have one of his cards."

I show her my 1987 Fleer basketball card, encased in Lucite.

"Are those worth a fortune now?" she asks me.

"Some are—not this one. But I thought it was pretty fucking cool when I was a kid."

Most of my old furniture is still here, exactly as it used to be, including my twin bed, which I used to sleep on with my feet hanging off the end. I feel like Yelena and I are both looking at the neatly tucked-in covers pulled tightly across the mattress. A funny tension arises between us.

I'm thinking how that youthful version of myself would have died to see a girl this gorgeous in my bedroom.

I'm not sure what Yelena is thinking.

We've kissed on every one of our dates, but neither of us has pushed it further yet. I'm trying to be respectful of her strict family situation. Despite my discipline, every time I get near her, I'm dying to put my hands all over her.

To distract myself, I say, "Let me show you the music room."

My mother's music room is on the top floor of the house. It's one of the prettiest and most sunlit spaces, with large colored-glass windows on three sides.

Her piano is a gorgeous Steinway—mahogany brown, the wood carved with scrolls and curlicues, flowers and vines. The room still smells faintly of her perfume and the papery scent of sheet music.

Yelena approaches the piano with an air of awe. "It's a beautiful instrument."

"We have it tuned every year," I tell her. "So it should sound all right."

She hesitates next to the plush leather bench. I say, "Go ahead, sit down."

Watching her slide into place gives me a chill.

The way that Yelena sits down and the way Aida does are completely different. Yelena sits with the same perfect upright posture my mother always had, with her lovely slim hands poised above the keys in exactly the same way.

They don't look alike—my mother was dark-haired and Yelena, fair. But I can tell at once that Yelena is a skilled musician, much as she downplays it.

Her fingers gently press the keys, testing the sound. The notes ring out clean and clear, echoing around this corner space with its vaulted ceilings.

Yelena starts to play from memory.

Her hands move flawlessly across the keys, no stumbling or hesitation. There's a flow to her playing—there's feeling. Her eyes are closed, and I can almost watch the music pour directly from her brain, down her arms, through her fingers.

I've never heard the song before. It reminds me of a cool, rainy night, of a person searching for something lost. As she plays, images rise before my eyes and fade away again: Light reflected on glass. Empty city streets. And the way my mother's hands used to move smoothly like that, when playing the piano or when tucking a lock of hair behind her ear.

♫ *"Naval"—Yann Tiersen*

I'm startled when Yelena stops, the song finished.

"What else do you want to hear?" she asks me.

"Play me something Russian," I say.

Yelena starts to play something light and rapid that somehow conjures the feeling of snowflakes swirling down and maybe a music box ballerina twirling slowly on a stand. It's wistful and plaintive.

♫ *"Once Upon a December"—Emile Pandolfi*

"What's that?" I ask her.

She laughs softly. "It's not really Russian," she says. "It's from an old animated movie—*Anastasia*. It's about one of the Romanov daughters. In the movie, she survives the revolution, but she hits her head and loses her memory. Later she realizes she's the missing princess and is reunited with some of her family."

She plays the refrain of the song again, soft and light.

"I loved that movie…" she says. "I thought how incredible it would be to find out you were a princess. To be plucked out of your old life, into a new one…"

In a way, Yelena is a princess. A Mafia princess. But I know that's not what she's talking about.

"Is it a true story?" I ask her.

"No. She was shot along with the rest of her family. It was confirmed with DNA testing not too long ago. That's why real life isn't a movie."

Yelena stops playing. Her hands drop into her lap.

"One more," I ask her. "Play me something you wrote."

Her cheeks flush pink. I think she'll refuse. But after a moment, she lifts her hands again, delicately pressing her fingers to the piano keys.

Yelena's song is the most beautiful of all. I don't know anything about music, so I can't describe why or how it has such an effect on me. It starts slowly, subtly. Then it builds and builds, with a pull like an undertow, dragging me under. The music swirls all around the room, filling every bit of space from floor to ceiling. It's wild and haunting, melancholic but insistent. It's something inside her calling out to something inside me, demanding I listen. Demanding I understand.

When she stops, I can't tell if she's been playing for a minute or an hour.

"That was incredible," I say.

My words seem weak compared to what she just did. She expressed something powerful, and I can't match it with a compliment.

All I can do is say, "I'm stunned, seriously. You wrote that?"

"Yes," Yelena says with a shyness that I've never seen in her before. "You really liked it?"

"Of course I did."

"My father says everything I play is depressing."

"Well…I wasn't going to say anything. But I'm starting to think your dad might be a bit of a dick."

Yelena snorts out a laugh from behind those supremely talented slim fingers.

She fixes me with her gorgeous eyes, the color of the sky right before it darkens.

"He's dangerous," she tells me seriously. "Very dangerous, Sebastian. He has resentments. Ambitions."

"I know what he is. That's why I didn't call you that first week. I wanted to, believe me. But I know this isn't exactly safe for either of us."

She drops her eyes, chewing on the corner of her lip.

"If he's all right with us dating, he can't be that pissed," I tell her. "Maybe we can bury all those past resentments. Move on, make some kind of deal. After all, if my family can make peace with the Griffins…" I wince, thinking of the sound of my knee shattering. "If we can do that, then anybody can learn to get along."

She doesn't answer me right away, twisting her hands in her lap. She looks upset. Maybe she thinks I'm too optimistic and her father is sure to lash out eventually.

"Hey." I grab her chin, tilting her face up so she has to look at me. "Don't worry about me. I told you, I can take care of myself. I can handle your father if I have to. I've been up against worse."

She shakes her head. "There isn't anyone worse."

To stop her worrying, I lean down and kiss her. Her mouth tastes as sweet as ever, even though we haven't been eating funnel cake this time. Her lips are the fullest I've ever touched—it makes kissing her incredibly satisfying. I could do it for hours.

But, god, I want to do so much more than that.

As we kiss, I can't help letting my hands drift down her body.

She's wearing a pale blue cotton sundress with buttons up the front. I let my fingertips trail down her long slender throat, to the shelf of her collarbone, and then a little lower to the top swell of her breast. I feel her suck in a gasp of air as I touch the space between her breasts, which is exactly the width of my middle finger.

Without the piano, the room seems intensely silent. All I can hear is her breath and my own heartbeat. Gently, I trace the shape of her breast, letting my fingers dip into the front of her dress.

She isn't wearing a bra. My thumb passes over her nipple, which is stiff, standing out against the thin material. Yelena lets out a little moan.

I can't stop.

I drop to my knees in front of her, so she's seated on the piano bench and I'm kneeling on the hard wooden floor. I unbutton the top three buttons of her dress, letting those beautiful breasts spill out.

Her tits are creamy white, teardrop shaped, with tan-colored nipples. I take them in my hands, and Yelena moans, pressing her breasts hard against my palms. I can tell she's incredibly sensitive.

I take her breast in my mouth and start to suck. Yelena moans again, grabbing my head and pressing my mouth harder against her chest.

"Oh my god," she groans. "Don't stop."

I go back and forth between her breasts, sucking one nipple and caressing the other with my hand, then switching places, until her nipples are swollen and throbbing and her pale breasts are flushed pink.

Yelena throws her head back, arching her back to present her breast to me more readily, groaning with pleasure.

I know she must be soaking wet. Kneeling between her thighs, I can smell the sweet, musky scent of her pussy. It makes me salivate.

I hadn't planned to take this further—not just yet. But I can't hold back any longer. I shove her thighs apart and push her skirt up. She is wearing panties—white cotton. I pull the crotch to the side, revealing a shell-pink pussy, gleaming wet.

I can't resist it. I bury my face between her legs, inhaling that intoxicating scent. It turns me into an animal. I have to lick and rub my face in that sweet cunt; I need to taste her, touch her, make her scream.

"Oh! Oh!" Yelena gasps, thrusting her hands into my hair. She doesn't have to urge me on—I'm eating her pussy like a starving man. I'm pushing my tongue all the way inside her, then gently sucking on her clit.

While I'm doing that, I reach up to caress those breasts again.

Yelena can barely stand the combination of the two. She tries to hold back her cries, but it's impossible. She's writhing and grinding on my face while I keep hold of both breasts, squeezing and tugging on her nipples, massaging the whole breast, and then pulling my fingers all the way down to the tip.

Her thighs are resting on my shoulders, and she's squeezing around my head, her clit grinding back and forth on my tongue. She's breathing faster and harder, crying out, "*Pozhaluysta!*"

She gives one last convulsive clench of her thighs, her back arched and her entire body taut and shaking. I squeeze her nipples hard, heightening the intensity and pleasure for as long as I can.

Then, at last, Yelena relaxes, her face flushed and her skin glowing warm.

"Ohhh, what are you doing to me...?" She groans.

"I need you," I tell her. "I need more of you. I can't wait any longer."

CHAPTER 8
YELENA

OH MY GOD, I'VE NEVER EXPERIENCED ANYTHING LIKE THAT.

I've never been touched like Sebastian touches me.

He sets every nerve in my body on fire. He's got me gasping, panting, desperate for more.

That wasn't an orgasm. It was a glimpse at nirvana.

When we leave the Gallo house, I can barely walk in a straight line. Sebastian can't stop grinning—he's pretty fucking pleased with himself. As he should be.

It's starting to get late. I should really head back home. My father knows I'm still seeing Sebastian—on his orders—but he doesn't know how often. I sneak out to meet Sebastian multiple times a week because I can't get enough of him. But I don't want my father to know how close we're getting. That's not part of his plan.

I don't know what his plan actually is—all I know is that it doesn't involve my falling head over heels for our enemy.

Still, I can't seem to stop myself.

I'm so confused. Part of me thinks I should break things off with Sebastian. I know this can't possibly end well. If I actually care about him, I should end it now and tell my father Sebastian doesn't want to see me anymore. That will put a stop to whatever idea he's got in his head.

But the idea of cutting this off...I can't stand it.

This is the first time in my life that I've ever felt happy. When I'm with Sebastian, I forget about my father, and his soldiers and lieutenants, and our house that's like a gilded prison. I forget about the constant pressure and constant disapproval. The unspoken threats. The total lack of privacy and the assumption that I'm just an accessory that can be used as my father sees fit.

Sebastian makes me laugh. He makes me feel safe. He takes me to beautiful places so we can experience new sights and smells and tastes together.

When I'm with him, I feel like myself. Not like a daughter, or sister, or *Bratva* princess. Just Yelena.

I want to tell him the truth. At the very least, I should tell him that it wasn't chance that we met that night. That I wasn't actually being kidnapped. I'm embarrassed by that deception. I was following my father's orders—he thought it was crucial that Sebastian and I seemed to meet by chance. And he thought the best way to captivate Sebastian was to make him think he "saved" me.

Now I realize it only worked because Sebastian is a good man. He intervened to help a stranger. He protected me before he knew a thing about me.

He had no idea that I was a shiny lure with a hook concealed inside.

I have to tell him.

But I'm afraid.

We've only known each other for a few weeks. If I tell him I was lying to him from the moment we met...why would he ever trust me again?

I'm in a hole, and I don't know how to get out. Every day that passes, I dig deeper and deeper. Every time I stay silent, it's like I'm lying to him all over again.

He'll be angry. I know he will. He won't want to see me anymore.

I can't go back to the way my life was before—dull and lonely, without even a glimmer of hope.

Besides, if Sebastian breaks up with me, if my father finds out I ruined his plans…I don't know what he'll do to me. His temper is horrifying. When he goes into a rage, nothing and no one is safe from him.

I'm in such an awful position.

"What should we do now?" Sebastian asks.

"I probably should go home…"

"Don't go yet," he urges. "Stay with me a little longer."

"What do you want to do?"

"Let's drive up to the dunes and sit out on the sand for a while. I've got some blankets in the back of the truck."

The thought of sitting on the lakeshore with Sebastian is a thousand times more enticing than the idea of going home. Even though I know it's a bad idea, I can't resist.

I climb into Sebastian's truck, which is becoming more and more familiar to me. I love the way it smells like him—like hawthorn and nutmeg, like fresh laundry and rubber. The seats are worn, and the windshield is cracked. I like that Sebastian doesn't care. Despite his good looks, he isn't vain. He doesn't wear brand-name clothes or an expensive watch.

In fact, the only jewelry he wears is the tiny gold medallion on a chain around his neck.

"What is that?" I ask him.

"It's Saint Eustachius. Patron saint of hunters, trappers, firefighters, and, uh…difficult situations."

"I didn't know you were Catholic."

"I'm not. My uncle was. He used to wear this every day. He said it was lucky. Then he gave it to me…and he died a month later. So maybe he was right."

I swallow hard, thinking of the Winter Diamond. Kristoff put it in a vault, and he was shot shortly thereafter. If my father's right, the Gallos don't have the stone anymore either. They sold it to fund their real estate development.

"How did your uncle die?" I ask.

Sebastian shifts uncomfortably in his seat, turning the wheel to head out of the city, toward the state park.

"Well…he was killed by *Bratva*. But I don't want you to feel bad about that. It was fifteen years ago, when the Chicago chapter was run by the boss before the last boss. So…I doubt it was anyone you know."

My stomach is churning, and my face is on fire. I should tell Sebastian. I should tell him.

But I can't. There's so much bad blood between our families. So much mistrust. He only likes me because he thinks I'm different from my father and his men. If he finds out I was part of their plan from the beginning…he won't forgive me. He won't be able to see past that. And his family won't either. They'll be certain it's proof that I'm *Bratva*, too. A liar and schemer. Full of ill intent and rivalry.

"Were you close to him?" I ask.

"Yes. He was my father's youngest brother—not that much older than Dante. So he kind of seemed like a big brother to me, too. He was competitive. He loved to take the piss out of people. But he wasn't cruel. You know, most people who like to tease and joke, they cross the line sometimes. They don't really care if you're laughing along with them. Francesco wasn't like that. He didn't hit you where it hurt. But he was overconfident. He never thought he could lose at anything. Even if he was ten pieces down playing chess against Nero, he always thought he was about to come back…"

Sebastian sighs, pulling into the parking lot next to the beach and turning off the engine. "That's probably what got him killed. When you're endlessly optimistic…you're going to be wrong eventually."

Sebastian climbs out of the truck, grabbing a couple of heavy outdoor blankets from the bed.

We take our shoes and socks off, leaving them in the truck, so we can walk across the sand barefoot.

The dunes aren't as crowded as the beaches close to the city, especially not in the evening on a weekday. Sebastian and I walk far up the shore, away from any other people. It's a little rockier here, but I don't mind. We have the blankets to lie on.

The sun has almost gone down. Heat is still radiating up from the sand. Even more heat comes out of Sebastian's body. I'm lying with my head on his chest, feeling the steady rise and fall of his lungs. Little waves break on the beach in almost exactly the same rhythm.

He's stroking his hands through my hair.

Sebastian has an incredible sense of touch. His hands are so large and long fingered that you'd think they'd be clumsy, but it's exactly the opposite. He's a true athlete, never uncoordinated. He touches me with the perfect mix of strength and delicacy, not too hard or too soft. Teasing out my most sensitive and responsive areas.

Even though he's so tall, his movements are smooth and precise. His reflexes are perfect. I think I could sweep an entire set of dishes off a countertop, and he'd catch every one before they hit the floor.

And then there's that face.

I roll over on my side to look at him.

His skin is so deeply tanned that you might think he was Latin American. His face is long and lean, with a little stubble that fails to hide the boyishness of his features. His eyes are the most striking part of him. They're brown, but not any brown I've seen before. The irises contain every shade of caramel and gold, bordered by dark smoky rings and framed by thick black lashes. His eyebrows are straight dark slashes, and his thick curls hang down almost over his eyes.

Then those lips…almost as full as mine. Finely shaped, but still completely masculine.

I lean over to kiss him.

Every time I kiss Sebastian, I think I'll get used to it. I think it will start to feel mundane. But that never happens. Every single time, he takes my breath away all over again.

The whole world falls away around us—the last rays of the sun, the warm rough sand, the sound of the water on the shore. It all disappears, and all I can feel are his lips and tongue and his strong hands gripping my shoulders.

Sebastian rolls on top of me. I realize how big and strong he really is with his full weight on me. I'm completely hidden beneath him. Completely trapped under him.

I don't feel afraid. Quite the opposite—it seems like the safest place in the world.

I want to stay in his arms forever.

He kisses me more deeply, his body grinding against mine. I feel his cock stiffening, pressing against my bare thigh with only his jeans between us.

I feel my own body responding. He made me come harder than I have in my life only an hour ago, but already I want more. Already I'm dying to feel that same sensation flushing through my system, wiping every fear and stress out of my mind.

His cock is getting harder and harder, until the pressure on my leg is almost painful. His arousal makes me aroused. It makes me want to touch him the way he touched me.

I reach down and snap open the button of his jeans. I tug down his zipper and reach inside his boxer shorts.

His cock is so hard that it's rammed down the leg of his jeans. I can barely slip my hand down to touch it.

I close my hand around his shaft, shocked by its thickness. His cock is bigger than a banana—it's almost as thick as my own wrist. And much warmer. I feel it throbbing against my palm. Sebastian groans with frustration.

Gently, I tug his cock upright, and it gets even harder now that the blood can flow freely. His erection juts out the open fly of his jeans, his cock brown and veiny, with a heavy head swollen with blood.

I stroke his cock with my hand, marveling that I'm doing

something completely forbidden out here in the open. I'm not allowed to touch a man like this. I'm not allowed to do anything sexual without my father's permission.

I can't believe how simultaneously soft and hard Sebastian's cock is. The skin is like silk, and the flesh beneath is iron. When my fingers catch the little ridge under the head of his cock, Sebastian moans into my mouth.

His cock is leaking fluid, which helps lubricate my hand. I slide my palm back and forth across the head, gently tugging and squeezing. Sebastian is thrusting into my hand, and those powerful thrusts make me soaking wet, imagining what it would feel like to have that cock penetrating another part of my body.

Sebastian reaches his hand under my skirt and slips his fingers inside my panties so he can touch me at the same time. My pussy is still swollen and sensitive from earlier. He rubs his fingers in gentle circles on my clit, then reaches down a little lower to slide his finger inside me.

Oh my god, just the feeling of that finger is exquisite. The warmth and pleasure are like an itch being scratched.

I want more. I want so much more than that.

Sebastian wants it, too.

Without speaking, I pull off my underwear and spread my legs a little wider. Sebastian positions his warm heavy cock at my entrance, looking down into my eyes.

"Are you sure?" he asks.

I'm not sure. Actually, if I'm sure of anything, it's that this is a terrible idea. I'm not supposed to even fool around with Sebastian, let alone let him take my virginity.

My father subscribes to the American idiom *why buy the cow when you can get the milk for free?* He intends to sell this particular cow for a hefty price. He'll be enraged if he discovers I've destroyed my value in his eyes.

But here's the problem. I want to fuck Sebastian. I want it more desperately than I've ever wanted anything.

If my father intends to sell me off at some point in the future…
then I want to lose my virginity right here and now with the person
of my choice. No one can steal what I don't have anymore.

"I want you," I tell Sebastian.

That's 100 percent true. No lies, no hidden motivation.

Sebastian pushes his cock inside me, slowly at first. Even though
I can tell he's being as careful as possible, it still hurts. He's just so
fucking big. A tampon or a finger isn't close. Not even a tenth the
size.

Seeing me wince, he pauses and says, "Do you want me to stop?"

"No." I shake my head. "Keep going."

Sebastian kisses me again, stroking my hair back from my face
with his free hand. That feels good. My body relaxes just a little,
and his cock slides in a little more. But it's not all the way in yet. It's
reached a kind of sticking point where it doesn't seem to want to go
any farther.

Sebastian doesn't seem impatient. He kisses and holds me, his
tongue soft and warm in my mouth, his breath sweet and sensual.
He touches my face; he caresses my breasts.

And then, finally, with one more thrust, he breaks through the
last barrier. I feel a sharp tearing sensation and a flood of warmth.
Now his cock is better lubricated. It slides all the way in, until I'm
completely filled by him.

He's all the way inside me, and I'm looking up in his eyes, thinking this is the closest I've ever been to another person. Whatever
happens after this, Sebastian will be my first lover, now and always.

My pussy is burning with pain and intensity. Tears leak out of
the corners of my eyes, running down toward my ears.

"Are you okay?" Sebastian asks.

I nod, saying, "I'm good. It's just…a lot."

"You feel incredible," Sebastian groans. "You're so beautiful,
Yelena…I know you know that, but I have to tell you anyway."

He starts to thrust in and out of me, slowly and carefully. Now,

finally, I feel something more like pleasure than pain. A warmth deep inside me, which spreads outward until my pussy feels that pleasant ache again, and my whole body relaxes and thrums with sensation.

I can hear the waves again. If the ocean were pleasure and my body were sand, then each time Sebastian thrusts into me, it's like a wave breaking on the shore, soaking me in bliss.

And like the tide, the waves are coming stronger and faster. I feel like I'm about to be submerged.

"Keep going," I beg him. "Just like that."

Sebastian wraps his arms around me, pressing our bodies tightly together. He kisses me, his tongue thrusting into my mouth at the same time as his cock penetrates deep inside me. My thighs are wrapped around his, and my clit is grinding against his body. Every inch of my skin is lined up with his. The more we touch, the more intense the sensation.

I can feel his breath speeding up in time with his thrusts. His ass is flexing against my calves, driving into me harder and harder. It doesn't hurt at all anymore—all I feel is warm liquid pleasure running through my veins like honey.

I already had the best climax of my life today.

What's building now isn't a climax—it's a fucking tsunami.

I kiss Sebastian ferociously. I'm biting at his lips, clawing at his back. I need more, more, more of him.

Sebastian squeezes me so hard, I can't breathe. He gives one last monstrous thrust into me, and he lets out a long strangled howl. I feel his cock twitching and pulsing, buried to the hilt in my pussy. That twitching tips me over the edge. With each pulse of cum, my pussy contracts. I'm clamped around him, my whole body shaking, my eyes rolled back in my head. I can't see, or feel, or hear anything except the brilliant flashes of color in my brain. I'm coming so hard that I think my soul left my body.

When I come to again, the beach is dark. There's no warmth

in the sand, and the sky overhead is black, studded with cool-white stars. They're the most stars I've seen since I came to this city.

Sebastian is warm. His heavy body blankets me, his cock still inside me. He has one arm wrapped tightly around me, and his other hand is cradling the back of my head. His face is buried in my neck.

"Look," I whisper.

He looks up at the sky, seeing the view you can never see when you're fully inside the city because the light pollution drowns it out.

"You like stars, don't you?" he says. "You always point them out."

"My mother got me a telescope. When we went out to the country, we'd go up on the roof to use it."

"Sometimes it freaks me out thinking about space," Sebastian says.

"I find it comforting. Everything out there is so much bigger than anything happening here. Nothing we do can move a single star by even an inch."

"You look like something that fell from heaven," Sebastian says, kissing me gently on the temple.

His arms are wrapped tightly around me.

I don't want him to ever let go.

But I'm realizing how late it is. The dunes are almost an hour from Chicago. We have to get back.

I start to sit up, and Sebastian gently disentangles from me. When his cock pulls free, I see there's blood on his shaft and on my thighs.

"Are you okay?" Sebastian frowns with concern.

"I'm fine."

Actually, I'm alarmed at the blood, worried I got some on my dress since I never actually took it off, only pulled it up around my waist. I have no idea where my underwear went.

"Here," Sebastian says. "Use the blanket to clean up if you like— it's old, it doesn't matter."

The blanket takes care of the worst of the mess, but I still can't find my panties. I either flung them somewhere, or they're buried in the sand.

"Never mind," I say to Sebastian. "We better just leave. I wasn't supposed to be out this late."

"Sure." He gathers up the blankets. "Let's go."

He takes my arm to help me back across the sand. I think I'm walking awkwardly as I do feel a bit raw and sore.

Once we're back in the truck, Sebastian turns to me and says, "That was incredible, Yelena. Just…incredible."

I feel suddenly shy, and yet I want to tell him what I was feeling in that moment.

Biting my lip, I say, "I wanted you to be my first."

Sebastian starts the engine.

"This is a first for me, too," he says, throwing a quick glance in my direction. "The first time I…the first time I'm falling in love with someone."

I'm so dumbfounded that for a moment I think I misheard him.

"Me?" I say. "You're falling in love with *me*?"

Sebastian laughs. "Yeah. I hope that's okay."

I've never felt two such opposing emotions at once: absolute joy at the thought that Sebastian could actually love me, and terror at the thought of losing him when he finds out what I've done.

Misreading my expression, he says, "It's okay, you don't have to say it, too—I know this is way too early. I just wanted you to know this isn't about sex for me. I mean, I wanted to sleep with you, of course. I was dying to. But it's so much more than that. From the moment I met you, Yelena, I was stunned. You're a fighter. You're ferocious, and proud, and brilliant, and I love that about you. You're brave."

I can feel tears pricking at my eyes.

He's wrong.

I'm not brave.

If I were brave, I would tell him the truth. I'd tell my father to fuck off and damn the consequences.

But I'm terrified of my father. He's the monster who's haunted my nightmares since I was a toddler. No one could understand what it's like to grow up in the shadow of a vengeful god—to know that at any moment, if you displease him, he could destroy anything and everything you hold dear. To know that he takes pleasure in hurting you, in crushing the last bit of your rebellious spirit.

Worst of all, my father isn't evil all the time. If I could just hate him constantly, that would be easier. He's so much more insidious than that. He's bought me gifts and allowed me favors. He's given me compliments and even good advice from time to time. He shows benevolence and humanity when it suits him.

He does that to find the weaknesses in my armor. To make me question my own judgment. He provides just enough hope that sometimes I think, *Maybe he'll let me apply to university. Maybe he'll let me marry a man I love, someday. Maybe he's growing kinder. Maybe he'll love me.*

He uses the carrot and the stick. And he saves the information he learns so he can hit me with it at the worst possible moment. I never know what he knows or doesn't. I never know if I'm safe. His manipulation is so entrenched that sometimes I believe he can read the thoughts in my head.

My mother used to bear the brunt of his abuse. But after she died, it focused almost entirely on me.

Now I feel like I'm bound in chains in the darkest of dungeons. Sebastian is offering me a key—a way to get out. But I'm so goddamned terrified that I don't know if I even have the strength to try the locks. Because my father is always watching.

So all I can do is shake my head silently, wanting to tell Sebastian everything but unable to do it.

"You *are* brave," Sebastian says, smiling at me. "You stood in the skybox. If you can do that, you can do anything."

———————

Sebastian drops me off at home. I was supposed to be out shopping, but there's no point continuing with that ruse, since the malls closed hours ago and I don't have any bags of clothing with me.

I can see that the light is off in my father's office, as well as on most of the main floor. A little kernel of hope blooms in my chest, thinking he must be out. I'll be able to sneak in unnoticed.

But as soon as I open the front door, I'm faced with the hulking silent figure of Rodion Abdulov.

Rodion has worked for my father for twelve years, since his last boss cut out his tongue.

Maybe that's why he's so relentlessly loyal—to rehabilitate himself in the eyes of the *Bratva*, to quash any suspicion that he might have resentment over losing the ability to speak. Or maybe it's just his nature. Whatever the reason, he follows my father's orders to the smallest degree, no matter how heinous they might be.

He seems to have decided his most important task of all is to keep an eye on me.

Adrian has a different theory. He thinks Rodion is fixated on me. He thinks Rodion believes that if he serves my father loyally, I'll be given to him as a prize.

It is true that Rodion watches me constantly, following me from room to room in the house. But the way he looks at me is nothing like love. It's more like suspicion or hatred. Maybe he knows how I feel about my father and thinks I'm dangerous.

I try to walk past him. He shifts his bulk so he's blocking my way.

Rodion is a beast of a man, with short dark hair almost exactly the same length as his beard. His small round head sits on a body the shape of a refrigerator, with no neck in between. His eyes are little slits in the puffy flesh of his face, and his nose has been broken several times. I don't know what his teeth look like because he doesn't speak or smile.

It's his hands that upset me the most. He has thick stubby

fingers that I've seen bathed in blood too many times. Even after he cleans up, the remnants of blood linger under his fingernails and in the deep crevices of his hands.

He uses those hands to make his own unlovely curt signs. It's not normal sign language—they're signs that he invented, that his *boyeviks* understand. I understand them, too, though I pretend I don't.

"Get out of my way, please," I say to him coldly. "I want to go up to my room."

Slowly, without moving, he points at the door.

He's asking where I was.

"None of your business," I say. I'm trying to keep my voice as haughty as possible so he doesn't see my nervousness. But Rodion doesn't shift his position in front of me. His piggy little eyes roam over my body.

I can feel his eyes like insects crawling on my skin. I hate it at all times, but it's particularly intolerable now when I'm already feeling nervous about what I've just done.

His eyes fix on the skirt of my dress. The hem is dusty from contact with the sand, but that's not what he's looking at. He's looking at the single spot of dark red blood on the skirt.

He turns his palm over, his hand open—his sign for *what?* He's asking me what happened.

"It's nothing," I say impatiently. "Just a little wine from lunch."

Rodion isn't fooled. He knows what blood looks like better than anyone.

Grabbing the front of my dress, he shoves me up against the wall. I consider screaming, but what good would that do? Any men who came running would be Rodion's soldiers.

I know Rodion has weapons on him at all times: A knife in his pocket and another strapped to his calf. Sometimes two guns in holsters beneath his jacket. And always a Beretta tucked in the back waistband of his pants.

He doesn't need any weapon to subdue me besides his own strength and size.

He's got me pinned against the wall with one meaty forearm, his glittering dark eyes staring down into mine. I can smell his cologne, which isn't warm and pleasant like Sebastian's—it's sharp and acidic, like alcohol. Beneath that, there's the musky animal scent of his sweat.

"Let go of me," I spit, trying to hide my terror.

Instead, Rodion forces my feet apart with his boot. He reaches under my skirt with one hand, keeping me pinned to the wall with the other. Now I do shriek, but it doesn't matter. He touches my pussy with his thick fingers, feeling the flesh that's still swollen and sore.

When he pulls his hand away, I see the gleam of blood and my own wetness on his fingertips—possibly Sebastian's fluids, too.

My heart stops dead in my chest.

If he tells my father about this, Papa will know what I've done.

At that moment, my brother comes into the foyer. For a moment he looks shocked, and then his face darkens with fury.

"GET YOUR FUCKING HANDS OFF HER!" he shouts.

Rodion steps away from me, taking his heavy forearm off my chest. I can breathe again, but just barely because my ribs are still tight with fear.

"What do you think you're doing?" Adrian cries. "How *dare* you touch her?"

Rodion looks between us with silent disdain. He respects my brother more than me, but ultimately, he answers only to our father.

He doesn't bother to make a sign to either of us. He just turns and walks away down the dark hallway.

As soon as he's gone, I sink against the wall, shaking with the difficulty of holding back my tears.

Adrian sits beside me, alarmed and confused.

"What's wrong, *fasol?*" he asks me. *Fasol* is "bean." It's been his nickname for me since we were children because we were two peas in a pod.

I want to tell my brother everything, but even here I can't be sure that no one is listening.

So I just press my face into his shoulder, sobbing silently.

CHAPTER 9
SEBASTIAN

THE NEXT TIME I SEE YELENA, SHE INSISTS I MEET HER AT A MOVIE theater on Southport Avenue.

She's already inside the theater when I get there, sitting all the way in the back row of a throwback showing of *The Grandmaster*. Because it's the middle of the day, only three or four other people are scattered through the seats, none close to us.

Her face looks paler than ever in the flickering light from the screen. She looks tense and frightened, her eyes large and dark in her drained face. I'm hit with a pang of guilt. The night I met Yelena, she looked as powerful as a Valkyrie. But the stress of our relationship has taken a toll on her.

I sit next to her, putting my arm around her shoulders and kissing her. "How are you?"

Without any preamble, she says, "I'm afraid my father is about to find out what we did."

"What do you mean?"

"When I came home last night, Rodion was waiting. He...I think he noticed something."

That doesn't make any sense to me. What could Rodion have noticed, besides maybe some messy hair?

"Are you sure?" I say. "No offense, but that sounds a little paranoid."

Yelena presses her pale lips together, looking down at her hands twisted in her lap. "Trust me," she says quietly. "He knows. And if he knows, it's only a matter of time until he tells my father."

She's upset, and whether she's right or not, I can't bear to see her like that.

I squeeze her tighter, and I say, "Yelena, you don't have to worry about anything. You and I are going to be together, do you understand that? Whatever your father says, whatever my family says, I don't give a fuck. I want you and only you."

Yelena looks up at me, her eyes wide and pleading. "You promise me, Sebastian? We'll be together no matter what?"

"Yes, of course," I say. "I promise."

Bright tears glint in the corners of her eyes, but as always, she's too stubborn to let them fall.

Instead, she kisses me.

Then she drops her head to my lap and starts to unbutton my jeans. I'm about to stop her because I don't want her to feel like she has to do anything for me when she's obviously upset. But she's already pulled out my cock and closed those gorgeous full lips around the head. With that one motion, all conscious thought leaves my body.

As soft as Yelena's mouth is when pressed against mine, it's infinitely softer while licking and sucking the most sensitive part of my body. She runs her tongue around the head of my cock, right under that responsive ridge of flesh that separates the head and the shaft. She sucks on the head, and then she relaxes her jaw to let more and more of my cock slide into her mouth, all the way back to her throat.

The sound of her mouth moving is drowned out by the theater speakers, but it's a lot harder for me to keep quiet. I lean my head against the back of the seat and close my eyes, trying hard to stop myself from groaning.

Yelena is using her hand and her mouth, moving them simultaneously up and down my shaft so her hand squeezes harder than her mouth does and her mouth provides that delicious warm, slippery sensation second only to her pussy.

I stroke my fingers gently through her hair, feeling like I'm floating on waves of bliss. The part of the movie is playing, where a woman and a man encounter each other in the snow next to a moving train. The flickering light, the drifting snow, and the ethereal music all combine with the sensation of Yelena's mouth until I feel like the movie screen is permeable and I've fallen right through it. I'm transported.

The best part about a blow job is that you don't have to work toward a climax. You don't have to hold back or try to time anything. You just lie back and let it happen.

When I feel myself getting close, I squeeze Yelena's shoulder to let her know so she can finish with her hand if she wants to.

Instead, she redoubles her pace, bobbing her head up and down on my cock, letting it hit all the way at the back of her throat so it feels like bottoming out.

This feels so fucking good that I have to grit my teeth together to keep from moaning. I'm squirming in the tiny theater seat, feeling like this constricted space can't possibly contain the volume of pleasure I'm experiencing.

My balls are boiling. With one explosive contraction, I feel the cum rocketing up through my cock and spurting into Yelena's mouth. She keeps sucking, a sensation that is exquisitely intense in the midst of climax. She's sucking out the cum, she's licking under the head of my cock, and I'm fucking dying of enjoyment, feeling a level of endless deep satisfaction that washes away every other care.

When she's finished, she sits up and wipes her mouth on the back of her hand. I don't have to clean up because she's licked me completely clean.

I'm feeling so good that I want her to feel the same thing. I want to melt away her fear and stress and show her that I'll do anything, anything at all for her.

But when I go to kiss her and I try to touch her like she touched me, she stops me with a hand on my chest.

"I can't," she says. "I don't have time. I have to get back."

"When can I see you again?"

"I don't know," she says unhappily.

"I don't want to sneak around," I tell her. "I want to make a formal agreement between our families. So your father knows I'm serious."

"Really?" The relief on Yelena's face is palpable. "Will your family agree?"

I think about Dante, gone to Paris with the love of his life, and Nero, immersed in his plans for financial domination on an unprecedented scale, and Aida, whose husband is about to run for mayor of Chicago.

They're too busy with their own concerns to care what I do. It's down to my father. I don't think he'll oppose me—not in this. After all, he gave Aida to our most hated enemy, so he's willing to make deals. And his own match to my mother wasn't strategic, so he knows what it feels like to fall in love.

I kiss Yelena again.

"They want me to be happy," I say.

She buries her face against my chest for one last moment. Then she hurries out of the theater to go back home to her father's house.

I hate to let her leave all on her own. I hate to let her go back there.

As much as I tried to reassure her, I am afraid of what Alexei Yenin might do to her. Which is why I need to get her away from him as quickly as possible.

CHAPTER 10
YELENA

MY FATHER CALLS ADRIAN AND ME DOWN FOR DINNER IN THE formal dining room. We don't eat in here very often, so immediately my nerves are on edge.

I've changed my clothes so that I'm wearing a sober high-necked dress, tights, and flat shoes, and I've brushed my hair and pinned it back with barrettes. This is what my father expects from us—that we dress and behave with the utmost respect for him at all times.

It reminds me of something I read a long time ago about the different types of respect. There's respecting someone as an authority and respecting them as a human. My father believes that if we don't respect him as an authority, he has no need to respect us as humans.

I hate the dining room. I hate all the ornate and elaborate furniture in this house. It makes me feel like I'm suffocating.

My father likes to think he's the tsar of his kingdom. He loves the luxury and history of our culture. Every room is full of plush oriental rugs, rich velvet antimacassars, cabinets painted with geometric Khokhloma folk art, and mosaic tiles in the bathrooms.

You would think that all these signs of home would help me not to feel the culture shock of moving to Chicago, but instead it gives me this sense that I can never escape the *Bratva*. Their tentacles extend through every major European city, and even here in America.

My father intends to take over Chicago like he's taken over

every other space he's ever inhabited. He thinks the Irish and Italian Mafia have become weak and complacent. He thinks they've forgotten how to rule.

When I sit down at the table, my father is already seated at the head, dressed in a dove-gray suit of impeccable fit. He's adopting the American style of suit, but he still hasn't cut his hair, which hangs lankly around his shoulders. I don't think he'll ever cut it. It makes him look like a warrior king, like a grizzled old lion. Like Sampson, he believes it's the seat of his power.

The *Bratva* can be extremely superstitious. Maybe that's a characteristic of all Mafia families—after all, Sebastian seems to believe in the luck of his gold medallion. Or, at least, that his uncle lost its luck by giving it to him.

That's why my father is so wound up about the Winter Diamond. It represents the luck of the *Bratva*, and their pride.

Perhaps he should consider the fact we don't have it anymore. Our luck has run out.

As Adrian and I sit down at the table, my father watches us with his blue eyes, cold as Siberian frost.

"Good evening," he says.

"Good evening, Father," Adrian replies.

"Good evening," I say.

"Look at my two children." He surveys us as we sit at his right-hand side. Adrian always sits next to our father. I sit next to Adrian, preferring to have a buffer between me and Papa. "Did any man ever have such impressive offspring?"

Adrian glows with pride. He has always had a different relationship with our father than I have. He's aware of our father's cruelty and sternness, especially as it related to our mother. But Adrian is treated differently as the son and heir, and that blinds him to the true depths of our father's selfishness. Adrian believes that our father loves us, that he would never actually harm us.

I think he's wrong.

Adrian defends him. He says, *We can't imagine what it was like growing up poor in Soviet Russia. He had to do whatever he could to survive. And look how far he's come. No one ever taught him kindness. He had to be harsh and violent to survive.*

The problem is there's a difference between doing what you have to do and enjoying it.

I saw my father's face as Rodion tortured the banker.

He definitely enjoyed it.

Just as he's enjoying this right now…making me squirm in my seat as he pretends to be in a good mood with us.

Rodion already told him what I did. I'm sure of it.

"What were you two doing while I was gone?" Papa asks.

"I spoke with one of our Armenian suppliers," Adrian says. "They have a new way of shipping product—they package it like a bath bomb. Scented and colored and wrapped in cellophane. Almost impossible for a sniffer dog to detect."

"What's the price?"

"The same. They save money because less is seized at the border."

My father nods slowly. "Very good. Double our order. We'll be expanding distribution on the west side of the city. I want a full presence in our old territory."

The *Bratva* used to have the exclusive run of that side of the city until the Gallos torched our warehouses and drove us out.

Now that I think about it, that happened twelve years ago. Right around when Sebastian's uncle was killed. Which action came first, I wonder?

It doesn't matter. Because the bloodshed and violence are a cycle. An ouroboros of revenge.

My father turns and fixes his eyes on me instead.

"And what about you, my daughter?" he says quietly.

I take a sip of my wine to stall for time. We're having prime rib and mashed potatoes with asparagus on the side. The prime rib looks raw. It turns my stomach.

I consider lying to my father—or attempting to lie.

It's pointless. He already knows. He's just testing to see what I'll do.

"I've been seeing Sebastian," I tell him.

No flicker of surprise on his face. He definitely knows.

"And what have you been doing with *Sebastian*," he hisses.

"I've been dating him," I say coolly. "Just like you told me to."

"Not *just like* I told you…"

Adrian looks back and forth between us, confused. I haven't told him that I slept with Sebastian. He doesn't understand the tension freezing the room.

The smile has dropped off my father's face. He's lowering his chin, getting that look like a bull about to charge. I have to head him off, immediately.

"He wants to marry me!" I blurt. "He wants to make a formal agreement between our families. This could be good for us, Father. Instead of fighting the Gallos, we could align ourselves with them. Like the Griffins did. Like the Polish Mafia. They don't have to be our enemies. It would be so much more profitable to—"

"Do you think you can school me on how the *Bratva* should operate in this city?" my father interrupts. He hasn't raised his voice, but his furious tone cuts through my words like a scythe through dry grass.

"No, of course not. I—"

"Quiet!" he barks.

I fall silent. Adrian finds my knee under the table, squeezing my leg in sympathy.

"This is why you can barely be trusted with the simplest of tasks," Papa says, his blue eyes boring into mine. "You're weak, as all women are weak. I send you out hunting, and not only can you barely secure your prey, now you're developing *feelings* for him."

I press my lips together, knowing I'm supposed to deny this but unable to even pretend. I have a lot more than *feelings* for Sebastian.

"And worse," my father hisses. "You've destroyed the only value you had to me."

Adrian's hand tightens on my knee. I'm sure he can guess what our father is referring to. He's flinching not out of disgust but out of fear for me.

"Oh yes," my father hisses, his eyes drilling into me. "You can't keep any secrets from me, Yelena. I know everything you think and everything you do. You will be punished, at a time of my choosing."

This is something new. Usually our punishments come at once, in the most painful and upsetting way possible. The fact he's delaying his discipline…that's the worst torture of all.

"I've tried to teach you two," our father says, including Adrian in his anger now. "I've tried to ready you for this world we inhabit. I've tried to harden you. You may think I've been cruel or demanding, but the world is infinitely crueler than I could ever be. If you can't make your skin into steel and your soul into iron, you'll be torn to shreds."

He takes a long drink of his wine, looking us up and down. This time there's no pride in his expression, only disgust for how we disappoint him.

"There is no stasis in crime," he says. "Your fortune is rising or it's falling. There's no middle ground. The Gallos believe they can transition from Mafia dons to wealthy citizens. They are *fools*!"

He bellows that word so loudly that Adrian and I jump in our seats, almost knocking over our wine.

"They think they've moved up a rung on the ladder with that South Shore development…but all they've done is announce their weakness to the world. Dante Gallo is gone—the heir of the family and their enforcer. Nero Gallo, that filthy thief, has ensconced himself in the world of so-called legitimate business. He thinks he's above *our* rules, above *our* laws. But he'll pay for what he did, stealing our crown jewel. And the youngest brother, the cripple." My father scoffs. "He has never been trained to take their place. He knows nothing about being a don."

I notice he doesn't mention Aida Gallo. She's only a girl and, therefore, of no interest or importance.

"There's blood in the water…" my father says coldly. "The sharks will come, whether it's us or someone else. The Gallos are bleeding freely, an invitation to all. They will be torn apart."

I don't understand any of this. I can't tell if he's being hyperbolic or if he actually has a plan. He wanted me to date Sebastian, but if he expected me to learn the Gallos' secrets and spill them to the *Bratva*, I haven't done that. I haven't met Sebastian's family. We don't talk about the Gallos' business. And even if we did…I wouldn't tell my father.

Actually, I do know one piece of information he'd love to have.

I could tell my father that Enzo Gallo lives all alone in that huge house, without any security besides the housekeeper. It would be child's play to send Rodion to that house to strangle them both in their sleep.

But I would *never* do that. Papa can't actually read my mind—that secret is safe with me.

Maybe he sees the look of defiance on my face.

He stares at me from the head of the table, his steak knife clenched in his fist and juice from the bloody meat gleaming on his lips. I can tell he's simmering with anger—at me, at the Gallos, maybe at Adrian, too. Papa has never been a happy man. The more he tries to squeeze out of the world, the less satisfied he seems.

He looks like he's about to explode into one of his rages.

Desperately, I try to think of a way to convince him that we don't *have* to fight the Gallos.

I blurt out, "To surprise the enemy is to defeat him. The Gallos know we have a grudge against them. They know our brutality and our fury. We could surprise them with magnanimity. They're in an unstable position—it's an advantageous time to make an agreement."

My father narrows his eyes at me.

To surprise the enemy is to defeat him—that's a quote from

Generalissimo Suvorov. My father's idol. He'll listen to those words, if not to mine.

To my shock and relief, he nods slowly. "Maybe you're right."

Even Adrian looks surprised to hear that.

My father sets down his knife and dabs his lips with his napkin. "This is what you want, Yelena? You want to align yourself with those Italian dogs?"

I don't know how he wants me to answer that.

All I can say is the truth.

"Yes," I whisper. "I want to marry Sebastian."

My father shakes his head in disgust. "He can have you. You're no good to me anymore."

With that, he pushes away his plate and stands from the table, leaving Adrian and me alone in the dining room.

Of course, I don't actually trust him. Not for a second.

I turn to Adrian, whispering out of fear that my father is still lurking, or one of his men is. "What is he doing? Tell me, Adrian. What is he planning?"

Adrian just shakes his head at me. He's not touching my knee anymore. He's looking at me with an expression I've never seen before. "Did you actually sleep with the Italian?"

"He's not an *Italian*," I say in irritation. "He was born right here in Chicago."

Adrian looks at me like I'm speaking gibberish. "He's our enemy, Yelena."

"Why? Because our father says so?"

Adrian frowns. What I'm saying is absolute treason. Our father's word is law. Loyalty to our family is supposed to be our highest priority.

"What he said is true," Adrian tells me. "We were born *Bratva*. We have countless enemies everywhere. Who do you think will protect you? The Italians? They barely know you. They don't care about you like we do, Yelena. Their loyalties are to one another. Do you think Sebastian would choose you over his own sister or brothers? Over his own father?"

I swallow hard. I believed Sebastian when he said he was falling in love with me. But could I really expect him to prioritize me over the family he's loved all his life?

"Would you choose *him* over *us*?" my brother demands. "Over me?"

I look into Adrian's face, so like my own. He's so much more than my brother. He's been my best friend and protector all my life. The other half of me.

But he's the other half of who I was.

Sebastian is the other half of who I *want* to be. The Yelena I could be if I were free.

I can't choose between them. I don't want to choose.

It's only my father trying to force that decision.

I want to explain this to Adrian, but all he hears is my silence. My refusal to assure him that he matters more to me than Sebastian.

His face darkens, and he pushes away from the table as abruptly as our father did. "You're making a mistake, Yelena. And you'll regret it."

CHAPTER 11
SEBASTIAN

IF WE'RE GOING TO MAKE A FORMAL AGREEMENT WITH THE Russians, I can't do that on my own. My father is still the *capocrimine*. No matter how far he's withdrawn, he's still the one in charge.

Which means I have to tell him everything.

I sit down with him over breakfast at the little table in our kitchen. Greta has made him a poached egg on toast with a side of fresh fruit. She offers me the same, but I'm too keyed up to eat.

Papa looks well rested this morning. He's freshly showered and already dressed for the day, despite how early I came to the house.

"What is it, Son?" he says. "You look excited."

"I met someone," I tell him. "A girl."

I see Greta perk up over at the stove top, where she's boiling water for tea. I know Greta has always had a soft spot for me. She always told me I was the type to make a woman very happy.

I think she was picturing some kind and gentle girl. Someone like my mother. I don't know what she'll think of Yelena.

With both Greta and my father listening closely, I explain how I met Yelena and how I've been dating her ever since.

"Alexei Yenin knows," I tell Papa. "I don't think he's happy about it. But he's willing to make a formal truce."

Greta sets down a steaming mug of tea in front of each of us. Papa lifts the cup to his lips, taking a long, slow sip.

His beetle-black eyes look troubled.

"I looked into Yenin when he took his position here in Chicago," Papa says. "He's violent. Cruel. Utterly ruthless. Feared even in Moscow. Not someone I planned to build a relationship with."

"I know, Papa," I say. "I don't like it either. But Yelena isn't like that. When you meet her, you'll see. And her brother isn't bad either."

Papa is quiet, his face still. I know his brain is ticking away, examining this development from every angle.

"We have unfinished business with the Russians," he says. "*Bratva* do not forgive easily."

"Our history with the Griffins was just as messy. And look how well that turned out—now they're our strongest allies. You never would have imagined that five years ago."

Papa presses his lips together, considering. "Fergus Griffin was my enemy, but I knew him. I respected him. I could trust his adherence to our agreement. I trusted him with Aida."

"It's Yenin who will be giving Yelena to us," I say. "She's his only daughter, too."

I can tell Papa doesn't like this idea, not at all. Still, he's considering it. For me—because he wants me to be happy.

I press him. "We have the advantage, Papa. We have the power, the money, the positioning. Yelena will be living with me. We give them nothing. We risk nothing."

Papa looks at me soberly. "Don't be overly confident, Sebastian. Yenin is not a fool. He does nothing without reason. If he agrees to this, it's because he sees some advantage."

"His advantage is partnership with us," I insist. "We'll allow them to expand their territory—it won't matter to us; we're making most of our money on the South Shore now. We can allow him to take over the parts of the business we wanted to jettison anyway."

"Don't make the mistake of thinking that Yenin will become our employee. If you think you can delegate to him, that he'll be happy with our scraps…you've misjudged him."

"I know all that!" I say, unable to hold back my frustration. "I know the risks. But this is what I want, Papa. I want Yelena."

Another long silence falls between us. This time I don't break it. I wait it out. Waiting to hear if I've convinced him.

"All right," my father says at last. "Set up the meeting."

Alexei Yenin agrees to come to the Brass Anchor restaurant, which is widely accepted as neutral ground for the gangsters of Chicago.

Almost three years ago today, my father sat across from Fergus Griffin at this same private table to negotiate the terms of Aida's marriage to Callum.

I waited in the next room during that meeting. Now I sit right next to my father, bookended by Nero and by Jace, who may not be Italian but can be trusted for an encounter as sensitive as this.

Nero likes this idea even less than Papa did. He's stiff and unsmiling in his chair, his narrowed eyes fixed on Alexei Yenin.

Alexei has brought three men of his own: his son, Adrian, the silent enforcer called Rodion Abdulov—whom I know Yelena despises—and a third soldier he introduces as Timur Chernyshevsky.

We all agreed to come unarmed, but I know Nero has his knives on him at the very least, and I have a gun concealed in my jacket. I'm sure the Russians did likewise. If we had intended to enforce that particular rule, we'd have met in a bathhouse instead.

Yelena isn't here. I had hoped Alexei would bring her. I wonder if she's sitting at home right now, wracked with nerves and praying everything goes smoothly.

The silence stretches out between our two groups as Yenin and my father consider each other.

Papa speaks first.

"Thank you for coming to meet with us today," he says politely. "As I'm sure you know, our children are eager to make an alliance.

The Italians and the *Bratva* have had a rocky history in Chicago. But with each new generation comes an opportunity for a fresh start."

"Who can stand in the way of young love," Alexei says, an amused gleam in his pale blue eyes. "Water will cut through stone, given enough time. My daughter is that water, chipping away at me."

My stomach clenches tight. I don't like how Alexei talks about Yelena. He's acting like she's a spoiled Mafia princess. Like he's a hard man whose only soft spot is his daughter. I don't believe that for a second. Yelena is no daddy's girl, and Yenin is no indulgent father.

"We all want happiness for our children," Papa says. "And we want security for *their* children. I believe an agreement can be reached, for territory and rights, that would benefit us all."

"That is my wish as well," Yenin says.

While he's talking, I'm looking at his men as well as Yenin himself. Watching to see if they give away anything in their expressions that betrays Yenin's words.

Though Adrian was so cordial the first time we met, he looks irritated today. He doesn't meet my eye but stares down at the table-top, scowling. Maybe he's unhappy at the thought of "losing" his sister. I know how close they are.

Rodion's expression is impossible to read. He keeps his jaw tightly clenched, probably because he's effectively mute and, therefore, doesn't open his mouth very often. Yelena told me his old boss cut out his tongue. Maybe he hates the idea of anyone glimpsing that humiliating injury.

Timur looks nervous and twitchy. He's the youngest of the Russians, with a smooth face and a slim build. He keeps looking across the table at Nero and then dropping his eyes again, cowed by Nero's furious stare.

It takes over an hour for Papa and Yenin to work out the precise terms of the agreement. They argue over a few of the particulars, but in general, Yenin is surprisingly amenable to the terms.

The only point on which he won't budge is that he insists the wedding take place immediately.

He fixes his cool-blue eyes on me from across the table, his face unsmiling.

"You may consider us old-fashioned," he says, "but the purity of our daughters is of high value to the *Bratva*. Were someone to take my daughter's virtue…then leave her defiled, without a husband… that would be a grievous insult."

He stares at me with a cold anger that assures me he knows I took his daughter's virginity. The implication is that he'll forgive my lack of patience as long as I rectify the transgression at once.

Papa looks over at me, his eyebrows raised. Yelena and I have only been dating for two months.

I don't care. I know who she is. And I know what I want.

I nod. "Let's set the date."

Nero writes two copies of the formal contract. His script is swift and slanted but surprisingly legible. He leaves space at the bottom for Yenin and my father to sign.

They each write their names twice: once on my father's copy, once on Yenin's. Then Nero hands my father his knife, and Papa slits the ball of his thumb with the razor-sharp blade. He presses his thumbprint onto the bottom of both pages.

Yenin does the same, cutting his flesh without flinching. He makes his marks right next to Papa's.

This is a blood oath—a tradition older than the Italian Mafia or the *Bratva*. It's our most solemn promise. We're allies now, and Yelena and I will be married with no option to back out.

I feel no sense of fear as I add my own prints and my own signatures.

Actually, I'm flushed with triumph.

Yelena is mine.

CHAPTER 12
YELENA

As soon as Papa steps out of the armored car, I see the contract in his hand, rolled up and sealed with his ring. My heart flutters wildly. He made a deal with the Gallos.

I can't believe it.

I knew he was going to meet them, but I didn't believe he'd actually agree to an alliance. I was sure something would happen to make it all blow up.

But there's the evidence, clear and irrevocable. This was no verbal agreement—he made a blood pact.

I'm up in my room, looking down from my window. I debate whether I should run down to thank him or whether I should steer clear for a while. He might be in a foul mood, depending on how well the negotiations went.

Even under the best of circumstances, I can't imagine he's thrilled about this. The Gallos could give him their most generous terms, and he'd still feel like a subordinate, forced to pay homage to the throne. He wanted revenge, not capitulation.

Adrian looks equally annoyed, stalking toward the house with his hands thrust in his trouser pockets. I expect him to come up to my room to speak with me, but instead he disappears inside our father's office for several hours, along with Rodion. I'm sure they're going over the details of how this new contract will work.

I pick up my phone to call Sebastian, noticing I already have a text from him.

It worked, he says. Come see me tonight.

I clutch my phone almost hard enough to break it, trembling with excitement.

I want to... I say. My father might not be in the best of moods...

That doesn't matter anymore, Sebastian replies. He promised you to me. You're safe now.

The relief I feel at those words is immeasurable. Sebastian is right—I don't belong to my father anymore. If he were to hurt or damage me now, he'd be breaking his agreement with the Gallos.

Thrilled beyond belief, I change my clothes. I put on a sage-green romper and a pair of gold hoops, then slip on my sandals. I pull on a kimono-style wrap over the romper in case my father sees me on my way out the door.

Sure enough, he intercepts me in the foyer. He has the ears of a cat—it's almost impossible to sneak out of the house unseen when he's home. Adrian stands just behind him, his face pale and somber.

"I assume Sebastian told you we reached an agreement," Papa says.

"Yes," I say, trying not to let my full emotion show on my face. I want to be grateful, but I don't want to annoy my father with something as distasteful to him as my complete and utter happiness.

"I expect you to remember your loyalties, Yelena. Even after you say your vows at the altar...you are still a Yenin. You always will be."

"Yes, Father," I say.

I wonder if he can see the lie on my face. I have no loyalty to him. I will always love my brother, but I intend to cut ties with my father as much as possible as soon as I'm wed.

Adrian will know I'm lying. I glance over at him to see if he's scowling. As soon as I try to meet his eye, he looks down at his feet instead.

"Is it all right...if I go see Sebastian?" I ask my father hesitantly.

"Why not?" he says, surprisingly amenable. "Enjoy your time with him."

I don't entirely trust this good mood. But I might as well take advantage of it while it lasts. "Thank you, Father."

I leave on foot, hurrying out through the open gates, down to the street. I walk a few blocks over to where Sebastian and I agreed to meet.

He's already waiting for me outside the café. As I walk up to him, he sweeps me up in his arms and kisses me hard.

"How did it go?" I ask as he sets me down.

"I wish you were there," he says. "I felt like an asshole signing for you like I was buying a car."

"It doesn't matter." I let out my breath. "This is what I want."

"Are you sure?" Sebastian says.

I see the concern in his dark eyes. He's afraid I'm only doing all this to get away from my father.

I grab his hand and squeeze it hard. "Completely sure."

"Good." He grins. "Me, too. Come on, then."

"Aren't we going in the café?"

"Nope."

I follow him back to his truck.

I usually hate uncertainty. My father likes to surprise me with the most unpleasant things possible. But already I've learned I can trust Sebastian—when he has something planned, it's always a good thing.

Sebastian drives us down to the lakeshore, to a building that looks like the Cathedral of Florence mixed with a spaceship. It's not until we're all the way inside that I realize it's a planetarium.

I feel a rush of warmth so strong, it frightens me. I can't believe Sebastian remembers all these little things I tell him. I never expected anyone to know me like this, to care about my interests and preferences. The only other person who treats me this way is my brother—and even he can be capricious.

I feel like a little kid, running around looking at all the displays, touching an actual chunk of meteorite that's apparently four billion years old. I lay my hand on the dense smooth metal, trying to imagine the timescale of this object flying around in outer space before it crashed down on this particular point of the galaxy.

Sebastian seems to be looking at me as much as any of the displays. He's smiling at my excitement—not laughing at me, just enjoying my pleasure at the exhibit on modern space travel and the scale model of the cockpit of the Apollo 13 rocket.

I'm disappointed when the docents begin ushering everyone out of the exhibits, telling us that the planetarium is about to close.

"We should come back another day!" I say to Sebastian.

"Sure," he says. "But come see one last thing before we go."

He grabs my hand and pulls me toward a set of doors that looks like some kind of theater.

"Aren't we supposed to be leaving?" I ask him.

"It's all right," he says. "Trust me."

Mystified, I follow him through the swinging doors.

The room beyond is completely dark, but I get the sense of vast open space over my head. When we speak, our voices echo through the air.

"Where are we?"

"In outer space," Sebastian says. I can hear his grin without seeing it.

At that moment, I hear a clunking sound and a whirring. Suddenly the whole room illuminates with a thousand pinpricks of light. I realize we're standing in the center of the vast dome of the building, and that dome is a model of the galaxy.

We're surrounded by stars, planets, nebulas, and the vastness of space. They float gently around us, so I feel like we're floating, too. The floor seems to have dropped away beneath me. The only thing stationary and close is Sebastian himself.

I look up into his face, illuminated by the pale blue light. His eyes look bright and clear, and when he smiles, his teeth flash white against his deeply tanned skin. It feels like we're the only two people in the universe. I wish that we were.

Sebastian drops down on one knee. My hands fly up to my mouth because I was not expecting this, not in the slightest.

"I know we went through the motions this morning to appease our families…" Sebastian says. "But I want you to know. Yelena, I'm not marrying you because of your father, or the *Bratva*, or anything else. I want to marry you because I want to be with you, always. You captivated me from the moment I met you. I'm fascinated by you, impressed by you, utterly infatuated with you. I love you, Yelena. I'll do anything for you."

He's holding up a box and opening the lid.

I didn't expect a ring. He signed the contract—that was the proposal and the acceptance, without me even there.

But now Sebastian is offering *me* the choice—not my father, just me alone.

I look down at the ring.

It's a teardrop-shaped stone on a delicate filigreed band of pale gold. The filigree looks like ultrafine lace, like frost on a windowpane. It's so lovely that I'm almost afraid to touch it. It's Sebastian who pulls it from its cushioned resting place and slips it on my finger.

The diamond gleams against my skin like Sebastian plucked one of those stars and set it on my hand.

"Will you marry me?" he says.

"Yes," I breathe, still unable to believe this is happening.

Sebastian sweeps me up in his arms, spinning me around so the stars whirl around us all the faster. He kisses me, his arms locked tightly around me.

I'm the happiest I've ever been in my life. I don't know how to handle this feeling. It's so overpowering that I feel like my body can't hold it all inside.

I keep thinking, *This can't be real. This can't be real.*

And then a cold, malicious voice whispers:

It isn't real. This whole thing is a fantasy. A lie you created.

Sebastian doesn't know that you set yourself out as bait. That you deliberately snared him. That you lured him into whatever trap your father's planning.

I shake my head hard, trying to force these thoughts away before they ruin this moment for me.

It doesn't matter that I lied before. It doesn't matter what my father planned…that's over now. He agreed to the alliance. He signed the contract in blood.

Once Sebastian and I are married, I'll tell him everything. And he'll forgive me, I know he will. He'll understand that my father forced me. I didn't know Sebastian back then—I didn't know we'd fall in love.

I can't risk telling him before the wedding.

Afterward, none of it will matter. We'll be safe together, the two of us. I'll be part of the Gallo family. They'll protect me. I'll tell them everything I know about my father, his business, and his resentments. They'll understand. They have to.

That's what I tell myself to keep my mouth shut. To keep myself from destroying this beautiful and perfect moment.

I tell myself that everything will be all right, as long as Sebastian and I are together.

CHAPTER 13
SEBASTIAN

WE HAVE ONLY A MONTH TO PLAN THE WEDDING.

That doesn't matter to me because I don't give a shit about the ceremony. It seems to matter a lot more to Alexei Yenin, who insists that it be a "traditional Russian wedding" in most respects.

To that end, he pays for a wedding planner to carry out his demands, and Yelena and I go along with it, not particularly caring whether we're married in an Orthodox Church, in a garden, or on a street corner.

Both families agree to keep it small to avoid any unpleasantness between the Italian families and the *Bratva*. If we invite one of the other Mafia families, we'll have to invite them all. And there's no way they'll be able to keep peace with the Russians, who have a complicated bloody history in Chicago.

Yenin doesn't even want the Griffins invited. He says it will be impossible for the soldiers who worked under Kolya Kristoff to stand in the same room as Fergus Griffin without seeking retribution.

Papa calls Fergus to discuss this problem, and Fergus agrees it's better not to risk sparking tempers.

"I'm not offended," he says to Papa. "I can send my congratulations from afar."

To me, Fergus says, "*Go maire sibh bhur saol nua.*" *May you enjoy your new life.*

The thorny part of this is that Aida is now, technically, a Griffin, too. Her husband, Callum, definitely is, and so is their little son, Miles.

I'm ready to argue with Yenin on this particular point—I don't want to get married without my one and only sister in attendance. But it's Aida who calls me, having heard about the issue from the Griffins.

"It doesn't matter, Seb," she tells me. "I really don't mind."

"Don't be stupid. I want you there."

"I know you do," she says. "And that's what matters to me. But the ceremony itself...trust me when I say it's not that important. Remember my wedding? It was a disaster."

I grin because she's right. Aida and Callum loathed each other on their wedding day. Aida was dolled up like a princess, which is basically the worst thing you could do to her, and she made Callum wear a hideous brown satin suit. You could see them glaring daggers at each other as she marched down the aisle. Then, when Callum seized her for the least-passionate kiss any of us had ever witnessed, he started to choke and collapsed in front of the altar because Aida had laced her lips with strawberries, to which Callum is severely allergic.

The wedding ended with a trip to the emergency room. And yet, three years later, they couldn't be happier together.

"It's the marriage that matters, not the wedding," Aida tells me. "I'll see you every day after. I mean"—she laughs—"not *every* day. But enough to watch you and Yelena fall more and more in love."

All through this conversation, my throat feels tight.

My wild and impulsive sister has changed.

"When did you get so wise?" I ask her.

Aida snorts. "I don't know about 'wise.' But a baby tires you out enough that you don't have quite the same energy to be an asshole."

The most annoying thing about the lead-up to the wedding is that Yenin seems determined to keep Yelena and me apart as much as possible. I don't know if he thinks it will prevent me from "getting tired of her" before the wedding day, but if that's the case, he's misguided. The more time I spend with Yelena, the more I want. I only find more things to admire about her.

She's extremely well-read, almost as much as my father. In fact, on one of the rare occasions where she's allowed to join Papa and me for brunch, they spend almost the entire time discussing Italian novels.

"I don't think you can beat *The Name of the Rose*," Papa says. "Literary theory, semiotics, medieval studies, and a mystery as well… what more could you want?"

"I would never argue against Umberto Eco," Yelena says, smiling. "Though I don't like *Foucault's Pendulum* as much."

"Why not?" Papa demands.

"I hate conspiracy theories."

"But he describes the descent into false belief so accurately—"

"I know! That's why I hate it. It's so depressing to see how irrational we can be as humans…"

I love watching them argue with each other. It reminds me of how Aida used to fight with Papa, or how my mother did. I've always loved women who aren't afraid to speak their minds, who know what they think and what they believe in.

In my family I've been considered the kindest sibling, the most amenable one. But I can be passionate, too, and insanely focused when it's something that really matters to me. I could never be with someone who doesn't have that same spark, that same fire.

I had hoped to get to know Yelena's brother better because I know how important he is to her. However, he refused the invitation to join us at brunch.

"Was he busy this morning?" I ask Yelena lightly.

She's looking particularly stunning today with her silvery hair loose around her shoulders, and her cheeks are flushed from sitting out on the outdoor patio, only half shaded from the sun.

She frowns at my question. "No," she admits. "He wasn't busy. I think he's sulking about the wedding. He's been avoiding me all week."

"Doesn't think I'm good enough for you?" I say, giving Yelena a quick kiss. "He's probably right."

Yelena smiles at me, but her eyes look troubled. "It's not that. Maybe it's because I'm escaping and he's not. But his situation isn't the same as mine. He's the heir, and I'm…the bargaining chip."

"Not to me," I assure her. "Not to my family."

Papa has gone to the restroom, so he isn't present for this part of the conversation. Yelena looks at his empty chair, then grabs my hand and squeezes it hard.

She says, "Will they really accept me?"

"Yes," I assure her. "We all love Callum now. Even me. And I've got more reason than anybody to hold a grudge."

Yelena gives a little sigh, not entirely convinced. "I wish we were getting married today."

"Me, too," I say, kissing her again. "Only a little longer."

If Adrian is the dark spot on Yelena's excitement, I soon get one of my own.

Dante calls me from Paris at midnight my time, seven o'clock in the morning for him.

"Hey!" I say. "When are you flying back for the wedding?"

"I'm not," he says gruffly.

"What do you mean?"

I can hear his disapproval radiating through the phone. "This is a bad idea, Seb."

I was expecting this, but still, my face gets hot, and I have to struggle to keep my tone even and unemotional.

"Why?" I say. "Because she's Russian?"

"Because her father is a fucking psychopath. He's got a reputation even among the *Bratva*. Do you know how far past the line you've gotta be for the *Bratva* to think you're scary?"

"He signed a blood contract."

"Yeah? And you think that wiped his memory?"

"He can't do anything. He has to abide by the agreement the same as we do."

I can hear Dante's slow heavy breath on the other side of the line. "We shouldn't have taken that diamond," he says. "We insulted their honor."

"They don't know we stole the stone."

"You don't know what they know," Dante growls.

"Well, you don't either!" I cry. "Because you're not here. You've got your wife and your kids and your new life. And I'm happy for you, Dante, I really am. But the rest of us are still here, doing the best we can. I love Yelena. I'm going to marry her. And I want you to be there."

There's a long silence in which I'm not sure if Dante is even going to respond.

At last he says, "I'm sorry, little brother. I wish you all the happiness in the world. But I promised Simone that I was done with violence. I want to move away from all that. And I can't help but think you're diving feetfirst into a whole new pile of shit."

I'm so angry that I think I'd hit him if he were standing here in front of me.

"Fine," I hiss. "That's your decision."

"Yes," Dante says. "It is. We all make our own decisions, and we live with the consequences."

I hang up the phone, tempted to throw it across the room instead.

God damn Dante with his stiffness and his obsession with caution. He's a fucking hypocrite. Simone's father hated him, too, and that didn't stop him from chasing the woman he wanted. He knows what it feels like to be in love! He could never walk away from Simone, and I won't give up Yelena.

If he wants to miss the wedding, that's his problem.

I'll be standing there at the altar, right where I'm supposed to be.

CHAPTER 14
YELENA

THE MOOD IN MY FATHER'S HOUSE IS STRANGE AND TENSE.

Adrian will barely look at me, let alone speak to me.

Rodion seems to shadow me more closely than ever. He's always lurking when I leave my room to eat or swim in the pool. He watches me with those piggy little eyes, like he's enraged that I'm about to slip away from him forever.

It doesn't help that it's swelteringly hot, hot enough that the air conditioner can't possibly cool all the space inside this house. I wake up sweating every night.

A few days before the wedding, I'm so hot in my room on the top floor that I have to pull on a swimsuit and go downstairs to the pool.

I let myself out through the patio doors, careful not to make too much noise. If I wake my father, he'll be furious.

I slip into the water, which barely feels cool compared to the muggy night air. Still, it's better than my stifling room. I stroke back and forth across the pool, thinking about the apartment Seb and I will be moving into on Goose Island.

It's a gorgeous industrial-style loft with a view of the water on both sides. It has a professional-grade kitchen, which made Sebastian and me laugh because neither one of us can cook for shit.

"We'll learn together, I guess," Seb said.

I can't believe I'll be living there in just a few more days. Him and me, all alone, without anybody looking over our shoulders.

Enzo Gallo already gave us our wedding gift: a brand-new grand piano, which is currently sitting in the living room of the loft. It's bright and gleaming and perfectly tuned. I can't wait to get my hands on it.

I don't expect any gift from my father, and I don't want one.

All I want is to be free of this place.

I roll over on my back and stroke across the pool, looking up at the sky. You can't see too many stars here—the city lights drown them out. But I can still pick out Ursa Major and a faint glimmer down near the horizon that might be Venus.

Looking up at the stars fills me with happiness, remembering how Sebastian proposed to me. He made the proposal feel special and intentional, not at all like he was forced into it by my father.

I don't understand how I got so lucky, meeting him.

I've never felt lucky in my life. Quite the opposite.

It's unbelievable to me that something my father orchestrated with such ill intent could turn out in my favor.

Sebastian said I should apply for a music program after the wedding. I'm thinking of applying to the Bienen School of Music at Northwestern or maybe DePaul.

Sebastian is going to keep helping run the Gallo empire. The truce between his family and mine is more of a formal ceasefire versus a collaborative partnership, but who knows—eventually Adrian will take over from my father. Maybe he and Seb will work together. Maybe my brother will get married, too. Maybe our kids will play together and eventually run this city together…

As I lie on my back looking up at the sky, the possibilities seem endless… Our futures unspool in front of my eyes, bright and shining as the moon overhead.

Until a shadow passes over my face and I realize Rodion is standing at the edge of the pool, looking down on me.

He looks as vast as a mountain, looming over me, and as displeased as some kind of volcanic god demanding sacrifice.

His silence is unnerving. It makes him seem without empathy, without any kind of soul, though I know he does feel things.

Lust, for instance.

I see the way he looks at me.

A lot of men look at me that way—almost all of them, in fact. But only he stares at me with resentment, as if I belong to him and have been unjustly taken away.

One of my greatest fears before this engagement to Seb was that my father truly would give me to Rodion someday, as a reward for his loyal service.

What bothers me most of all is how well I understand him. I'm used to picking up the meaning of small signs and gestures because of my mother. She communicated silently to avoid the attention of the *bratoks* or my father himself.

I hate that Rodion reminds me of her in a strange and twisted way. He's like a monstrous, bizarro version of her. Large and hulking, where she was gentle and petite. Malevolent, where she was fundamentally kind. Menacing, when she would have done anything to protect me.

I hate that I understand him, without meaning to and without wanting to. I know what all his signs mean, though I never meant to learn them.

Perhaps that's part of why he's fixated on me. Because he knows that I *do* understand him. He thinks there's some kind of connection between us.

Maybe I should pity him. After all, losing your ability to speak is awful, particularly in such a humiliating way. Honor is everything to the *Bratva*. Rodion was stripped of his honor and his authority. He's labored relentlessly for years to recover his leadership position under my father.

But I can't pity him. Because he has no pity for anyone else. I'll never forget the hour of torture he inflicted on Raymond Page while I was forced to sit watching. I saw the pleasure on Rodion's face and on my father's.

And that's why I will despise them both, always.

I understand violence out of necessity. But to enjoy it…that I'll never understand. And I'll never respect it.

I've stopped swimming. I bob in the water like a buoy, looking back at Rodion with every ounce of disdain I can muster. I can't let him see how much he terrifies me. I know he feeds on fear.

Instead, I demand, as sternly as I can, "What do you want? You're bothering me."

Rodion looks down at me, unsmiling, his arms crossed in front of his broad chest as he refuses to answer with even a sign.

My heart is beating hard, but I tilt up my chin, pretending I'm looking down at him instead of him looking down at me while I float, half naked and vulnerable, in the water.

"Go away," I say as if commanding a dog.

Rodion just tilts his head slightly to the side, his eyes narrowed, his lip curled.

"If you come near me again after I'm married, my husband will kill you," I hiss at him.

Without waiting for a response, I force myself to start swimming laps again. I feel horribly exposed, knowing we're all alone in the backyard. He could jump in the pool and drag me down with his massive bulk, drowning me silently in the chlorinated water.

But I keep swimming anyway, refusing to stop, refusing to look at him. And when I finally glance up again after twenty laps or so, he's disappeared.

CHAPTER 15
SEBASTIAN

IT'S MY WEDDING DAY.

I feel an excitement so acute, it's almost painful. My chest is too tight to breathe. I feel tense and feverish.

Yet I'm happier than I've ever been.

I had my bachelor party last night with Nero, Jace, Giovanni, and Brody. Brody was my roommate in college and the shooting guard on the basketball team. After graduation, he played a year in the Chinese league. Now he's back in Chicago, flush with stories of how many girls in Beijing wanted to try out a six-eight white dude, even with the ugly mug he's carrying around.

Giovanni is one of my lieutenants, generally in charge of the high roller poker ring. And, of course, Jace was both my roommate and soldier up until this week. After today, he'll be living alone in the apartment in Hyde Park, while I move in with Yelena.

The thought of waking up to her every morning, seeing her every time I come home, makes me happier than I can express. I wouldn't give a fuck if we were moving into a cardboard box if she would be there.

But I wanted to get her the most beautiful apartment imaginable, something that had space and light and, most of all, belonged to her. I want her to pick the paint color, the furniture. I want her to feel that it's all her own, not imposed by anyone else, for once in her life.

Unfortunately, we haven't had time to pick out much of anything just yet because of how rushed the wedding has been. But there'll be plenty of time afterward. All the time in the world.

I told my groomsmen I had no interest in strippers, so instead we went drinking at the Blarney Stone. If I had been getting married a year ago, I'm sure Nero would have fought me on that. But he's been shockingly faithful to Camille and seemed perfectly satisfied to slug down a few shots, then challenge Giovanni to a game of pool, without even bothering to check out the coeds lined up at the bar who kept throwing hopeful glances in his direction.

Jace leaned on the table with both elbows, glumly slugging down a beer.

"I can't believe you two are in committed relationships before me," he said, casting a disbelieving look at me and then Nero.

"I'm still single!" Brody piped up from the pool table.

"Of course *you* are!" Jace shouted back. "Just look at you!"

Brody shrugged and grinned. He's got a head the size and shape of an overgrown potato and one of the scraggliest, patchiest beards I've ever seen, so he's used to taking shit about his looks.

"And you…" Jace shook his head in disbelief. "You're just walking down the street, and you happen to bump into a Russian goddess. Some guys have all the luck."

"Maybe Yelena has a cousin," I told him, trying to cheer him up.

"Really?" Jace said, perking up a little. "Like, coming to the wedding tomorrow? 'Cause I'm gonna be lookin' pretty fucking spiffy in my new suit."

"I don't know." I laughed. "It's going to be a tiny ceremony. Just a dinner after, no reception."

Jace pouted at the idea of no reception where he could dance with the gorgeous Russian cousins of his imagination.

"What about the honeymoon?" he said. "You going back to her home country? You could take me with you…I could carry your suitcases…"

"We're going to Switzerland. But not for a couple of months. We want to backpack in the Alps, and we need more time to plan it all out."

Despite the disappointments of my wedding and honeymoon plans, Jace cheered up pretty well once he got a couple of more beers in him. He even snagged a phone number from one of the coeds at the bar after she realized no amount of hair tossing or lip biting was going to get Nero to pay attention to her.

Brody likewise enjoyed himself, despite losing four games in a row to Nero. He managed to beat me at darts, and that seemed like more than enough victory for him, ignoring the fact I'd never played darts before in my life and only had the shakiest understanding of the rules.

Nero was quiet, though not in his usual sullen, glowering way. He just seemed lost in thought.

When he stepped outside for a smoke, I followed him, wondering what he was thinking about.

He lit the cigarette, the flare of his lighter briefly illuminating the sharp planes of his face. His hair hung over his eyes, casting them in shadow.

He took a long pull, then exhaled, the smoke forming a wreath around his face.

Without prodding, he said, "I wish Dante were here."

"Me, too," I said. "It doesn't feel right without him."

"Have you talked to him?"

"Yeah. He said exactly what you'd expect. That this whole thing is a bad idea."

I expected Nero to give an impatient snort. I thought he'd agree with me—he was always the most annoyed of anyone when Dante tried to exert his stodgy big-brother conservatism on the rest of us.

But to my surprise, Nero just took another long exhale and said, "I understand him better since he's been gone."

"What do you mean?"

"The weight of it. Of all of it. It's heavy and it's relentless."

I nodded slowly.

I've been feeling it, too—the sheer mass of responsibility Dante had been shouldering all that time, now falling onto me and Nero instead. Nero covering the South Shore, me running the rest of our territory. Papa retreating further and further from all of it.

"Your mistakes aren't your own," Nero said. "They affect everyone. And that's terrifying."

I didn't know if he was referring to me embroiling us with the Russians or if he was talking about himself and the risk he'd taken in stealing that diamond. Either way, it shocked me to hear Nero admit anything scared him.

"It'll be all right," I told him. "You and I can handle it, with or without Dante."

"Yeah," Nero said. "But it does make me appreciate him just a little bit more."

"Who knew he really was doing a fuck ton of work and not just complaining about it?"

We both laughed.

We already knew that, of course. Theoretically. But reality hits harder.

"How's the shop?" I asked him.

Nero and Camille opened a custom car modification shop over on Howe Street. They live above it in a tiny apartment that always smells a little bit like fresh paint and gasoline fumes, which I think they like.

"Flourishing," he said. "Camille's brilliant. Some of the shit she can do with an engine...I hate to admit it, but she might be better than me."

He said it like it shamed him, but I could hear the obvious pride in his voice.

"Think you'll be following me down the church aisle?"

"One hundred percent," Nero said without hesitation. "Very soon. Her dad's been sick—"

I nodded, remembering her father had lung cancer.

"We're waiting for him to be completely recovered. Or recovered as much as you can be with that kind of thing."

"I'm happy for you, man," I told him.

"Likewise," Nero said with a little half smile.

Now my groomsmen are probably getting dressed just the same as I am, in pewter-colored suits. I hadn't planned to have any groomsmen since Yelena doesn't have any bridesmaids, but she said she didn't care—"Adrian will stand up with me."

It won't really matter for the ceremony. It's not arranged like a Catholic wedding. Only Yelena and I will stand at the altar, along with the priest and Adrian, who will function as something called a *koumbaros*.

Instead of sleeping at my apartment with Jace, I spent one last night at my family home. I don't know if I'll ever sleep in this narrow twin bed again, under this steeply gabled roof with its posters and familiar scent of cedarwood.

I take a long time getting ready, wanting everything to be just right, down to the last hair on my head. Unfortunately, my hair rarely cooperates when I want it to. The curls seem just as excited as I am today, and I wish I had gotten my hair cut shorter this time around so I could be sure of managing it.

As I'm buttoning up my crisp white dress shirt, I see the gleam of the tiny gold medallion on my chest. I press it between my thumb and index finger, wondering what Uncle Francesco would say if he could see me marrying a daughter of the *Bratva*. Would he see it as a betrayal? Or would he understand?

It's impossible to know. That's the trouble with losing the people you love. You can't ask their opinions anymore. You can't make them happy or unhappy with your choices.

My mother isn't here either. She never got to see a single one of us married.

Her opinion, at least, I can be sure of. She married for love, damn the circumstances. She wanted to be with my father, no matter his history.

She would have loved Yelena. She'd be glad I was marrying someone who loved music like she did. She would have been the one to pick the piano for our wedding present.

When I'm shaved and brushed and dressed to perfection, I meet Papa and Greta downstairs in the kitchen. Papa is wearing his finest charcoal suit, double-breasted, with an almost-invisible pinstripe—the one Mama had made for him for their fifteenth anniversary. Greta looks very nice as well. She's got on a navy blazer and skirt, with a little matching hat pinned in her reddish hair.

"You look like you're going to a royal wedding," I tease her.

"At least one of us does!" she snaps back, never at a loss for a response. "What happened to men wearing proper tuxes for their weddings?"

"A lot of people wear suits now," I say, shrugging.

"A lot of people get married in Vegas." Greta sniffs. "That doesn't mean it's good manners."

"You look very handsome," Papa assures me. He lays his hand on my shoulder, something he has to reach up to do these days. "I'm proud of you, my son."

"Thank you, Papa."

He knows I mean thank you for all this, not just for the compliment.

Nero pulls up front of the house in one of his nicest cars—the oxblood Talbot-Lago Grand Sport. It's freshly washed and waxed, gleaming in the bright morning light. It's such a boat that Papa, Greta, and I can all fit in the bench seat in the back, while Camille rides up front with Nero.

"Congratulations, Seb," she says, turning around in her seat to squeeze my shoulder.

Her dark curly hair is pulled up in a bun on top of her head, and her pretty sundress almost exactly matches the shade of the car.

"You finally finished this thing!" Papa says to Nero, admiring the buttery leather seats and the vintage dashboard with its round dials and knobs.

"*We* finished it," Nero says, throwing his arm around Camille's shoulders. "Camille helped me swap out the alternator. It's her car, by the way. She's just letting us borrow it today."

"That's brave of you," I say to Camille. "Have you seen him drive?"

Camille grins. "If he runs into anything, I know how to fix it."

We speed off toward the church, swift and smooth as a bird in flight. For all I like to give Nero shit, he's an excellent driver. I'd trust him to take me anywhere, even in this ancient car without a single modern safety feature.

The closer we get to the church, the less I can listen to the conversation swirling around me. All I can think about is what Yelena will look like in her wedding dress.

We're getting married in the Orthodox Cathedral in Ukrainian Village. Technically, my family is Catholic, but that was one of the many concessions we were willing to cede to Yenin to make this whole thing go smoothly.

Nero pulls up in front of the church, which is a white-plastered building with a large octagonal dome and a bell tower. It looks simultaneously grand and provincial, with its painted woodwork and its rustic shapes, so unlike a Catholic cathedral.

As we walk inside, it seems even more exotic. A massive triptych stands behind the altar, painted in red, turquoise, and gold. The mosaic angels on the walls look decidedly Byzantine. The interior of the dome is likewise painted turquoise, spotted with stars. I smile at that, thinking Yelena will like it.

Greta looks around at the scarlet carpet and the gilded wood.

"It's very...Russian," she whispers to me.

I stifle a laugh. "I think that's the idea."

Yenin comes striding around the triptych, flanked by an Orthodox priest and his son, Adrian.

"Good morning," he greets us politely. "What a perfect day for a wedding."

"You couldn't ask for better," Papa says, holding out his hand to shake Alexei's.

Yenin looks over at Greta with mild curiosity.

Papa says, "Allow me to introduce our...Greta."

He doesn't like to call her our housekeeper because Greta is so much more than that to our family.

Greta likewise shakes Yenin's hand, with less than her usual enthusiasm. I'm sure Papa told her all about Alexei. Or else she just dislikes the look of him, with his wide smile that doesn't extend to his eyes.

"My son, Adrian," Yenin says. Adrian likewise shakes hands all around, with about the same enthusiasm Greta showed.

When he comes to me, I say eagerly, "Is Yelena here?"

"She's getting ready in one of the side rooms," Adrian says.

He looks pale and solemn in his dark suit. I have an automatic liking for Adrian because he looks so much like Yelena. But I don't think that feeling is returned. Today he meets my eyes, but not with any warmth. He looks unhappy and slightly ill.

"I have a question," Greta says to the priest. "Where are the pews?"

"We do not sit during sermons," the priest explains. "But you may bring forward the chairs from along the wall, if you wish."

He points to the ornate high-backed armchairs lined along the walls. They look heavy and difficult to move. Catching sight of Jace, Giovanni, and Brody coming into the church, I say, "Just in time— I've got a job for you."

"Already?" Brody grins.

Greta directs us to where she thinks the chairs should go, and Jace, Giovanni, Brody, and I move them into place.

Nero sits in one of the chairs along the wall, watching us.

"You should be doing that, not your brother!" Greta scolds him. "It's *his* wedding day."

"Yes, but he's not as hungover as I am," Nero replies.

Nero didn't actually drink enough to be hungover. I think he's more interested in keeping an eye on the rest of Yenin's men who have come into the church. I see the big silent one, Rodion, who appears to be in a particularly foul mood, and then three others behind him. One is the baby-faced kid who was at the negotiating table. I believe he's Yenin's driver and a distant cousin of Yelena—his name is Timur something. The other two I don't recognize. They might also be relatives or just *bratoks*. I get the feeling Yenin has more soldiers than family.

The tension is palpable, even in the open space of the chapel. Yenin and his men take the seats we arranged on the left side of the space, and my family sits down on the right. We're all facing forward, toward the altar with its massive painted triptych almost two stories high. But we're glancing sideways at each other, no one entirely comfortable.

For all they might not like the idea of this wedding, the Russians dressed up just as nicely as we did. Yenin is wearing a rich-blue suit with a single white lily in the buttonhole, and Adrian wears a black suit with the same.

I didn't get boutonnières for myself or the groomsmen. I wonder if that was a mistake. I hope Yelena won't mind.

I keep checking my watch, counting down the minutes until the ceremony is supposed to start. At five minutes to noon, the priest gets up to close the doors to the chapel. Right before he can pull them shut, a burly arm shoots through, blocking their path.

The priest startles, stumbling backward in his long black robes.

"Sorry," a deep, rumbling voice says.

I jump up, shocked and pleased. "Dante!"

He pushes his way inside, dressed nicely in a dark suit and tie, with his black hair freshly combed back.

Yenin frowns at the sight of him. "I thought you weren't coming," he says in an irritated tone. He seems offended that Dante refused to attend initially and even more offended that he showed up now at the last minute.

Dante ignores him. He does allow me to hug him and clap him on the shoulder.

I say, "I'm glad you came."

"I thought I'd regret it if I didn't. I am happy for you, Seb."

"I know you are."

My side of the church now includes both my brothers, Papa and Greta, Giovanni, Brody, and Jace. On the opposite side are Yenin, Adrian, Rodion, Timur, and the other two men.

The only person missing is my bride.

The priest closes the doors, then takes his position behind the altar.

He motions for me to join him, and Adrian as well. Adrian is going to be our *koumbaros*, which Yelena told me is an essential part of the ceremony and a sort of godfather to the couple for the rest of their lives.

Adrian looks less than pleased about his position next to the priest, but one quick glance at his father seems to remind him of his duty. He straightens, his shoulders back, readying himself for the task at hand.

Now, at last, I hear the doors behind the triptych creak open as Yelena enters the chapel. Unlike in a Catholic ceremony, she comes from behind the altar instead of walking up the aisle.

It doesn't matter—she doesn't need a grand entrance to blow my fucking mind. There's no music playing, no path of rose petals for her to walk along. And yet she is so intensely, ethereally beautiful that my heart stops dead in my chest.

Her dress is so light and transparent, it seems to float around her body. I can just make out the shape of her long slim arms and legs as she moves, the gown swirling around her like fog. Her hair is half pinned up, with a thin silver circlet on her head, and then her long pale hair tumbles down her back in waves. The silver of her crown is picked up in the tiny pinpricks of silver on her gown, glimmering like stars in the translucent material.

Her skin is as luminescent as the moon. Her eyes are the brightest I've ever seen them—clear and unearthly. For a moment I wonder if Yelena really is human at all because I've never seen a woman like this.

All of us are stunned to silence, even the priest.

As Yelena joins me at the altar, all I can do is take her slim cool hands in mine and whisper, "*Incredible.*"

The priest begins the long and convoluted ceremony, which I can only stumble through, since I've never seen a Russian Orthodox wedding before. The priest recites his blessings and Bible passages, then takes our rings so he can press them to our foreheads three times each. It seems like everything happens three times over, to represent the trinity, I'd guess. Adrian passes the rings between our hands three times and then finally sets them on our fingers.

Next we do a ceremony with lit candles that Yelena and I each hold in our hands. And then we share wine from a cup and walk around the altar together three times over. At last the priest gives us his final prayers, saying the words "*na zisete,*" which Yelena had told me before is an ancient blessing meaning, "May you live!"

With those words, Yelena and I become man and wife. She looks up into my face, her eyes brilliant with tears. I bend down to kiss her. Her lips are just as sweet as the very first time I tasted them.

We turn to face our families, her hand locked in mine, both of us smiling with all our might.

What happens next seems to happen in slow motion, like a nightmare. And just like a nightmare, I'm frozen in place, unable to move.

In one swift motion, like the swell of the tide, Alexei Yenin and his men rise from their seats. They pull their guns from their suit jackets, pointing them across the aisle at my family.

Before I can move, before I can shout, before I can even take a breath, they begin to fire.

My father is the first one hit because he's the slowest to react and because he's the one they're targeting. The bullets hit him in the chest, the neck, and the jaw, blowing bits of his flesh onto Greta's horrified face. His body jolts from the impact, betraying how frail he's truly become. I can tell from the way he falls that he's dead before he hits the ground.

At the same moment, I see a blur of motion in my peripheral vision as Adrian Yenin raises his gun and presses it against my temple. He hesitated just a moment—he didn't pull his weapon as fast as the others.

That hesitation is the only reason I'm not dead. Had he raised his gun while I was looking at my father, I never would have known what hit me. His bullet would have torn through my skull while I watched Papa die.

But I see his arm move up, and I react without thinking. My knee may be fucked, but I still have all the reflexes of an athlete. My right hand shoots up, hitting him in the elbow and knocking his arm upward. The gun explodes an inch above my head, deafening me. I bring my left fist swinging around, crashing into Adrian's jaw.

The cathedral rings with a long, long, unbroken shriek, as loud as a siren—Yelena is screaming, her fingernails digging into her cheeks.

Two more Russians come around the side of the triptych, both armed. One I've never seen before, but the other looks oddly familiar. He's got a squashed nose and a tattoo of an arrow running down the side of his shaved head. With a sickening jolt, I realize he's the man who was trying to shove Yelena in the trunk of his car the night she and I first met.

Everything that happens next I see in split-second snapshots. It all happens simultaneously, but my brain registers it as still images, captured between chaotic flashes of light.

I see Nero flinging himself on top of Camille, shielding her with his body as he's shot in the back three, four, five times. I see Brody pick up one of the heavy chairs and fling it at Yenin before he, too, takes a dozen bullets to his lanky frame. Giovanni is shot while charging at the Russians. He manages to barrel into two of them and knock them over, even after being hit several times.

The priest tries to run and is shot in the back—either by accident or to eliminate any witnesses. I rip the gun out of Adrian's hands and turn it on the men who have just entered the room. I shoot the pretend kidnapper right before he can fire at Greta.

The other man snarls and points his gun at me, pulling the trigger before I can swing my gun around at him.

I hear Yelena's scream at the same time as the gun fires. She slams into me, knocking me backward. My bad knee folds beneath me, and we both go tumbling. It's only when I try to shove her off me and I feel how limp she's become that I realize she's been shot.

Rodion is hit in the shoulder, and another of Yenin's soldiers fall—the baby-faced driver called Timur. I realize Jace is shooting back, and Dante, too. They weren't stupid enough to come unarmed like I did.

But Dante's been hit himself. He stumbles toward the triptych, bleeding from the leg and hand.

Snarling, Yenin tries to shoot Dante in the back. It's too late— Dante has braced himself against the massive wooden triptych and he's shoving it with all his might. With a strangled roar, Dante manages to tip the two-story screen. It falls toward the seats with sickening force. It must weigh two thousand pounds, like the front of a house falling down—anyone beneath it will be crushed.

The shooting stops as everyone scatters.

I grab Yelena's limp body and fling her over my shoulder. Camille is dragging Nero, her teeth bared and the tendons standing out on her neck. Dante has grabbed Greta, who alone seems unharmed.

The triptych crashes down with a thunderous impact like a bomb exploding, shards of wood shooting off in all directions. I don't know if it hit the Russians or not because there's no time to look back. We're fleeing out the back of the cathedral, Dante limping on his injured leg but still helping Camille support Nero's bleeding

body, me trying not to trip over the long train of Yelena's gown as it hangs down over my shoulder.

In the darkened apse, I hear footsteps pounding after us.

I spin around, Adrian's gun still clutched in my hand. I can barely see, and my finger jerks convulsively against the trigger. Right before I fire, I realize it's only Jace.

"Don't wait for me or anything!" he pants, highly incensed.

I have no words to answer him.

I just turn and flee the church, leaving my father's body behind.

CHAPTER 16
YELENA

I wake up, cold and stiff, in a dark room.

It smells damp in here, and a little bit like diesel fumes.

When I try to move, I hear a clinking metal sound and the rustling of fabric. My whole body feels heavy and aching, the throbbing pain seeming to radiate from my left shoulder all the way down to my toes.

My head is heavy and dull. I can't seem to understand what the fuck is happening.

And then it all starts to come back to me.

Sebastian standing at the altar, looking the most handsome I'd ever seen him in that perfectly fitted suit.

His family, arranged in the tall high-backed chairs, looking pleased and expectant.

And then my father and his men. He brought Rodion, Timur, Vale, and Kadir. Other than Rodion, the *bratoks* were technically related to me, Vale being my uncle through marriage, and Timur and Kadir distant cousins. Still, it felt strange to have my side of the wedding party staring at us so coldly, without any hint of happiness. Only a kind of stiff expectation.

Then there was Adrian, who looked strangest of all. As he led us through the ceremony in his position of *koumbaros*, I kept thinking how pale he was and wishing that he would look me in the eye and give me one of his irreverent smiles, to let me know he wasn't taking the whole thing too seriously. I've never seen him stand inside a church without a single eye roll or wink in my direction when the priest is droning on.

At the very least, I thought he'd hug me that morning and tell me that he loved me, that he'd miss me, but he hoped I'd be happy with Sebastian.

He did none of that. When I went to his room early in the morning to speak to him, his bed was empty. Usually it takes a brass band to wake him up.

I felt a prick of unease, but I told myself it was nothing. I tried to look only at Sebastian, at his handsome face and his excited expression. I looked at his height, his broad chest, and his air of utter confidence, and I told myself, *Seb will protect me. His family will protect me. Once we're married, nothing can hurt us.*

Then, at last, the ceremony was over, we were man and wife with rings on our fingers, and he kissed me... It was the warmest and happiest kiss of my life...

And then...

It all turned to blood, and terror, and misery.

That perfect moment shattered like glass, splintering into a thousand pieces that cut every part of me as they tumbled down.

My father betrayed the Gallos. He betrayed me, too.

And my brother tried to kill the man I love.

He put a gun to Sebastian's head. He tried to pull the trigger.

And the rest of them...

I don't know how many died.

My hand flies to my mouth as I realize I don't even know if Sebastian is alive. The last thing I remember is one of my father's soldiers pointing his gun at my husband and me jumping in front of the barrel...

I touch my shoulder, which is so stiff and aching that it feels like stone. Again I hear that clinking sound that follows me every time I move.

I feel a thick bandage wrapping from my chest all the way over my shoulder to my back. Also, I feel the tattered and filthy remains of my wedding dress. And then, encircling my wrists and my ankles... manacles. Iron bracelets, attached to chains.

I lift my wrist again, tugging.

I only have limited mobility because these chains are apparently bolted down.

I let out a little moan. It sounds very pathetic in this dark, gloomy space.

I have no idea who's put me down in this dungeon and chained me to the wall. I don't know where I am, if I'm even still in Chicago. I feel the cold stone walls more than I see them.

All I know for certain is that I'm sitting on a mattress with a single thin blanket over my legs.

I'm still wearing my wedding dress, but the tiara I wore in my hair, the one that belonged to my mother—that's gone. So are my shoes.

Feverishly, I feel my left hand with my right.

My ring is still there, at least. I touch that little circlet with its beautiful diamond, twisting it on my finger.

I don't know what I would do if I'd lost that, too.

I want to cry, but I won't allow myself to do it.

I don't know who could be watching or listening.

So, instead, I curl up in a ball, feeling the relentless throb of my shoulder and hoping against hope that Sebastian is still alive.

I don't know if I lie in the dark for hours or days.

I know that I slept several times and became very thirsty.

Finally, after what seems like forever, the door scrapes open, and a light snaps on.

I sit up on the mattress, blinking against the blinding glare.

Standing in the doorway is a figure I recognize immediately: my tall, strong, immeasurably handsome husband.

I try to jump to my feet so I can run to him, but the chains tangle me up, and my legs wobble beneath me. I feel a spike of pain in my shoulder and a thick wave of nausea that makes me sit down hard on the mattress.

It's better for me that I can't throw myself into Sebastian's arms because he's already cringing away from me with a repulsed expression on his face.

"Don't touch me," he says through lips as white as chalk.

His expression is unlike anything I've seen before—furious and disgusted, like he fucking loathes me.

It's so unlike how Sebastian usually looks at me that I can only blink up at him in confusion, wondering how this man who was willing to go to the ends of the earth for me just days ago could now regard me like shit on the bottom of his shoe.

Then I look a little closer at the deep, bruise-like smudges under his eyes, and the gauntness of his cheeks, and the misery in his eyes beneath that fury. And I know someone has died. Maybe a lot of people.

"Sebastian," I croak. My throat is dry, and so are my lips. It's hard to speak.

He winces, like even hearing his name on my lips is too much for him. "*Don't*," he says again.

I don't know what he's forbidding me from doing this time. Speaking? Looking at him? Maybe just existing…

"What happened?"

He's so angry that he's shaking down the whole length of his considerable frame. "*You know what happened.*"

"My father betrayed you," I say. "But Sebastian, I didn't know! I—"

"DON'T LIE TO ME!" he roars.

His face is congested with rage, his fists clenched at his sides. He takes one jerking step toward me before stopping himself, as if he wanted to tear me apart with those hands.

I flinch back from him, and maybe it's that flinch that stops him because he pulls himself up short, and I see the tiniest flicker in his eyes, as if his fury surprised even him.

He looks down at me. I know I must look filthy, pained, pathetic. But whatever sympathy that might have engendered before, whatever wispy memory of love resides inside him, he crushes it ruthlessly. He blinks, and his face is like a stranger's again. Worse than a stranger—it's the face of an enemy.

"You set me up," he says, his voice colder than these stone walls. "From the moment we met, you were lying to me. There was no kidnapper. That was one of your father's men. And then, when I didn't call you afterward…" He's watching my face, confirming every word as it comes out of his mouth. "Then you threw yourself at me again, at the date auction. That was no coincidence. You knew I'd be there."

It's been years since I've let tears flow freely. But I feel them running down my cheeks now, silent and hot.

"I'm sorry," I say. "I wanted to tell you—"

"You're a *fucking liar*," Sebastian says. "I don't believe a goddamned word that comes out of your mouth."

I can't deny it.

I should have told him the truth as soon as I knew I was falling in love with him.

I should have told him when he showed me his mother's piano.

I should have told him that night on the beach when he took my virginity.

I should have told him at the planetarium when he proposed.

I had so many opportunities, and I never took them. Because I was a coward. And selfish. I was afraid my father would hurt me—and even more afraid that Sebastian would leave me.

I told myself it wouldn't matter after the wedding.

But it always mattered, and it always will.

"You're right," I whisper. "I lied to you. I knew it was wrong,

but I kept doing it. I'm so sorry, Sebastian. I didn't know this would happen. My father—"

"I DON'T WANT TO HEAR ABOUT YOUR FUCKING FATHER!" Sebastian bellows. "MY FATHER'S DEAD!"

It's like a spike to my chest. I fall silent under the enormity of what I've done.

I suppose I knew that, if I'd tried to remember. I saw my father and his men open fire on Sebastian's family. I saw Enzo Gallo—that warm and well-mannered man who treated me with more respect than my own father has ever done—I saw him hit in the face and the chest.

No one could have survived that. Especially not a man his age.

My face crumples like a paper bag, and the tears fall faster.

It only infuriates Sebastian more.

"*Don't you dare cry for him.* It's your fault he's dead."

"What about the others?" I ask, unable to help myself. I have to know if his brothers are all right, and Camille and Greta.

Sebastian stares at me coldly, not wanting to answer. But at last he says, "Nero was shot six times. But he isn't dead yet. Camille, Greta, and Jace are alive. Giovanni and Brody are dead." He swallows hard, then says, "Brody wasn't even a fucking mafioso. He was just a friend."

I don't know what to say.

There's nothing that can be said. Nothing will wipe away what I did. Nothing will bring Sebastian's father back, or his friends.

I look up at him, feeling like my heart is tearing in half. "I'm sorry," I say. "I'd give anything to take it back."

"Well, you can't."

With that, Sebastian turns to leave.

But first he throws a water bottle down on the bed, the one and only hint of mercy he's given me.

He turns and slams the door, locking it behind him.

CHAPTER 17
SEBASTIAN

I STAND OUTSIDE THE CELL WAY DOWN IN THE BASEMENT, MY whole body shaking with fury and hurt.

I feel betrayed. I feel like a fool.

And most of all, I feel horribly, sickeningly guilty.

I told Yelena it was her fault that my father's dead and my brother is lying in an intensive care unit with tubes going in and out of his body.

But the truth is, it's my fault.

I knew Alexei Yenin hated us. I knew he wanted revenge on my family. I knew he exerts incredible pressure and control over his children.

And yet I told myself it would all be fine. Because I wanted to believe it would be fine. I wanted to believe I could fall in love and be happy and that all the wrongs of the past could be swept under a rug.

Of course, Yelena and I didn't meet by chance. It's ludicrous now to think I ever believed that.

The way we connected with each other, the way we fell in love so quickly felt so fated, so absolutely right, that it made me believe in destiny. I never questioned how we kept crossing paths. I believed the universe was bringing us together.

Those are the delusions of a fool. Someone who thinks that karma is real, that things always work out right in the end. How could I ever have believed that when I've seen a thousand times that it isn't true?

My uncle was burned alive by the fucking *Bratva*. My mother died of an infection that was random, capricious, and totally preventable. And now my father is dead because of my mistake. There's no justice in any of that.

I shouldn't have gone in that cell.

I can't get the sight of Yelena out of my mind: Her beautiful wedding dress now dirty, torn, and stained with blood. Her face stricken and pleading. Chains on her hands and feet. And that bandage covering her shoulder where Dr. Bloom plucked out the bullet and sewed her up again.

The bullet she took for me.

When she told me that she knew nothing, that she had no idea what her father had planned, I didn't believe that for a second. She knew that he was out to get us from the beginning. She knew it was a setup.

But one thing I know for certain is that she jumped in front of that gun...

Nobody made her do that.

It was instinctual, immediate.

She wanted to save me.

Which means that whatever else she might have done, she does care about me. That part wasn't entirely a lie.

But it can't bring my father back from the dead.

I just came from the morgue. The police recovered Papa's body from the Orthodox Cathedral. They found it under the triptych, along with the bodies of three of Yenin's *bratoks*. They ran Papa's prints through their system, finding his old record from his younger years when he was arrested on charges of racketeering and money laundering. They called me in to identify the body.

My father looked so much smaller than usual, lying on that slab under a sheet, his suit and dress shirt stripped off him. His skin was the color of cheese, with marks all over from the heavy wooden frame falling on top of him. And his face…it was almost completely destroyed. Not from the triptych—from the *Bratva*'s bullets. All that was left was one beetle-black eye, open and staring.

The police already knew who he was. They brought me in to shock me. Hoping that when they took me into the room next door, I'd spill the details of exactly what had happened at the cathedral. They must have recognized the other bodies as *Bratva*. Maybe they thought I'd tell them everything, motivated by revenge.

I refused to answer a single question. I said I didn't know what had happened, why my father had been at the church that day. Worst of all, I couldn't tell them that the bodies lying next to my father's— one tall and lanky, the other broad and bulky, belonged to Brody and Giovanni.

Giovanni didn't have much family, only a brother in prison. But I thought of the bewildering call Brody's parents were sure to receive later today or tomorrow as they sit calmly in their little house in Wilmette, reading the paper or watching television, never suspecting that anything had happened to their only child. I wanted to slap my own face over and over in pure shame and anger.

I lean against the basement walls—plain concrete, damp and chilly because this little dungeon is the lowest level of our house, below even Nero's old garage. I wish I could disappear off the face of the earth. Because I can't face all the things I've caused to happen.

But that would be the coward's way out.

I'm not going to kill myself.

I'm going to get revenge.

So I climb the stairs back up to the kitchen. Greta is sitting at the little table, dressed in clean clothes, her hair neatly brushed and tied back as always, but her face puffy and swollen from crying.

It's strange to see her sitting. Greta is always bustling around, keeping her hands busy. She's never idle. She hates to sit down even to watch a movie.

When she sees me, she jumps up and throws her arms around me. It hurts to accept her hug. I don't deserve it—I don't deserve her comfort.

"How's Nero?" she asks.

I went to the hospital before the morgue. That was the strangest sight of all. Nero is the id of our family—primal, ferocious, and intensely alive. To see him lying there, pale and motionless, only breathing because of the machines keeping him alive…it was unbearable.

Camille was sitting right next to him, almost as pale as Nero himself. She hadn't changed out of the pretty red dress she'd worn to the wedding. She hadn't left his side for a single moment except for when he was in surgery, and even then she'd sat in the waiting room, crying until she had no more tears left in her body.

The dress looked wilted and sad, stained all over with my brother's blood just a little darker than the material itself. I remembered how he'd flung himself on top of Camille, without even attempting to protect himself or to fight back against the Russians.

I could never have imagined Nero behaving that way. I don't think he would have sacrificed himself for Papa or Aida or any of us. Only for Camille.

"They don't know anything yet," I say to Greta. "He survived the surgery, though."

"He'll pull through," Greta assures me, letting go of me so she can blow her nose into one of the many tissues she keeps tucked in her pockets. "Nero is too stubborn to die."

"I told Jace to guard the hospital door. I told him not to leave for any reason."

I'm trying to justify myself to Greta, even though we both know how insufficient it is to try to protect Nero now, after I almost cost him his life.

Greta is too kind to accuse me. She already knows how much I'm blaming myself.

I have to discuss something else with her, but I don't know how to say it.

So I take her hand and ask her, "Will you sit down with me for a minute?"

"Should I make us some tea?"

"Not for me. But if you want some…"

"No." She shakes her head. "All I've been doing is drinking tea, until I'm shaking. It's not calming me down anymore."

She sits down across from me at the tiny slightly wobbly table that's been sitting in this kitchen since before I was born. So many things in this house were here before me and will probably be here long after I'm gone—a duration of time that might not be as long as I think with the plans I intend to execute over the next few weeks.

Which is what I need to discuss with Greta.

Once we're both seated, I look her in the eye. It's hard to do that because Greta's face is so kind and sympathetic, so full of love for me. I've always been her favorite, I know that. And I've never deserved it less than today.

"Greta," I say. "This isn't over with the Russians."

Her bottom lips trembles, and she presses her mouth into a firm line to keep herself from letting out a sob. I assume she's remembering her terror in that moment when the *Bratva* stood from their seats and pointed their guns at her.

"You know what I have to do now."

Greta slowly shakes her head, her clear blue eyes fixed on mine.

"You don't *have* to, Seb," she says quietly.

"Yes, I do."

"Why?" she says. "Because you think your father would have wanted revenge? Is that why?"

"No—" I say, but Greta pushes on, overriding me.

"Because I wouldn't be so sure of that, Seb! Enzo told me a lot of things these last few years. Things he had done. Things he regretted. His hopes and dreams for you children. And especially for you, Seb.

He said you were a good man. He said you weren't like him—you're more like your mother—"

"He was wrong," I cut her off. "I'm no different from Dante or Nero, or even my father. In fact, I might be worse."

"You don't mean that—"

"YES, I DO!" I bark, startling Greta into silence. "Greta, I *hate* Yenin. I'm going to find him, and I'm going to blow his fucking face off his skull, just like he did to Papa. He broke a blood contract, and he'll pay for that, no matter what I have to do. I'm going to kill him, and his son, and every one of his men. I'm going to wipe them off the face of this earth, so anyone who even dreams of raising a hand to our family again will remember what happened to the Russians and shake with fear."

Greta is staring at me wide-eyed. She's never heard me talk like this before.

"You heard Papa," I tell her. "For every blow, return three more. Our fury overwhelms their greed."

"He wasn't himself that night!" Greta cries. "He never wanted that for you."

I'm silent for a moment, remembering the thought I had as we finished our chess match.

I thought, *Some night we'll play our last game. And I won't know it's the last game when it's happening.*

That was the night. That was the last time. And just as I thought, I had no premonition that it would be the last.

"It doesn't matter who he expected to take his place. I'm the only one who can do it. I'm going down a path, and I don't expect you to follow me. I don't expect you to support me. You know Papa left you five million in his will—"

"I don't want that money!" Greta cries.

"You're taking it. It's yours. You've loved us, you've raised us, and you've cared for us. You've been our family. You made Papa happy when almost nothing else could. You should take care of yourself now. Travel, see the world, do all the things you put aside when you put us first."

Greta looks angry—and when Greta is angry, you better watch out. She has a thick fuse with a lot of dynamite behind it.

"I don't give a damn about traveling," she says. "This is my home. You are my family. Not sometimes—*always*."

I shake my head. "I can't protect you. I couldn't protect Papa or anyone else. This is a war, Greta. There's no possibility of a truce anymore. We eradicate the Russians now, or they'll pick us off one by one. One of us will destroy the other. It's win or die."

Greta looks at me, her face blotchy and her eyes full of tears. Her hands are folded calmly on the table in front of her.

"I never married," she says. "I never had children. I never made a family of my own. I threw my lot in with the Gallos, for better or worse. I helped raise you and your siblings. And I'll help raise *your* children, too."

"I'm not having any children."

I thought I would when I was dreaming of what my life would be like with Yelena. But now my wife is locked in a cell in the basement, and those dreams are torn to shreds and drenched in blood. There's no future for either of us. No babies to renew this family—not from me.

"You don't know what's to come," Greta snaps. "You're not a boy anymore, but you're not a man either, if you still think you can predict the future."

"You should at least leave until this is settled—"

"*No!*" she cries, her cheeks flaming with bright spots of color. "I'm staying right here! And I'll work however I can. That's what brings me happiness, Sebastian, for as long as it lasts. I don't care about traveling, and I don't care about being safe. If I did, I never would have taken this position to begin with. Do you know, your father told me the truth about his job the day he hired me? He never lied to me, Sebastian. Don't think I've been some blind fool, protected from the truth! What I do is humble, but I am one of you and I always have been."

I've never been able to win an argument with Greta. She never backs down when she's sure she's right.

And in this instance, what am I even trying to prove? That she'd be happier alone in Italy or sunny Spain?

"Now," Greta says firmly, deciding that her point has been made, "who have you got locked up below the garage?"

I look at her, startled. I didn't think she even knew about the cell beneath the garage.

She rolls her eyes at me. "I know every part of this house, boy. Remember that I've cleaned it since before you were born."

"It's Yelena," I admit.

"SEBASTIAN!" she shrieks.

"Don't argue with me about this," I say furiously. "She lied to me, and she betrayed us all. We have no idea what she's told her father or what she'll tell him next if we let her go."

"You can't keep your wife locked in a dungeon!" Greta shouts.

"Yes, I damn well can, and if you're so determined to stay here, you're going to help me."

"Help you how?"

"She needs food and antibiotics. And you might need to change her bandages."

"Bandages! Have you—"

"I didn't hurt her. She was shot at the wedding. Dr. Bloom came to see her; she's going to be fine."

Greta scowls at me, not liking this one bit.

"Don't let her go," I warn Greta. "I'm serious. I'm not the only one fucking pissed at her. The Russians might be, too, because she did stop them from killing me. She's safest exactly where she is."

Greta presses her lips together but doesn't argue. That means she'll do it, even if she doesn't like it.

With that settled, I get up from the table.

I have another conversation I've got to get through, which will be worse than the one with Greta.

I've got to talk to Dante.

CHAPTER 18
YELENA

I don't know how long it is between when Sebastian came down to visit me and when the door to the cell creaks open again. It's hard to judge time when you're in a windowless room that's almost completely dark.

I sit up as I hear the latch turning, thinking of all the things I want to say to Sebastian, the words I've been agonizing over during the time I've been trapped in here. But it isn't Seb who opens the door—it's Greta.

I search her face to see if she hates me, too, as everyone must.

She doesn't look angry—only sad.

She regards my ruined wedding dress with a pained expression—whether because the dark blotches of blood remind her that her friend and employer is gone, or perhaps because she started that day with the same sense of optimism and joy I did, only to watch it all burn before her eyes.

"Please don't attack me," she says. "I haven't got the key to those manacles, so it would be pointless."

"I wouldn't anyway," I tell her, and that's true. Even if I knew Seb were on his way down here with a gun in his hand, I still wouldn't hurt Greta. I've already done enough to tear the Gallos apart.

Of course, Greta has no reason to believe me, but she comes into the cell without fear. She's carrying a huge tray that must weigh almost as much as she does. On it I see a basin of hot water, a washcloth, soap, a toothbrush, toothpaste, fresh bandages, scissors, ointment, a bottle of pills, and a folded pair of clean pajamas. Then, next to that, a sandwich and a glass of milk.

I want all those things badly.

A wave of gratitude hits me, almost as painful as pleasant. I don't deserve Greta's kindness. I got Enzo killed, and Greta was probably closer to him than to anyone.

I can't even apologize for it. That only enraged Sebastian.

So all I say to Greta is, "I didn't know what was going to happen."

Greta nods. "I know. You saved Sebastian's life. You could have been killed yourself."

"I wish I were," I say dully.

I'm not being dramatic. I had one brief shining period of happiness with Sebastian. And now it's destroyed. I can't go back to the way my life used to be. Yet there's no way he could ever love me again.

"Don't say that," Greta says. "As long as you're alive, you don't know what could happen."

I don't want to argue with her, so I just look down at the faded mattress.

"I need to check your wound," Greta says. "I'll try to be careful..."

She removes the old bandages, which are dark with blood on the side closest to my body. I look down at the place where I was shot, morbidly curious.

The wound is surprisingly small—at least on the front side, which is all I can see. It's just below my collarbone, sewn shut with maybe a dozen stitches. The flesh around it is puffy and red, but it doesn't look infected.

Greta gently applies the antibiotic ointment, on the front side and the back, then rewraps my shoulder with clean bandages. She instructs me to take two of the pills, which she shakes out of the bottle into my hand.

I swallow them with milk, then take a bite of the sandwich for good measure. I hadn't realized I was starving.

"Go ahead," Greta says. "Eat."

I devour the sandwich in less than a minute. It's a club sandwich, toasted, cut in half, and speared with toothpicks to keep it together. I'm not surprised by how delicious it tastes—Greta doesn't strike me as a person who does anything halfway.

I finish all the milk, too, then turn my attention to the hot water. I'm filthy, and I badly need a wash.

"Should I help you take off the rest of the dress?" Greta says. "I don't think it can be saved…"

My wedding gown was already cut away all around the wound. Not to mention torn and bloodstained everywhere else. Still, it pains me to watch Greta cut through the remaining fabric with her large sharp shears. When she's finished, I'm left in only a strapless bra and panties.

Greta doesn't seem embarrassed by that, and neither am I. I use the soap and washcloth to give myself a bath as best I can, and then I brush my teeth and spit into the basin. It works reasonably well—I suppose this is how people did things in the olden days. And here I am in a dungeon, just like a medieval peasant who pissed off the king.

When I'm finished with all that, Greta offers me the clean pajamas, but we both realize I can't actually put them on with my arms and legs attached to the wall by long chains.

"It doesn't matter," I tell her.

Greta frowns, obviously displeased with this entire situation. "I'll bring you another blanket," she says.

By groping around, I discovered a small toilet in the corner, so I at least don't have to burden Greta with anything worse. There's a sink next to it, but the water tastes rusty, and it only runs cold.

I do have one last favor to ask her.

"Could you leave the light on, please?" I say.

"Of course," Greta says, frowning even more. "I'll bring you some books to read, too."

That's almost too much for me. I have to look down at my hands again, clenched tightly in my lap.

"Thank you," I whisper.

CHAPTER 19
SEBASTIAN

I find Dante in his hotel room at the Drake.

He chose to stay there instead of coming back to our family home. Another sign that he doesn't really want to be here at all.

I can hear his heavy bulk moving around inside the room, but when I knock, it's a long time before he answers. Maybe because he has to limp over on his stiff leg.

He was shot in the thigh by one of Yenin's men—who knows which. The bullet landed an inch from the femoral artery. If the *bratok*'s gun would have been pointed a millimeter to the left, Dante would have bled out in seconds.

Worse is the damage to his hand. He was hit in his right palm. The doctor said his pinky and ring finger might not ever regain their function.

All these things are added to the list of the damage I've done.

Dante hasn't shaved since the wedding. His stubble looks thick and bluish, and his ink-black hair is messy instead of combed back from his brow like usual. The deep lines on his face make it look as if he's aged ten years.

I don't bother to greet him with any of the usual questions, like, *How are you?* I know how he's doing—the same as me: fucking horrible.

As I walk into the hotel room, I can see he's already made the bed with military precision. His suitcase is packed and zipped on top of the coverlet. Dante himself is dressed in fresh clothes, including his shoes.

"What are you doing?"

"I'm leaving," Dante says.

"What do you mean you're leaving?"

"Exactly what I said."

He's standing next to his suitcase, his arms folded across his broad chest. His jaw is tightly clenched.

"What about Papa's funeral?"

"You shouldn't have one," he says bluntly. "That would be an open invitation to the Russians to come finish what they started."

"And what about us?" I demand. "Aren't we going to finish it?"

Dante says. "I'm not."

"How can you say that? Don't you care what they did to Papa?"

A dark fire comes into Dante's eyes. For the first time in a very long time, he loses his temper. In one motion, he seizes me by the throat and throws me against the wall. He's not as tall as I am, but he's still plenty big and the strongest man I've ever met. It's like being charged by a bull. He knocks the air out of me with the force of the impact, rattling my brain around in my skull when the back of my head hits the wall.

"Don't talk to me about our father," he hisses, right in my face. "You don't get to do that when I told you this was a bad idea from the very beginning."

Maybe he sees me wince with guilt because he lets go of me and steps away again almost immediately.

"I know it's my fault!" I cry. "But you have to help me, Dante. We can't let Yenin get away with this. He signed a blood oath. He has to pay for breaking the agreement."

"He'll pay when no one will do business with him again," Dante says. "Not the Italians, not the Irish, not the Polish, not the Asians, not the MC clubs, not fucking anyone, Seb. That's what it means to break a blood oath. You're cast out. Your honor is gone. He won't be protected by the *Bratva* in Russia or by anyone else. He can try to build his business, but it will wither and die without support, without anyone to trade with. And eventually, without protection, somebody will pick him off. He made his decision in anger, and he will pay for it."

"That's not good enough!"

"And what will be?" Dante demands. "You want to kill him and his men? How many more people will we lose trying to do that?"

"I don't know. But you're insane if you think they're just going to leave the rest of us alone. They meant to kill every single one of us. We only survived because you were there and they didn't expect it."

Dante shakes his head. "I shouldn't have come. I promised Simone I was done with this. I promised her I wouldn't come home covered in blood ever again. Now look at me." He holds up his bandaged hand with its two useless fingers. "I'm not starting another cycle of violence."

"It's already started!"

"I don't care." His voice is firm and final. "I have two children, Seb. I hope to have more. I missed out on nine years with Simone. I want to live every second I have left by her side. If anything had gone differently at that wedding…Simone would be getting a phone call instead of her husband home on a plane. I won't do that to her, or to Henry and Serena. My daughter doesn't even know me yet, Seb. I won't have her grow up with just a photograph for a father."

"And what about the rest of us?"

Dante looks at me with his black eyes so like our father's. "I love you, Sebastian. I always will. But Simone and my children are my family now. I have to put them first."

I can't believe he's actually leaving. Not now, when we need him the most.

But he's already hoisting his suitcase, picking it up as easily as if it were empty.

"Be careful, Seb. This isn't like robbing that vault or even your wedding. I won't be there to save the day. I'm not coming back this time."

I stare at him, unbelieving.

He starts walking toward the hotel room door. I watch his broad back striding away from me.

Then, right as he turns the knob, I call out, "Wait!"

He pauses, looking back over his shoulder without letting go of the door.

I say, "I love you, too, Brother."

CHAPTER 20
YELENA

GRETA COMES BACK DOWN TO THE CELL SEVERAL MORE TIMES TO bring me warmer blankets, food, drinks, and an assortment of books from Enzo Gallo's library.

One of them is *The Name of the Rose*, a mystery novel Enzo and I had discussed at length when we went for brunch together. I can tell from the creasing on the spine and the soft, slightly battered pages that he must have read it many times.

It feels wrong to hold Enzo's book and read through it when he won't ever get the chance to enjoy it again.

Yet reading it is strangely comforting, too, in a way I probably don't deserve. It brings back our conversation so vividly: The way Enzo spoke to me, as if I were an equal, and listened to my responses with real interest. The way he put his warm dry hand on top of mine and said, "There's no pleasure quite like reading, is there? Sometimes it's the only thing that eases my mind."

Now I feel how true those words were. Reading this book is easing my mind when nothing else could. I get lost in the fourteenth century, in the world of the Italian monks. And finally, I'm calm enough to sleep again.

When I wake, it's impossible for me to tell what time it is, day or night. There are no windows, no natural light whatsoever. And, of course, no view of the stars.

In the artificial light of the cell, I remember how comforting astronomy always was to me. I looked up at the sky, and it was so infinite and vast that it made even my father seem insignificant by comparison. The stars were so beautiful and so untouchable by anything on earth. They represented the idea of something more... of endless possibility.

And then, that night Sebastian kissed me on the Ferris wheel, they came to symbolize Seb himself. He was that hope, that love I'd looked for. He came into my life like that first glimmering star I glimpsed right above our car. I lost my virginity to him on the beach, under a sky studded with stars. And he proposed to me in the dome of the planetarium, with the whole universe whirling around us.

That's why I chose the dress I did—because it reminded me of a little piece of the cosmos. It seemed to symbolize how powerful our love was. That it was untouchable by my father or anything else.

But I was wrong.

My father destroyed it all in one moment.

And now I'm down here in this cell without any sun or moon or stars. Because they're snuffed out. Because Sebastian doesn't love me anymore.

I hear the creak of the latch, and I sit up, thinking Greta has come back with tea or soup.

Instead, Sebastian opens the door.

Even though I know he hates me now, the feeling that springs up in my chest isn't hate in return. It's swift and desperate longing. I still love his face. I still love his frame. I still love those dark and searching eyes, even if they're scrubbed of all affection for me.

"Where are your clothes?" Sebastian says.

He glances at my near-naked body, then quickly looks away again.

"I can't put on the pajamas. Because of these." I hold up my hands to show the manacles around my wrists and the chains that extend outward to the wall.

"Oh," Sebastian says.

He considers for a moment, then strides toward me. He takes a key from his pocket and unlocks the four manacles, one by one.

He has to come close to me to do it. Close enough that I can smell the achingly familiar scent of his skin. My heart hammers against my ribs like a fist beating against the bars of a cage.

As the restraints snap free from my wrists, Sebastian sees that the skin is red and raw in the places where it rubbed. I see the wince of guilt that flashes across his face before he smothers it.

"Has Greta been feeding you?"

"Yes. She's taking care of me."

I see his eyes flit over to the bandage on my shoulder. This time he can't quash the look of unease on his face. I was shot trying to save him, and he knows it. It doesn't make up for what I did. But it means something, all the same.

"Why are you keeping me here?" I ask.

I want to know if he plans to kill me. Because if he does, he might as well do it now.

"Why?" he snarls. "You want to go home to your father and brother?"

"No."

"Why not?"

"Because you're my husband," I say quietly. "Whether you like it or not. I belong to you...or to no one. I'm never going back to that house."

I still have Sebastian's ring on my finger. He didn't take it off me. It glimmers there...one tiny star that has yet to be snuffed out.

Sebastian's face is a maelstrom of emotion. I can't read them all. There's definitely anger there. And maybe, maybe...sadness, too.

He takes a moment to compose himself before he says, low and cold, "I want you to tell me everything you know about your father's business. The name of every one of his *bratoks*. Every one of his holdings. I want to know where he operates, how he operates, where he stores his drugs, his guns, his money. I want to know his friends and his enemies. Every secret he's let slip. And don't tell me you don't know, Yelena—I know how clever you are. Whether he's explicitly told you or not, I know you've seen things. If you lie to me about one single thing..."

The threat hangs unspoken in the air, even more ominous because Sebastian doesn't bother to give it form. He doesn't have to. We both know that if I betray him again, he'll kill me.

It doesn't matter. Whether Sebastian believes me or not, I'll never lie to him again.

For over an hour, I tell him every detail I've ever observed of my father's business. Sebastian only interrupts to clarify certain points. When I'm done, he nods slowly but doesn't thank me.

I probably should keep quiet, but I can't help asking him, "What are you going to do?"

Sebastian looks me dead in the eye, his face a pitiless mask. "I'm going to kill every fucking one of them."

It's what I suspected, but his words still hit me like a slap.

One of those men is Adrian.

Despite the fact he went to my wedding to murder my husband...I still love my brother.

I don't bother to plead for his life. I know Sebastian won't listen.

All I can do is watch him leave the cell, my guts churning with misery.

I can't see a scenario where both my brother and the man that I love walk away from this alive.

CHAPTER 21
SEBASTIAN

IF I DON'T HAVE DANTE OR NERO BESIDE ME, I NEED ANOTHER ally.

The obvious choice is the Griffins. Even with my father dead, our alliance still stands—particularly since the current heir of both our empires is Miles Griffin, Callum and Aida's son.

The problem is that the Griffins are trying to move into full legitimacy. Callum is running for mayor of the whole damned city. The last thing he wants is to be embroiled in a bloody battle with the Russians.

But there is someone else I can turn to. Somebody with his own grudge against the Russians. Someone likely to feel Alexei Yenin's wrath turned onto him next, after I'm killed...

I drive my battered truck out to the edge of the city and then down the long, winding drive to the secluded mansion of Mikolaj Wilk.

It's a spooky-looking place, even in broad daylight. It's surrounded by so many thick and overgrown trees that the sunlight can barely penetrate down to the driveway. It's a Gothic manor house, dark and sprawling, with a large glass conservatory on one end and endless towers, gables, and chimneys along its length.

I park next to the empty, leaf-filled fountain, then walk slowly toward the front door so Mikolaj's men have plenty of time to get a good look at me via the security cameras. The Polish Mafia is vicious and insular, and Mikolaj himself is hardly social. He and Nessa tend to stay locked up in their house, with very few visitors.

I knock on the door, expecting it to be opened by one of the *braterstwo.*

Instead, I'm greeted by Nessa Griffin herself.

She pulls the door open, her cheeks flushed pink and her light brown hair pulled up in a messy bun on top of her head. She's wearing a leotard and tights and an extremely battered pair of ballet shoes. She's sweating slightly, probably not just from the run down to the door.

"Sebastian!" she cries, her face alight with pleasure and surprise. Then the smile falters on her face. "I'm so, so sorry about your father…"

"Thank you."

Nessa hesitates, like she wants to do something but isn't sure what. Impulsively, she throws her arms around me and hugs me tightly.

It's a nice hug—warm and genuine. I always liked Nessa. I've never met someone so completely and truly kind.

The only thing that makes me stiffen in her arms is the knowledge that her husband is both dangerous and intensely obsessed with his wife. I'd rather not start my interaction with Mikolaj with the sight of me embracing his beloved.

So I give her a pat on the back to let her know I appreciate the gesture, and Nessa lets go of me. Looking up into my face, she says, "Are you here to see Miko?"

"Yes." I nod.

"I'll get him. Come inside!"

She pulls the door wider, inviting me in. She leads me to a dark and gloomy formal sitting room with several sofas, a writing desk, and a cavernous fireplace.

"Make yourself comfortable," Nessa says kindly. "Can I get you a drink?"

"No," I say. "No thank you."

"I'll be right back."

She runs out of the room in those scuffed and torn ballet slippers. Nessa is a choreographer, so I assume she goes through plenty of shoes while working on her arrangements. She must have a studio somewhere in this place.

Sure enough, after a few minutes, I hear music on the upper floor—distant and scratchy, like an old phonograph. Accompanying that, the sound of lightly thumping feet.

A moment later, Mikolaj comes into the sitting room. He moves almost silently. He's tall and slim, fair-haired and sharp featured. He's tattooed across every inch of his skin: The intricate designs run down his arms to the backs of his hands and even his fingers. They rise over his neck all the way to his chin, like a high collar. Only his face is unmarked.

I've only ever seen him smile looking at Nessa. But I know he's brilliant and utterly ruthless. He took on my family and the Griffins simultaneously and caused a fuck of a lot of trouble until he was ensnared by the gentle heart of the youngest Irish princess.

"Good morning," Mikolaj says politely in his slight accent. He grew up in the slums of Warsaw, and you can still hear it in his voice. Dante said Miko almost exclusively speaks Polish with his men and even with Nessa, who learned it during her captivity in his house.

"Good morning," I say.

Mikolaj moves to the bar beneath the dusty leaded-glass windows to pour himself a drink of scotch. Without asking, he pours one for me, too.

I take it from him.

Mikolaj raises the glass and says, "To Enzo."

I raise my glass in return, my throat too thick to speak.

We both drink.

Mikolaj sits on the sofa across from mine, setting his glass down on the side table. "My condolences," he says.

"Thank you."

It occurs to me that out of all the people I know, Mikolaj might understand the pain I'm feeling the best. After all, he lost his adoptive father, a man he loved and respected.

I don't know if that will motivate him to help me, however—considering it was Dante who shot Tymon Zajac.

"What can I do for you, Sebastian?" he says.

I had considered many ways I could broach my request. I turned it over and over in my head during the long drive over here.

In the end, I decided to be blunt and completely honest. I knew Mikolaj would see through anything else.

"I want to kill Alexei Yenin," I say. "Also his son, Adrian, his lieutenant Rodion, and as many of the rest of his men as I can. I want revenge for what they did to my father, and to Nero, and to my friends Giovanni and Brody. I want justice for the blood oath he broke."

Mikolaj listens, motionless and expressionless. He doesn't answer, waiting for me to continue.

"Yenin is a mutual enemy of ours. He's a grudge holder and an oath breaker. He probably blames you for the death of Kolya Kristoff as much as he blames my family. He probably blames the Griffins even more. I believe he'll try to attack you and the Griffins in turn, once he's eradicated my family."

Mikolaj takes another sip of his drink while he considers. He swirls the glass gently, so the amber liquid spins around.

"It was me who broke my agreement with the Russians," he says, "when I fell in love with Nessa."

"That's what I mean," I say. "Alexei Yenin is not forgiving."

"Neither am I," Mikolaj says coldly. "The *Bratva* made a deal with my lieutenants behind my back. They convinced some of my men to betray me."

He considers his drink again, though I know he's actually considering my proposal. He sets the glass down on the end table with a sharp click.

"I met Alexei Yenin once," he says. "In Moscow. I was there with Tymon Zajac. Yenin barely looked at me, and to Tymon, he was arrogant and rude. I'm not surprised he broke the blood oath— he has no respect for tradition. And no honor either. You know he worked for the KGB, hunting *Bratva*? Only to become a *pakhan* himself. They ought to have cut his hands off and gouged his eyes out of his head before tattooing those stars on his shoulders."

His voice is icy, without a hint of emotion. He rises from the sofa, and I do the same. Mikolaj holds out his slim tattooed hand to me.

"I will help you get your revenge. I want all of Yenin's territory added to my own. That's my price."

I shake his hand immediately, with no desire to bargain. His offer is more than generous. "I think we'll work well together."

Mikolaj gives me a thin smile. "If we don't, we'll both end up dead."

CHAPTER 22
YELENA

I HADN'T INTENDED TO ESCAPE FROM THE CELL. I WAS WILLING TO put my fate in Sebastian's hands, one way or another.

But now I can't stop the fear gnawing at me.

Sebastian is about to go on a bloody rampage, seeking his revenge. I can't blame him for that—he deserves retribution.

But I can't just sit by waiting to see who will live and who will die.

At the very least, I could find my brother. I could beg Adrian to get away from my father. Maybe if Sebastian kills Papa and Rodion and the rest of the *bratoks*, he'll be satisfied. After all, Adrian didn't shoot anyone Sebastian loved.

I know my brother regrets what he did. I saw the hesitation in his eyes as he raised his gun to Sebastian's head. It's why he avoided me in the weeks before the wedding. He didn't like the plan. He didn't really want to be a part of it, I'm sure of that.

I think he would leave now, knowing that my father is doomed.

Or at least I hope that's what will happen.

I can't even entertain the possibility that it might be Sebastian who falls by my father's hand.

So, as soon as Sebastian leaves my cell again, I start looking for a way to escape.

My options are limited.

I've been unshackled from the wall. But there are no windows to climb out and no possibility of tunneling through the walls or floor. I'm deep under the Gallo house in a room made of solid cement.

The door seems to be my only option. It's made of steel. When it unlocks, I can hear the thud and clunk of a heavy magnetic lock.

Sebastian is careful when he comes in and out. Greta less so.

I have no intention of attacking her—she's been much too kind to me to do that, not to mention the fact it would enrage Sebastian. But it's possible I could use her indifference to my advantage.

The next time Greta brings me food, I take a long time eating the chicken and risotto she's so expertly prepared.

"Don't you like it?" Greta asks.

"I do," I say. "I'm just getting full. Do you mind if I keep it to eat a little later while I'm reading?"

"Of course." Greta stands, dusting off her hands. My mattress is set directly on the floor, and the floor seems to have a perpetual powder of concrete dust, despite the fact I'm sure the industrious Greta has swept it.

She leaves me alone to read.

I have no intention of picking up a book. As soon as she's gone, I take the dishes off my tray and turn it over.

Sure enough, I find a large rectangular sticker adhered to the bottom of the tray, with the name of the brand and place of manufacture printed on it. Very, very carefully I start to pick it off. It's difficult because the glue is strong, and I don't want to tear the sticker. But millimeter by millimeter, I'm able to pry it off the tray.

Once I've gotten the sticker free, I hide it under my pillow.

I don't know for sure if I'm going to use it or if it will even work.

But I have the option now.

CHAPTER 23
SEBASTIAN

Visiting Mikolaj and Nessa's house had a strange effect on me.

As I left, Nessa came down to say goodbye to me. She stood in the grand entryway, panting with exertion, a wisp of damp hair hanging over one eye, shaken loose from her bun.

Mikolaj reached out with one of his slim tattooed hands and tucked it gently back behind her ear. That hand has probably killed a hundred men, but Nessa didn't flinch away from it even for a moment. She looked up into Mikolaj's face, her eyes shining with trust and adoration.

Who would have thought a monster like Mikolaj could be loved by an angel like Nessa?

Yet it's clear they share a bond that can't be broken.

I thought that's what Yelena and I had.

Now, driving back toward my father's house, I realize we *do* have something.

Because deep inside me, I feel a pull stronger than magnetism, stronger than gravity. The closer I get to the house, the more powerful it becomes. I'm compelled to go back down the long, winding staircase to the cell.

I want to see Yelena.

I need to see her.

I told myself my previous visits were to rage at her and then to get information.

But if I'm being honest with myself, I need another look at her face. At those eyes the color of twilight, and those lips softer than anything I've ever touched, and that body that haunts my dreams when I lie sweating in my bed, unable to sleep.

I want her and I need her, worse than ever.

As I stride into the kitchen, I almost run into Greta carrying a basket of clothes out of the laundry room.

Greta sets it down on the kitchen table, eyeing me warily. "Where are you going?"

"Downstairs."

"How long do you intend to keep her locked up down there?" Greta demands. "This isn't right, Sebastian."

I whirl around to face her, trying to hold back this fury that's continually simmering right below the surface. "What do *you* think I should do, Greta?"

"Forgive her or let her go!" Greta cries.

"I can't let her go. And I will *never* forgive her."

I say that with total certainty. But as the words leave my lips, they don't ring true.

What would it take for me to forgive her?

She already risked her life to save mine. What more do I want from her?

Do I want her to beg? To grovel? What would prove to me that she's truly sorry?

While I'm wondering, Greta throws her hands up in frustration. "This isn't you, Sebastian! What are you doing? You're letting Yenin turn you into some kind of monster."

I can tell she didn't want to say that to me—her expression is miserable. But she means it, all the same.

I look at Greta without anger—only seriousness. "There was always a monster in me. Yenin just let it out."

Greta shakes her head at me, her pale blue eyes accusing. "You'd better not hurt her."

I sweep past her without making any promises.

I pause momentarily at the door of the laundry room. I see the heavy industrial-size washer and dryer and Greta's neat row of jars containing detergent pods, fabric softener, and clothespins.

Impulsively, I open the last jar and grab a handful of pins, stuffing them in my pocket alongside my switchblade.

Then I stride down the stairs, past the garage, all the way down to the lowest and most hidden level of this house. Beneath our weaponry, beneath our safe, way deep in the earth.

That's where my bride is waiting.

I wrench open the door, startling her so that a book falls from her hands. It was one of my father's—I recognize the cover, with its image of a rose and a skull in the style of an illuminated manuscript.

As she always does, Yelena searches my face, trying to read my intentions before I even open my mouth.

She won't guess them today.

I stride toward her, and she rises to meet me, her hands held up in an instinctive protective gesture. I shove them aside. I grab her by the back of the neck, seizing her and kissing her roughly.

She stiffens with shock.

I shove my tongue between those tender, soft lips, kissing her so hard that I taste blood in my mouth.

When I release her, she looks up at me, anxious and confused.

"Do you still love me?" I demand.

"Yes," she breathes.

"What would you do for me?"

She answers without hesitation. "Anything."

"Are you sure?"

"Yes."

"Don't say it unless you're really sure."

Yelena regards me with an expression as clear and serious as I've ever seen it. "I made a mistake, Sebastian. I was selfish and foolish. But I love you. And I will do *anything* to prove it."

I look at her standing there—the most beautiful woman I've ever seen, and the most ferocious. Even half dressed, locked up in a cell for days, she remains unbowed and unbroken. She won't submit. Not to that beast Rodion, and not to her psychotic father.

But she just might submit to me.

I push the cell door shut behind me. It closes with an ominous clank of metal. The room is lit by only one flickering overhead light. It's a dank and depressing space. But right now, it feels perfect. If feels right.

I take a step toward Yelena. She looks nervous. Which is also right—she should be nervous.

Even exhausted, recovering from a bullet to the shoulder, and locked in this basement for days, Yelena is so beautiful that it hurts to look at her. Her silvery hair hangs loose down her back, tangled but still lovely. She's paler than ever, with concrete dust smudged across her skin and dark circles under her eyes. It only serves to highlight how clear and luminous her skin actually is under the dirt. Her eyes look bigger than ever under the straight dark slashes of her brows, and her full lips are trembling slightly.

She's wearing the pajamas Greta brought downstairs—soft cotton with buttons up the front.

"Take those off."

Watching me warily, Yelena starts to undo the buttons. She fumbles with the first few because her fingers are unsteady. But she manages to get them all undone, and she slips out of the top, then the bottoms.

Now she's standing there in only her bra and panties, showing a body that men would fight and die to possess. A body that's strong, tall, and rebellious, and completely under my control at the moment.

I thought from the minute I met her that she looked like a warrior princess.

Well, now she's been captured from the barbarians. Now she belongs to me.

I took her. I married her. And now I own her.

She says she loves me?

Well, she can fucking prove it.

"Stand against the wall," I order.

I see a flutter in Yelena's throat as she swallows hard. Still, she obeys me, stepping away from the mattress and pressing her back against the cold concrete wall.

I pick up the manacles off the floor where they've been lying since I unlocked her.

I close them around her wrists and ankles again. They shut with a metallic snap. I can see the little goose bumps rising on her arms, from the chill or from nerves. I pull the chains tight so she's bound to the wall, her ankles apart and her hands only able to move a few inches.

I can see her pulse jumping in her throat. I hear her rapid breath, though she's trying to stay quiet. I can even smell the sharp tang of her adrenaline, laced with the enticing natural scent of her skin.

She's afraid, and that's exactly how I want her. I want her to feel just the smallest bit of the anguish I experienced over the past few days. I need to know if she truly wants to give herself to me or if she'll crack under pressure.

So I take my knife out of my pocket and snap open the blade.

Yelena eyes the razor-sharp edge as I bring the knife up to her ribs. She doesn't flinch. She stays perfectly still, her jaw clenched.

I lean over and put my lips right next to her ear.

"I'm going to push you to the limit, Yelena. Anytime you want, you can tell me to stop. I'll stop, and I'll leave. But if you want to me to stay…if you want to be mine…it's not gonna be so easy this time. I want *all* of you. I want every last fucking shred of you. Body and soul, you belong to me. I want you bare, vulnerable, and willing. I want to know you aren't holding anything back from me this time. Do you understand?"

She nods slowly, her eyes wide and unblinking.

She doesn't really understand.

But she will soon enough.

With one quick slash of the knife, I cut through the band of her strapless bra. The bra falls away from her body, baring those soft warm breasts. The moment they're exposed to the chilly air of the cell, her nipples harden and point slightly upward, like they're inviting me to take one in my mouth.

I will. But not yet…

Instead, I cut through her underwear, too, tearing the remains of her panties off her hips. Now her tight little pussy is bare, the lips slightly parted because her ankles are chained to the wall two feet apart. She can't close her legs. She can barely move at all.

It's incredibly erotic to have her chained up, completely at my mercy. It's even more erotic to see the look of determination in her fiercely narrowed eyes.

She thinks she's going to rise to this challenge.

I think I'm going to break her.

We'll soon know who is right.

Roughly, I grope her bare breasts with my hands. I press her against the wall with the weight of my body. I squeeze her nipples hard until she gasps, and I growl in her ear, "Does that hurt? Do you want me to stop?"

"No!" she cries, her stubbornness rising to meet mine.

I take the clothespins out of my pocket. I open one, and then I let it close around her left nipple. Yelena sucks in a sharp breath of air, but she doesn't cry out. I see her fists clench where they're chained to the wall at her sides.

Her nipple turns from its normal light tan color to dark pink, the same shade as her lips. It stands out from her breast, caught tight in the grip of the clothespin. I pinch the other wooden pin around her right nipple.

The pressure is steady and relentless. Her nipples are turning darker by the minute, and I know they must be aching. Yelena doesn't complain. When I kiss her, she kisses me back twice as hard. When I reach down to slide my fingers between those slightly parted pussy lips, I can feel that she's slick and wet.

Well, well, well. Either my bride has been missing me, or she's finding her own catharsis in the rough treatment.

I slide my fingers back and forth across her clit, using her wetness as lubrication. I feel her clit start to swell and stand, just like her nipples. Yelena tries to grind against my hand as best she can from her constrained position.

She's moaning and rubbing against me, trying to use the pleasure to distract herself from the nagging pain of her breasts.

I keep rubbing her pussy, increasing the pace and pressure until that pink flush comes into her cheeks, and her breathing quickens, and I know she's starting to build to orgasm. Then I withdraw my hand and step away from her.

Yelena lets out a groan of frustration. She wants me to keep touching her. She wants it badly. But I'm just getting started.

Her nipples are deeply flushed now. Slowly, achingly, I depress the spring to release the clothespin's grip on her left breast. As soon as I've removed it, I put my mouth around her puffy, swollen nipple, and I suck.

The noise Yelena makes is like nothing I've heard from her before. It's a deep groan: part pain and part exquisite relief. I'm soothing her sore nipple and stimulating it while it's sensitive and engorged.

I know she's dying for me to do the same on the other side, but I make her wait. I tug on the clothespin without removing it. Yelena arches her back, her eyes closed, whimpering softly.

At last I remove the pin, and I take her right nipple in my mouth, savoring how swollen and hot it's become and how Yelena writhes against the wall, barely able to handle the intense stimulation of me suckling on her tender breast.

Standing up straight again, I unzip the front of my pants. My cock springs free, rock-hard and throbbing. I press the head up against her entrance, and I watch her face as I ram it inside. Yelena groans and bites down hard on my shoulder. She bites me so hard that she almost draws blood.

I don't give a fuck. The only sensation I can feel is my cock sliding all the way inside her tight warm cunt. Even though it's been less than a week since the last time I fucked her, it feels like it's been a hundred years. My longing for her, my obsession with her, it all comes roaring back, stronger than ever. I thrust into her harder and harder, and it's not enough; I want more. I fuck her relentlessly against that wall, rocking her whole body against the concrete.

The rough cement is probably scratching her back. I don't care.

In this moment I want Yelena to feel every sensation to a fever pitch, just like I am. Whatever it takes, I have to get her to understand how she puts me through a shredder every time I see her, how my bond to her is painful and terrifying, how she hurt me worse than my knee, worse than losing my mother, worse than anything that's happened to me in my life. And yet I still fucking need her. I can't stop it; I can't turn it off.

She has this power over me, and I need to exert my power over her. I need to know that she wants me just as badly, that she'll tear herself to pieces for me, just like I'll do for her.

Feverishly, I unlock the manacles so I can take her in more positions. I throw her down on the mattress, and I mount her from behind. I grab that long silvery hair and I wrap it twice around my hand, seizing it tight. Then I yank her head back as I enter her from behind, using her hair to hold her fast.

I'm fucking her hard and rough, my hips slamming into her ass. I can never decide my favorite position with her because each one feels the best in the moment. Right now, the sight of her tight waist flaring out to that luscious heart-shaped ass brings out a primal lust that makes me grunt and rut like an animal.

I'm already sweating, and I'm dying to explode inside her, but I refuse to do it.

I'm taking everything tonight.

I pull out of Yelena to take a short break, my cock gleaming with her wetness.

I've never seen it so hard. It's standing straight out from my body, thick with veins.

Yelena turns around to look at me, sitting back on her heels. Her face is flushed, and her eyes look wild.

"What do you want now?" she asks.

She's trying to be submissive. She's trying to show that she's sorry.

But I still see that fire in her eyes. That look like when she stepped out into the skybox. She likes a challenge.

"Suck my cock," I order.

Yelena looks down at my cock that's still warm and wet from being inside her.

She doesn't hesitate. She lies down on her stomach and takes my cock in her hand, looking up at me. She licks all the way up the length of it, from base to head. She keeps eye contact with me the entire time while she swirls her tongue around the head and then takes the whole thing in her mouth. She licks and sucks eagerly, using her other hand to gently cradle my balls.

It feels outrageously good. She looks up at me, watching my face to see if I like it, watching to see if she's pleasing me right.

I roll her over on her back, and I shove my cock inside her again. I thrust into her ten, twenty times, and then I pull my cock out and bring it up to her mouth again so she can suck me off.

I alternate between her pussy and her mouth, using them each as long as I please. I go back and forth, feeling the softness and warmth of each, bringing myself to the edge of climax over and over.

I've never felt anything like this. It's insane and filthy, and I never want it to stop.

CHAPTER 24
YELENA

I LIE ON THE MATTRESS, LETTING SEBASTIAN ALTERNATE BETWEEN fucking my pussy and fucking my mouth. At first it was strange because I could taste myself on his cock, but it's not actually unpleasant. I taste musky and slightly sweet. The feel of his cock thrusting into my mouth is almost as pleasurable as when he goes back to my pussy again.

My lips and tongue are swollen and sensitive, and my nipples still ache from the clothespins. Every time he starts fucking me again, my bare breasts rub against his chest, sending sparks of pleasure down my body.

I don't know what the hell is happening to me.

I've been missing Sebastian so badly, I've been so fucking miserable thinking that he'd never touch me again, that I'd let him do anything to me. Every time he touches me, I feel such a powerful relief that it doesn't matter if he's rough or angry, it all feels good.

Actually, I want it rough.

I want to know he's feeling this just as hard as I am.

If he came down here and fucked me coldly, clinically, I couldn't stand it.

I want to know he still has desire inside him, even if it tears me apart.

I hear him panting and grunting; I see the sweat on his skin; I see that crazed look in his eye like he wants to devour me whole. I want it all, more and more and more.

I feel half out of my mind myself. I'm clawing at his back, biting his shoulder, urging him on to fuck me harder and deeper. I want the pleasure, and I want the pain. I want the punishment. I deserve it.

Sebastian kisses me ferociously, biting my lip.

"Tell me you'll do anything I say," he growls.

"I will."

"Tell me you need me."

"More than anything."

"Then turn over and put your face down and your ass up."

Obediently, I flip over, putting my face down against the mattress, kneeling with my hips raised.

"Pull your cheeks apart," he orders.

For the first time, I feel a shiver of real fear.

I was willing to please Sebastian any way I could. But I wasn't expecting this.

All of a sudden, I feel horribly exposed.

I'm embarrassed to do what he asked and afraid of what he'll demand next.

"Do you want me to stop?" Sebastian says coldly.

My eyes squeezed shut and face burning, I reach around to cup my ass cheeks in my hands, pulling them slightly apart.

Now I'm totally exposed, and I almost want to tell him to stop. But another part of me, the deeper part, the part that refuses to give up or give in, has decided I'm going all the way to the end of the line. Whatever that may be.

I let out a little shriek as I feel Sebastian bury his face in my pussy. His tongue feels almost unbearably hot and eager. But the surprise of his tongue against my clit is nothing compared to the surprise I feel as he starts to work his way upward...

He eats my pussy, and then he eats my ass. It's simultaneously humiliating and incredibly erotic. I've never been touched there in my life. I should be disgusted, but instead I feel the shockingly pleasurable sensation of his hot, warm tongue stimulating me in the most forbidden place. I relax a little. Sebastian uses his fingers to rub my clit while his tongue massages my ass. And it feels *really* fucking good.

I press my face harder into the mattress to stifle my moans. I can't admit how much I like this.

Sebastian rubs my pussy with one hand, and with the other, he slides a finger into my ass.

I stiffen, and he barks, "Relax!"

I try to do as he ordered. I try to accept what he's doing while my body revolts against being penetrated in this brand-new place.

The feeling is intense and mildly uncomfortable. Sebastian keeps massaging my clit at the same time. And relentlessly, inexorably, my body seems to decide this whole area is erotic, inside and out. All of it is sensual, all of it feels good.

The more I relax, the more I can accept his finger sliding gently in and out of my ass. It's weird, but it actually feels pretty fucking incredible.

That is until Sebastian presses the heavy head of his cock against my ass instead.

"Don't!" I gasp. "You're too big!"

If his finger was that intense, I can't even imagine how his cock will feel.

"You want me to stop?" he asks again.

I hesitate.

I don't know what will happen if I tell him to stop. Maybe he'll leave, and this whole encounter will be over. This could be my only chance to reconnect with him. Or maybe he'll forgive me either way. There's no way to know for sure.

The truth is, I'm not actually trying to prove anything to Sebastian.

I'm proving it to myself.

What I said was true—I'll do anything for him.

Before, I made a decision based off fear and selfishness.

I won't do that again. Even if it scares me, even if I'm embarrassed...I want to see what will happen if I give myself to him, without holding anything back.

I say, "I'm yours—fuck me any way you want."

Sebastian rubs his cock between my pussy lips to get it wet and slippery. Then he presses the head against my ass again. I take a deep breath, trying to relax.

Slowly he starts to push his cock into my ass.

It's like taking my virginity all over again, but ten times worse. The tightness of the fit is insanity. It seems to take forever just to get the first few inches in.

Sebastian goes slowly, but it's just so fucking intense. I can feel every millimeter of his cock. He's stretching and filling me like nothing I've experienced before.

My ass is even more sensitive than my pussy. I can feel everything more. Sebastian has aroused this whole area, so it's experiencing sensation in an entirely new way. But it's still making my body sweat and shake because my brain doesn't quite know how to interpret this kind of sensory input.

Finally, Sebastian's cock is all the way inside. It feels enormous, the size of a baseball bat. It feels impossible.

He stays still for a moment to let me get used to it. Then he starts fucking my ass with slow shallow thrusts.

It's tight going in and tight pulling out. The tightness never relaxes, not for a second. It means I can feel every part of his cock, head and shaft, every ridge and vein. I can feel his cock twitch and pulse deep inside me.

Sebastian drops on top of me, his weight on his elbows on either side of me, his chest pressed against my back. He's still thrusting into my ass, trying to be gentle, but I can hear from his groans how good this feels for him, how hard it is to hold back.

"You like that?" I whisper.

"It's fucking unreal..." he groans.

"Then come up my ass, Daddy...I want it..."

Sebastian pulls me on my side so he's spooning me, still inside me. He starts to rub my clit with his long strong fingers while he keeps thrusting shallowly in and out of my ass.

It's so intense that I can hardly think, can hardly breathe. The noises coming out of me are raw and guttural. I feel dirty and naughty and wildly aroused. I want to make Sebastian come this way, as the ultimate submissive act. But it's me who starts to shiver and clench, my body so full of pleasure that it can't be contained any longer. I need release.

I grind my pussy against Sebastian's hand. That makes my ass squeeze all the harder around his cock. Sebastian starts to thrust a little faster, and I grind a little harder, my whole body burning with this new combination of sensations.

The orgasm builds hard and fast, doubling and doubling again, until I can't hold it back a moment longer. I press my clit against his palm, and I feel a deep and wrenching climax that hits me inside and out, that makes my whole body vibrate.

At the same time, Sebastian explodes. I feel his cock twitch, and then I feel the distinct pulses of his cum shooting inside me. The molten cum pours out of him, hot and thick. Sebastian lets out a roar.

We both collapse on the mattress, panting and sweaty, scratched and bruised. The sex was aggressive and animalistic. Rough and dirty.

And yet...I don't feel upset. I don't feel used.

I feel strangely satisfied. Like I was given something I didn't even know I needed.

For the first time since our wedding, I'm not thinking about the mistake I made and all the awful things that happened afterward.

My brain seems washed clean of all that, at least for the moment.

I'm only listening to Sebastian's breath and my own. I feel his heavy arms wrapped around me. He hasn't let go of me yet—I'm praying he won't.

With Sebastian holding me, I can finally fall into a deep and lasting sleep.

CHAPTER 25
SEBASTIAN

WHEN I WAKE UP, YELENA IS SLEEPING BESIDE ME, CURLED AGAINST me like a kitten.

Her face doesn't look tense with strain anymore. Instead, she's relaxed and peaceful. Like she used to be when we were alone together, just the two of us, before we were married.

The sight of her lying there, happy in her sleep, away from the reality of our situation, makes my heart seize in my chest. The love I feel for her is still there, stronger than ever. But it's drenched in pain and regret. It hurts to look at her, and yet I can't look away.

Gently, I smooth her pale hair away from her face. I kiss her softly on her forehead.

Then I get up from the mattress.

She doesn't stir a muscle. She doesn't hear me leave.

I close the door behind me, listening to the magnetic bolt slide into place.

It's for Yelena's own safety.

My mind is clearer and more focused than ever. I can see what I have to do, laid out before me like a chessboard.

I was never the planner, the strategist. I was never meant to lead this family.

But my father is dead. Dante is in Paris. Nero is lying in a hospital bed.

I'm the only one left. The only one who can finish this.

I remember what Papa said, that last night we played against each other, up on the roof: *Play the opening like a book, the middle game like a magician, and the endgame like a machine.*

When this whole thing began, I played by the rules. I did everything the way I was supposed to—I met with Yenin, and I signed the contract.

Now it's time to become a magician instead. It's time to surprise and shock him. It's time to make everything he holds dear turn to dust in his hands, without him understanding how it's even happening.

And then in end…I'll kill them all, as cold and relentless as any machine. Without hesitation, without mistakes, and without mercy.

I'm not angry at Yelena anymore. I understand she was as blinded by love and hope as I was. But she's safest exactly where she is. She can't be a part of what happens next.

I run over the information I confirmed with Yelena the day I interrogated her down in the cell.

I picture the chessboard, with Alexei Yenin in the center as the king, safely surrounded by his men who will protect him to the death. In a chess match, the object is to capture enough of your opponent's pieces that the king becomes vulnerable. You have to lure him out of safety.

In a chess game, each piece is assigned a point value. The points have no bearing on the game—capturing the king is all that matters. But it gives you a sense of how well you're doing, of how much you've managed to reduce the other player's forces.

I picture Yenin's men as those pieces.

His low-level *bratoks* are the pawns, of course. He has a dozen or so of these men, and I'll kill as many as I have to, though they aren't my main focus. If Yenin is dead, they won't come for revenge on their own. One was already shot at the wedding: the baby-faced driver Timur.

On the next level up, Yenin has his *boyeviks*, his warriors. Those would be his knights. Yelena says he has four main enforcers: Iov, Pavel, Denis, and Pyotr. Two were killed at the church: Iov, the pretend kidnapper I shot with Adrian's gun, and Pavel, who was crushed by the triptych. The two remaining are Denis, a former bare-knuckle boxer from Saint Petersburg, and Pyotr, who Yelena tells me was a freelance killer for hire before her father recruited him to come to Chicago.

Then Yenin has his brigadiers—the lieutenants in charge of a particular aspect of his business. Yelena says his most trusted lieutenants were likewise at the wedding: her uncle Vale and her cousin Kadir. Vale handles bookkeeping and bribes, while Kadir is in charge of stocking Yenin's sex clubs and strip joints with a fresh supply of girls from Ukraine and Belarus. Those two men are Yenin's bishops.

Adrian Yenin could be considered the queen—Yenin's right hand. But in truth, Adrian is young, and inexperienced, and not particularly vicious. He's more like a rook: important for certain maneuvers but not truly crucial.

It's Rodion who's the queen—Yenin's most powerful and dangerous asset. He's also the greatest threat to Yelena. If I don't eliminate him, then even if Yenin and I are both killed, Rodion will come for her. I'm sure of it.

I compare my forces to Yenin's.

I have Jace, who escaped from the wedding completely unharmed through sheer dumb luck. Since he's the person I trust most, I've sent him to the hospital to guard Nero's room. I told him not to leave my brother's side for any reason and to shoot anyone who tries to come through the door who isn't a doctor or nurse.

In addition, I have Matteo Carmine's two sons stationed in the hallway outside Nero's door, watching the elevator and the stairs. With Nero sequestered on the top floor, this should keep Yenin's men from finishing what they started.

The Carmines are one of the three Italian families most loyal to my father. The other two are the Marinos and the Bianchis. Bosco Bianchi is a fucking idiot, but he owes us for getting him out of a jam last year. Antonio and Carlo Marino are both strong fighters. I'll use them and my father's top three enforcers: Stefano, Zio, and Tappo.

Stefano is a ferocious fighter even though he's pushing fifty—he's been collecting debts on my father's behalf for the past thirty years. Zio is the youngest of the bunch and relatively inexperienced, but he's my cousin and intensely loyal to Papa, who paid every expense for his baby sister's heart surgery a few years back. Tappo is surprisingly small for an enforcer, but he's vicious as they come. He was a lightweight MMA champion, known for knocking out his opponents with one punch. Even I'd think twice before squaring up against him.

It's not a very big army. I'm realizing now how many of my father's men have grown old, settling into less demanding duties. Most of them work in the construction or hospitality arms of our business now. They're barely even gangsters anymore.

I'd be worried—but I also have Mikolaj Wilk and four of his men.

I'd put the *braterstwo* up against anyone, and I'd put Miko against all of them. They're just as vicious as the Russians and even more cunning.

So, early in the morning, while Yelena is still sleeping down in her cell, I drive back to Mikolaj's mansion so we can launch our attack.

CHAPTER 26
YELENA

When I wake, Sebastian is gone.

There's nothing as empty as a bare stretch of mattress where you hoped to see the person you love.

I stare at that space for a long time, wondering where he went—and wondering if he'll return.

I roll over into the dent where his heavy body lay, and I bury my face in his half of the pillow, trying to see if the scent of his hair and his skin is still lingering.

The night before seems like a dream.

My aching muscles remind me that it was all real. Sebastian and I fucked like animals for hours. I gave myself to him, fully and entirely, holding nothing back. He took everything he needed from me and gave himself back in return. The real Sebastian. Dark and angry, but still in love with me.

I know he is. I don't see him leaving as a sign that he doesn't care. He wouldn't have come down here at all, if that were the case. He couldn't have fucked me like that, with such fixation and desperation.

He was doing what he had to, to forgive me. To take me back again.

I understand all that.

And I understand where he's gone now.

The sex healed the rift between us. But it hasn't satisfied his need for revenge.

I sit on that mattress, facing my fundamental dilemma once more.

Sebastian has gone to kill everyone I know and love.

Most of them I could lose without blinking. Some I might even like to see die—Rodion, for instance.

I won't enjoy hearing that my father's been killed, but I accept it. He signed his own death warrant when he broke the blood contract.

But Adrian…Adrian is still my twin. After my mother died and before I met Sebastian, Adrian was the only person on this planet who loved me. He has his faults, but he always tried to comfort and protect me. He's my brother, and I can't stop loving him, no matter what he's done.

So I sit here wondering what I should do.

Should I stay exactly where I am and let fate decide?

Or should I intervene and risk losing Sebastian once and for all?

He forgave me for what I did before, despite the damage I caused. Despite the trust I broke.

But if I interfere in his revenge…

I'm sick at the thought of fucking things up all over again. I should stay put, exactly where I am. I can't ruin anything if I'm here, right where Sebastian wants me.

That's what I tell myself. Until my brain starts tormenting me with thoughts of where Sebastian might be right now, what he might be doing—and what my father might be doing in return.

What if Sebastian gets himself killed? What if they all do?

I can't just sit here while the world burns around me.

I jump up from the mattress and pace the room. Then I force myself to sit down again. Then I jump up once more.

I'm tormented, my mind swirling around and around in my skull like my body paces around and around in the cell.

Hours pass this way. I know Greta will be coming down with lunch. If I'm going to act, I have to do it soon. Assuming I can do anything at all.

I sit on the mattress for the last time, forcing myself to decide. Stay or go? Act or wait?

At last, I realize there is no right choice. I have no ability to save Sebastian and my brother, not really. And I have no ability to avoid regret. The outcome isn't in my hands. All I can do is try.

So I sit quietly on the mattress, my brain and body calm at last. I slip my hand under my pillow and find the sticker, still tacky on one side. Luckily, I didn't lose it while Sebastian and I destroyed this room last night. I hold the sticker in my hand, hidden between my palm and my thigh.

Only a few minutes later, I hear the creak of the door as Greta comes into the cell. Because her arms are full with the heavy lunch tray, she doesn't close the door behind her. She carries the tray over to the bed and bends her knees to set it down.

Pretending to reach for the tray, I knock over the glass of milk.

"Oh, sorry!" I cry. "Let me grab a towel."

I jump up from the bed, pretending to grab a washcloth from the sink. As I pass the open doorframe, I press the sticker over the hole where the magnetic bolt slides into place. Greta—busy righting the glass and trying to salvage my sandwich—doesn't notice a thing. I bring her my washcloth and help her to mop up the spilled milk.

She sits with me while I eat. She seems a little nervous. I think she's concerned for me.

Greta asks tentatively, "Did you speak to Sebastian last night?"

"Yes," I say. "He came down here."

"Was it…a productive conversation?"

My face burns with a flood of memories. I'd die if Greta could see inside my head right now. "I think we'll come to an agreement, eventually."

"Really?" Greta's face is full of relief. "I knew Sebastian would be able to move past all this, given time. He has a good heart, Yelena, and he loves you intensely. I know he does."

I feel bad for deceiving Greta after all she's done for me.

I put my hand over hers and squeeze it.

"I love him, too," I tell her. "No matter what happens."

Greta nods, then leans over and hugs me, careful of my bandaged shoulder.

"Thank you for taking care of me," I tell her.

"Oh," she says, flapping her hand to swat away my gratitude like she's swatting a fly. "It's nothing."

"It's something to me."

Greta picks up my tray, which I've cleaned in minutes, ravenous from the activities of the night before.

"Do you want any more milk?" she asks.

"No," I say. "That was perfect."

She leaves the cell, closing the door behind her. She doesn't notice—though I do because I'm listening carefully—that the magnetic lock makes its normal whirring sound but without the accompanying clunk of the bolt sliding into place. It's blocked by the sticker on the doorframe.

I wait a full twenty minutes to make sure Greta is all the way upstairs and not coming back.

Then I walk over to the door and pull.

It swings open easily on its hinges.

I look out into the dark hallway, my heart rising in my throat.

I don't have to think about it—I already made my decision. Taking a deep breath, I slip out of the cell.

CHAPTER 27
SEBASTIAN

IT'S TIME TO BECOME A MAGICIAN.

It's time to take everything Alexei Yenin owns and make it disappear.

He expects me to attack him outright. He thinks I'm so blinded by bloodlust that I'll do anything to find him and kill him.

Instead, I'm going to launch an attack on three targets simultaneously. None of them are Yenin.

During my conversation with Yelena, I realized how little my family had actually understood Yenin's operations. We thought of him as small-time because his drug and arms trade were constrained to the west corner of the city—the surrounding territory controlled by other factions.

However, his operation is much bigger than I thought.

He makes his money in three main ways: illegal gambling, porn production, and a wind farm west of the city.

The gambling we knew about because my family runs the biggest poker ring in the city. We knew Yenin was running a sports betting operation on the side, but we underestimated the scale.

Yelena told me Yenin doesn't make his money off the bets themselves. He makes his profit by loaning additional money for betting at a 200 percent interest rate. Then he ruthlessly collects from the hapless gamblers who inevitably lose it all.

Even though he lends the money locally, his operation takes place almost entirely online. He has a team of Russian programmers who work out of a warehouse in Bensenville, while his enforcers handle the collections.

Already, I'm missing Nero—he'd know exactly how to royally fuck up Yenin's network. He could probably hack into it remotely. But Nero is barely conscious and definitely not able to work. So I'll have to figure it out myself.

The porn production was likewise a surprise. We knew Yenin imported girls from the poorer regions of Ukraine and Romania, but we thought it was only to stock his depressing little brothel. It was Yelena who told me the girls are actually used to make fetish videos, which he likewise sells online through OnlyFans and Pornhub.

Finally, there's the wind farm. This is, apparently, a brand-new venture. Yelena explained it to me, based off snippets she'd overheard and things her brother had told her.

"It's a new industry," she said, "so it's poorly regulated. You've got high prices, complicated financing. And then there are the government subsidies. Adrian told me he's skimmed off ten million this year alone taking green energy grants and pocketing the funds. He's supposed to have eight windmills out there, but only two of them actually work."

I plan to wipe out all three of his cash sources, all at once. Mikolaj and I timed the attack down to the minute.

Mikolaj and his men will take down the sports betting ring.

"Make sure you wipe the system before you destroy the servers," I told him. "We don't want him back and up and running with just the cost of a few new computers."

"Don't worry," Miko said carelessly. "I'm bringing a kid from Wroclaw. He was stealing weapons schematics from the Department of Defense by the time he was fifteen. So I'm sure he can handle whatever Yenin is running."

I sent Antonio and Carlo Marino to Yenin's brothel to clear out the girls and torch his makeshift film studio.

"Bring Bosco Bianchi," I told them. "But don't let him near the girls."

"What do you want us to do with them?" Antonio said.

"Let them go. Or tell them they can go to Bareback on Forty-Eighth Street if they want a new job—Lorenzo is always hiring."

"Do we have to bring Bosco at all?" Antonio frowned.

"Yes," I said. "He's better than nothing."

"We'll make him go in first"—Carlo grunted—"so he doesn't shoot one of us in the back by accident."

I'll be taking Stefano, Zio, and Tappo to the wind farm.

Before we head out west of the city, I take my three enforcers over to the last phase of construction on the South Shore development. We pick up two unmarked white vans and a whole shit ton of nitroglycerin.

The nice thing about having demolition licenses is legal access to a wide variety of explosives.

Now, I'm no construction expert—Dante's the one who oversaw most of our crews, not to mention liaised with the various unions and subcontractors. But if there was one thing I was always interested in, it was blowing shit up.

We had to demolish all the existing steelworks structures before we could start the fresh build on the South Shore. I was there for all of it—setting charges, synchronizing the timing, and detonating.

Bringing down a building isn't just about setting a bomb. You have to work with the existing structure so you can bring it all down as cleanly and effectively as possible.

There are four main ways you can bring down a structure—telescoping, implosion, progressive collapse, and the technique I'll be using for the wind turbines: toppling. I want to bring those fuckers all the way down, and I don't want to do it quietly.

As we drive out to the field full of its eight turbines, I tell Stefano to stop and pull over. Only a single-lane road heads in this direction, with fenced-off fields on both sides. The turbines share space with a pasture full of docile brown cows peacefully grazing on the cropped grass. A cattle grid across the road deters the cows from wandering out where they don't belong.

The cattle grid is a simple structure: a depression in the road covered by a transverse grid of metal bars. I pop it up easily, revealing the empty space beneath. Zio helps me pack the area with gelatine explosives connected to a remote detonator.

"You gonna blow up some cows?" Zio asks me, his shaggy hair hanging down over his eyes. Zio's only twenty, and he has the perpetually sleepy look and rumpled clothing of an all-day stoner. But he's a lot sharper than he looks.

"Something like that," I say.

We set the heavy metal grate back in place then continue down toward the turbines.

Splitting up, we set our charges around the base of each structure. I check each one myself, noting that the blades of only two turbines are spinning in the light breeze. The others are dead, just like Yelena said. All eight look battered and dented, and not well maintained. These are three million-dollar machines—or at least they were when they were new. I'm sure Yenin bought them for a steal when he set up his bullshit energy operation.

Though I've seen turbines from a distance many times, I've never been this close to one before. They're much bigger than I expected— almost three hundred feet tall and fifteen feet across at the base. I'm glad I brought plenty of nitroglycerin.

"We all set?" Tappo asks me nervously.

He's eyeing the explosives with great mistrust. No one is a more fearless fighter than Tappo, but he prefers to work with his hands. He doesn't trust the explosives and almost jumped out of his skin every time Stefano drove over a pothole, thinking the nitro in the back of the van was going to obliterate us all.

"Yeah," I say. "You stay here to set off the charges while the rest of us take cover."

"Are you serious?" he cries, looking green.

"No, you idiot, I've got a detonator," I tell him, holding up the remote.

"Oh, fuck off," he grumbles, scrambling to get behind the vans, which we've parked a respectable distance away.

While the others take cover, I climb on top of the van so I can get a better view. I'm pretty sure we're far enough back that I won't risk any shrapnel, and I want to enjoy the show.

The turbines stand in the field, pale and eerie from this distance, like a graveyard of propellers silhouetted against the sky. I press the detonator.

For a moment, nothing happens. Then explosions bloom along the base of all eight turbines, like brilliant flaming flowers unfurling in the air.

We drilled boreholes on the bases, concentrating the explosives on the east side of the towers so the turbines would all topple in the same direction. The noise of tearing steel is like an outraged scream—then the thunder of 164 tons of metal tumbling down. Eight columns of smoke rise into the sky.

Zio has climbed next to me, wanting to see the aftermath clearly.

"Fucking hell," he says in his mellow voice. "Sort of beautiful, isn't it?"

"It is to me," I say.

"'Cause of the fire, or 'cause it's really gonna piss off Yenin?"

"Both." I grin.

"What do we do now?" Stefano pipes up from the ground.

"We wait," I say.

Forty minutes later, a black Mercedes SUV comes roaring up the bumpy road. I watch it speeding along. I recognize the vehicle, but it's too far away for me to make out who's driving.

Honestly, I don't really give a fuck.

Right as the SUV passes over the cattle grid, I press the button on the second detonator.

The explosion launches the car in the air, flipping it nose over end. It rolls four times before coming to a stop in a ditch.

"Let's go see who that was," I say to the men.

We pile back in the two vans and drive over to the wreck.

I approach the crumpled Mercedes with my gun in hand, even though I doubt anybody inside is in any shape to be shooting back. Sure enough, the driver is dead, his head twisted against the steering wheel and his blank eyes staring out at me. The passenger next to him is in similar shape, pressed against the airbag that failed to keep his skull from connecting with the side window at high speed.

But I hear someone groaning in the back.

The door is deeply dented and almost impossible to open. It takes Stefano and me pulling together to wrench it open.

The man in the back seat is covered in cuts embedded with chunks of glass. His face is so bloody that it takes me a minute to recognize him. It's Uncle Vale, Yenin's brother-in-law.

I grab him by the arm and yank him out of the vehicle, ignoring the fact said arm is broken in at least two places. He screams, rolling across the gravel, unable to stand.

I use my boot to shove him onto his back.

"Get his phone," I say to Tappo.

Tappo searches his pockets with no luck.

"It's in here," Zio says, plucking the phone out of the wreckage of the back seat.

The screen is cracked in a dozen places but still operational.

"What's the pass code?" I ask Vale.

"It's burn in hell with your fucking cunt mother," Vale snarls through bloodied teeth.

I raise my gun and shoot him in the right kneecap.

He howls like a wolf, writhing on the road.

"I've got eleven more bullets," I tell him calmly. "No need to die like a dog over something that won't help your brother anyway."

"You fucking *guido* piece of—"

I raise the gun again.

"One, two, seven, four!" he shouts.

I lower the gun and nod to Zio, who plugs in the code. The phone screen unlocks.

"Good choice," I say.

I shoot him in the head, right between the eyes.

"No mercy, huh?" Stefano says, one dark eyebrow cocked.

"That *was* mercy," I tell him.

My phone is buzzing in my pocket. I pull it out. Mikolaj's number is on the screen.

"How did it go?" I ask.

"Flawlessly, of course. We wiped their servers. Torched the warehouse. And transferred every penny he was keeping on the books over to my personal account. It was almost twelve million— I'll wire your half."

"Very generous."

"Simple fairness," Mikolaj says in his cool clipped voice. "I'm sure you'll do the same with whatever other spoils you recover."

"I will," I agree.

I can see Carlo Marino on the other line, so I switch over to his call. He sounds out of breath and pained.

"Problems?" I ask him.

"A few," he admits. "They had more men than we expected. Bosco blundered right into a room full of *Bratva* playing Durak."

"Did they shoot him?"

"No. He ran across and dove out the window. Cut the ever-living shit out of himself and dislocated his shoulder, but otherwise he's all right. Actually—it was a pretty good distraction. While they were trying to grab him, me and Antonio started shooting."

"You sound like you got hit," I say, hearing the strain in Carlo's voice.

"Yeah," he says, "but not by the *Bratva*. We went downstairs. Most of the girls had already run away 'cause they heard the shooting upstairs and got scared. But one of 'em hit a guard over the head with a fry pan and took his gun. She's the one who shot me. Felt bad about it after once she saw we weren't trying to kill 'em. Sorry doesn't put the bullet back in the gun, though."

"Where are you going now?"

"To see Dr. Bloom."

"Good." I nod.

"Bosco's driving me one-armed, so we'll see if I make it. I'll send Antonio back your way."

"All right. Talk soon."

I hang up the phone. Not too bad so far. But this is just the beginning. I've made my move. Now it's Yenin's turn. If I've threatened him sufficiently, it should be time for him to send out his power pieces.

Once they've been eliminated…the king will be unprotected.

CHAPTER 28
YELENA

Sneaking out of Sebastian's house isn't too difficult. It's easy to hear Greta because she makes no effort to be quiet while she's bustling around cleaning, especially when she's humming to herself.

Right now, she's all the way up on the top floor, probably dusting the music room from the sounds of it. Picturing that bright, sunny space, with its faint remnant of floral perfume, makes me wince. Sebastian took me into his mother's room, into the most cherished space in this house. He didn't hold anything back from me. He shared it all, right from the beginning.

I wish I had done the same.

I intended to walk out the front door, but now I'm reconsidering that plan. I'm dressed in a set of floral pajamas. Granted, the streets of Chicago have seen far stranger things, but I don't fancy walking around barefoot.

Moving as quietly as possible on the creaking stairs, I make my way up to the second floor, where most of the bedrooms are located. I saw from my visit to Sebastian's room that all the Gallo siblings still retain their childhood bedrooms in much the same state they used to be when they all lived at home.

I'm looking for the room that belonged to Aida Gallo.

I still haven't met her in person since my father didn't want the

Griffins at the wedding. Now I realize he banned them to keep the numbers in his favor. I suppose he didn't want to make the same mistake that got Kolya Kristoff killed, attacking both rival families at once. I wonder if he's deluded enough to believe the Griffins would make an alliance with him after he broke a blood oath with their closest allies or if he simply thinks it will be easier to fight them one after another.

I'm hoping he'll never find out. I'm hoping Sebastian will crush him once and for all before he even has the opportunity to face off against the Griffins.

But I can't think about that now. I've got to finish my escape.

I slip into the bedroom right next to Seb's, the smallest in the house.

You'd never know this room belonged to the only Gallo daughter—it doesn't contain anything overtly feminine. From the scuffs and dents on the walls and a patched-over hole on the back of the door, it looks more like a Tasmanian devil lived here. One leg is broken off the bed, an upended milk crate shoved in its place to keep the frame upright. The wall to my left is covered with stapled-on album covers, and the one to my right features a stolen street sign from Hugh Hefner Way. Whether this indicates that Aida was a fan or felt Hefner was undeserving of a sign, I couldn't guess.

I saw Aida and her husband, Callum Griffin, the night of the date auction. They shared a table with Seb. I was distracted looking at Sebastian, but even so, Aida had a kind of galvanic energy that pulled the eye in her direction. I can feel it now in this room—like the charge left in the air after a lightning storm.

I thought when she and I met at last, it would be as friends. Maybe even as sisters.

Instead, she'll hate me, like all the Gallos must. She's an orphan because of me.

I open her closet. Most of her clothes have been cleared out, but a few T-shirts still dangle from crooked hangers, and a pair of filthy old sneakers are jumbled in the corner. Oddly, one sneaker is much dirtier than the other.

I put on an old Van Halen T-shirt, torn on the shoulder, and the battered Converse. They're too small—Aida isn't a giant like me. But they're better than nothing. My pajama pants will have to suffice because she didn't leave any shorts.

With that sorted, I poke my head out the door and listen for Greta. She's still on the top floor, humming "You Can't Hurry Love" while she cleans. I hurry back down the stairs, trying not to step in the center, where they creak the most.

I'm about to head for the front door when I remember the Gallos have an entire garage full of cars below their house. Sebastian didn't include that on the tour, but he told me all about his brother Nero's fascination with all things mechanical. In fact, that's probably why my cell always smelled slightly of gasoline—it must have been directly underneath the garage.

Heading back down the stairs gives me a shiver of dread. It wasn't exactly pleasant being locked up down there. Well…with a few exceptions.

I take one wrong turn that leads me to some kind of vault, and then I retrace my steps and find the garage.

It's well lit and scrupulously clean with every tool neatly lined up in its proper place. A dozen separate berths each contain a vintage car or motorcycle.

I don't know how to drive stick, and I have no interest in trying to figure out a Mustang older than I am. So I'm relieved to see there's a perfectly normal BMW parked down here, too. I open the door, praying the keys are in the ignition. I find them waiting for me in the cup holder instead.

I slip into the cushy leather seat, a woodsy citrus scent filling my nostrils. I freeze with my hands on the wheel, realizing I've climbed into Enzo Gallo's car. I remember that cologne. It brings back vividly the vision of a distinguished older man in a fine wool suit, with shocking streaks of white in his dark hair. I remember how his smile lifted the corners of his mustache while dropping his heavy eyebrows over his eyes. He smiled when he bought me the grand piano for my new apartment. The apartment I should have been staying in right now, with Sebastian...

My hand shakes as I fit the keys into the ignition. I start the engine, the garage door opening automatically to let me ascend to the street.

I'm not sure where to go.

Adrian could be anywhere right now—the same with Sebastian and my father.

The only thing I can think to do is head toward my father's house.

I don't consider it *my* house anymore. It never felt like home to begin with. When I left, I had no intention of ever returning.

Driving back toward that house is worse than descending the stairs toward the cell.

The peaceful tree-lined street doesn't look attractive to my eyes. It fills me with dread, like its manicured perfection is a sign of the corruption hiding behind my father's high stone walls.

I had planned to pull into one of my neighbor's driveways so I could hide and wait. Instead, I have to snatch up a pair of sunglasses and shove them on my face and pull down the sun visor because I see Rodion's Escalade driving straight toward me. I can't stop my car or turn around, it's too late—he'll notice if I do anything besides keep driving along at a steady pace.

It's torture drawing closer and closer. Our vehicles are going to pass with only a couple of feet between us. I can't decide whether to look over at his car or keep my eyes straight ahead.

It's impossible not to look.

To my surprise, I see my brother, Adrian, driving and Rodion sitting in the passenger seat. They're punching something into the GPS, so they don't glance over as our cars pass.

I pull into the next driveway, my heart hammering wildly against my sternum.

I know where my brother is now—but I don't know how the fuck I'm going to talk to him with my father's attack dog riding shotgun.

I take several deep breaths, trying to calm myself. Then, when I think they're far enough away that they won't notice, I reverse out of the driveway and follow them.

Tailing another car is nerve-racking. If I get too close, they're sure to notice. But if I lag too far behind, I'll lose them at the next light or when they turn a corner.

If Rodion were driving, he'd be sure to notice the BMW continually in his rearview mirror. Luckily, my brother is less experienced and less observant.

Why Adrian is driving is a question all its own. Mystified, I can only follow along as they head toward Old Town.

Finally, the Escalade pulls up against the curb. I pull over as well, hiding my car behind a delivery van. I have to clamber across to the passenger seat so I can see what the fuck is happening.

Rodion gets out of the Escalade, a long rectangular black bag slung over his shoulder. He starts walking toward the alley between a fish-and-chips shop and an apartment building.

I feel a swift sweep of relief—with Rodion gone, I can drive up next to my brother and get him to pull over. If we can talk alone, I'm sure I can convince him to give up on whatever shambolic plan my father is trying to piece together in the aftermath of the wedding.

I'm sliding back across the seats, ready to start the car engine once more.

Until I glance across the street and see something that freezes my blood in my veins.

We're right across the street from Midtown Medical.

Nero Gallo is in that hospital in a private room on the top floor. He's lying in a bed recovering from six bullet wounds, basically helpless.

I'm sure Sebastian has plenty of guards stationed around his brother.

But I'm equally certain Rodion intends to finish what he started and kill Nero. Why else would he be here?

Adrian's car is pulling away from the curb. If I'm going to follow my brother, I have to do it now. This is my chance to speak to him.

If I do that...I'll be leaving Nero to Rodion's mercy. And Rodion doesn't have any fucking mercy.

Before I've even fully decided, I'm shoving open the passenger side door and jumping out of the car. I hurry down the alley, following the direction Rodion disappeared.

For a moment I'm confused—I can't see which way he went. It's a long alleyway. He shouldn't have disappeared so quickly. Maybe he started running as soon as he was out of sight?

I'm about to sprint down the alley myself, thinking he already turned the corner, but then I hear a scuffling sound overhead. Looking up, I can just make out the bulky dark shape of Rodion scaling the fire escape of the apartment building.

Fuck. He's going up to the roof.

The fire escape is partially retracted. I have to jump as high as I can to grasp the ladder, then pull myself up. If I weren't so tall, I wouldn't be able to reach it at all.

I try to keep my grunts to a minimum so Rodion doesn't hear me. I wait until he's all the way up before I start scaling the wobbly, rattling staircase. If he looks down and sees me, I'm fucked.

With each floor I ascend, my hands get more and more sweaty. The building has to be twenty stories high. I don't like being way up here, not one bit. It was bad enough going up in the Ferris wheel or the Skydeck, but at least those were enclosed spaces. The railing of the fire escape barely comes up to my waist. I'm horribly aware of how easy it would be to topple over the spindly metal edge.

I try not to look down as the pavement recedes below me. I try not to feel the breeze up here or notice how close the clouds look overhead.

I peek up onto the roof, trying to see where Rodion went. After a moment, I spot him all the way over on the far side of the building, setting up some kind of tripod device.

My mouth goes dry as a desert as he pulls a sniper rifle out of his bag. Rodion plans to shoot Nero Gallo through his hospital window.

Wildly, I consider running back down the fire escape so I can find a phone to call someone: the police or Sebastian. But I already know how useless that would be. Nero will be dead long before anyone can get here.

The only person who can help him is me.

I don't even want to step onto the roof. My whole body is screaming at me not to do it.

The roof is flat and open, with only a two-foot raised concrete ledge running around the perimeter. There are no walls, no railing, nothing to stop me from tripping and falling off the edge. A couple of vent hoods poke up from the building below, but otherwise there's nothing up here.

Well…almost nothing. The building is old and in poor condition. In a couple of places, the perimeter is crumbling away. In the corner closest to me, I see a loose chunk of concrete about the size of a brick. I creep over to it, trying to move silently, my eyes fixed on Rodion as he sets the sniper rifle into place on its tripod.

I'm also trying not to startle the pigeons strutting around on the roof. Their cooing and fluttering help disguise the noise of my creeping around. For that I'm grateful. But if I startle them into flight, Rodion is sure to turn around.

Quietly, I wriggle the chunk of concrete free. It's hefty in my hands, but I wish it were bigger. Rodion is a beast. I'm only going to get one chance to take him down.

He's lying prone on his belly now, peering through the sight of the rifle. He's looking across the road, all the way over to the hospital. It's too far away for me to see, but I can just picture Nero Gallo lying in his bed, pale and motionless, maybe with Camille right beside him.

She might be holding his hand, totally unaware that at any moment her lover's head could disappear in a mist of blood.

I sneak closer and closer to Rodion's massive frame. It's the worst possible version of Red Light, Green Light. Any moment my shoe could crunch a pebble or a bit of broken glass, and Rodion could turn.

Luckily, he's immersed in adjusting his barrel, checking the sight again, and curling his finger around the trigger.

I'm so close that I can smell the stale scent of cigarettes on his clothing and his hateful cologne. I grip the concrete tightly in both hands, raising it, readying to bring it smashing down on the back of his skull.

At that moment, one of the pigeons takes off from the roof with a percussive explosion of wings. Maybe something scared it. Maybe it just wanted to see me dead.

Rodion's head whips around. He fixes me with his puffy, blood-shot glare. I try to smash his head regardless, but he rolls away from me, and the concrete only hits him a glancing blow on the shoulder. Not even close to enough to disable him. Meanwhile, I'm off-balance from the force of my swing.

I stumble, trying to snatch up the sniper rifle instead, thinking maybe I can shoot him at close range. The weapon is heavier than I expected, bulky and awkward. Rodion has jumped to his feet. He easily wrenches it out of my hands, yanking so hard that he almost breaks my fingers.

Instead of turning the gun on me, he tosses it aside. His mouth is slightly open, showing the dark emptiness within. He isn't making any sound, but from the shape of his lips, it almost looks like he's laughing.

He circles around me, half crouched, daring me to make a move.

I know I'm doomed. Rodion is bigger than me, and stronger. He knows how to fight—I don't. He feints at me. When I stumble backward, trying to get away from him, his mouth opens again, and he makes a quiet huffing sound that I'm certain is his version of laughter.

His dark eyes are gleaming, and his ugly round face is red from the sun and the exertion of climbing up here. He holds up one big scarred hand, beckoning to me, daring me to attack him.

Instead, I dive for the dropped piece of concrete and snatch it. I throw it at him as hard as I can, trying to smash his teeth out. He bats it away easily, then charges at me.

I manage to slip his arms by an inch, but he grabs hold of my ponytail and yanks me back. I hit him in the face as hard as I can. It's like punching a sack of sand. He barely seems to register the blow. Instead, his piggy eyes gleaming, he pulls one fist back and pops me in the shoulder, right where I was shot.

He didn't even hit me full force, but the pain is explosive, blinding. I crumple to the ground, gasping, my right hand clamped over the spot that has become a flaming ball of agony. I felt the stitches tear, and I'm sure I'm bleeding again.

Rodion seizes me by the throat and hauls me upright again. He lifts me off my feet, Aida's too-small sneakers dangling while I kick helplessly. Rodion starts to carry me toward the ledge.

It's my worst nightmare: he's going to fling me off the roof, and there's nothing I can do to stop him. I'll feel his hands release; I'll feel myself floating weightlessly through the air, then rushing with sickening force toward the unforgiving concrete.

Maybe this is why I've always been so afraid of heights. Some part of my brain looked into the future and saw that this is how I die.

I'm clawing at his arms, kicking and squirming, but his hand is locked around my throat. Already my vision is blurring, my head getting dizzy and light.

I look into his cold, dead eyes, and I wonder if there's anything I could do to make him stop.

I stop scratching his arms. Instead, I bring my right hand up to my face. I raise my first two fingers and touch them to my forehead in a motion almost like a salute.

It's one of Rodion's signs—the one he uses to refer to my father.

I've never used his signs before. Never even admitted I knew them.

I can see the surprise in his eyes.

He hesitates, and I do the sign again, as if I have a message for him. A message from my father.

He lowers me slowly, relaxing his grip on my throat so I can speak.

"My father says…" I croak, and then I give a fake little cough, stalling for time.

The moment my feet touch the ground, I lunge forward and reach around his back. My hands close around the handle of the Beretta tucked in the waistband of his pants. I yank it free and throw myself backward as Rodion's fist comes swinging around an inch in front of my nose.

I thumb the safety and point the gun right at his chest. I shoot him three times in rapid succession, the bullet holes disappearing in the featureless expanse of his black T-shirt.

Rodion barely jolts. For a moment I think he truly is invincible. I think he'll keep coming at me like the Terminator.

So I shoot him twice more. This time he staggers back, the back of his knees meeting the concrete barrier. He's top-heavy, his vast bulk concentrated in his chest and shoulders. He topples backward, tumbling off the roof to the pavement below.

I'm still holding the gun in both hands, pointing it at the place where he was standing a moment before.

I have to force myself to lower it, my breath ragged and nearly hysterical.

I do not like being on this roof. Not one fucking bit.

I have to crawl back over to the fire escape because I'm too weak to walk.

Climbing down is almost the worst part of all. I'm shaking so hard that the rickety metal structure won't stop rattling beneath me. I keep thinking that if I look down, I'll see Rodion waiting below, bloodied and limping, but still somehow alive, like a horror movie monster.

I wasn't able to force myself to look over the concrete barrier so I could see his broken body in the street. I heard the screech of tires, though, and the shouts of the people who saw him land.

I can still hear shouting as I finally drop from the fire escape. A siren wails, far off and coming closer.

I run back to Enzo's BMW, my knees shaking beneath me.

I did it. I saved Nero.

But I have no idea where Adrian went.

CHAPTER 29
SEBASTIAN

I RENDEZVOUS WITH MIKOLAJ SO HE CAN TRANSLATE THE TEXT messages coming into Vale's phone. He reads Russian as well as Polish, and he scans them quickly, a thin smile playing on his lips.

"They're freaking the fuck out," he says. "Yelling at Vale to answer his phone. Then they stopped texting—must have realized he's dead."

"Did they say anything useful first?"

"They said for him to come to Bond Street," Miko says, raising one pale eyebrow. "What's on Bond Street?"

"A weapons cache, most likely. I assume they plan to retaliate by attacking the South Shore development."

"Should we go to the South Shore, then?" Miko says.

"Not if we can get them at Bond Street."

It's only been fifteen minutes since their last message. I think there's a good chance they're still arming themselves, and I'd rather bring the fight to their warehouse, not to my family's most expensive asset.

Sure enough, when we drive over to Bond Street, we see two black SUVs parked out front of a dingy brick building.

"You want to wait for them to come out?" I say to Mikolaj.

He shakes his head. "Then they'll be fully strapped."

"They might already be geared up in there."

"With guns, maybe," Miko says. "Not with these."

He opens the trunk of his Range Rover and rummages around. After a moment, he pulls out a gas mask and tosses it to me.

I grin, slipping the face shield over my head. Mikolaj pulls his on as well. He looks eerie enough under normal circumstances, let alone with his ice-blue eyes peering through tinted glass, the lower half of his lean face covered by dual filters like he's some kind of apocalyptic plague doctor.

He passes two more masks to his *braterstwo*.

"What about me?" a tall dark-haired soldier says. If I remember correctly, his name is Marcel.

"Hold your breath," Miko says. "That's all I've got."

"I'll go in, you cover the back door," his comrade says, slipping his own mask over his head.

Mikolaj's *braterstwo* go around the back of the warehouse while he and I approach the front.

"Ready?" he says.

I nod.

Cocking back his arm, he pulls the pin on the first tear gas canister and hurls it through the nearest window. The canister sails in a neat arc, smashing through the glass and tumbling inside. I throw mine through the window on the opposite side of the door.

I can hear the hiss of gas, then startled shouting and running. Too late—the shouting turns to hacking coughs and the barking sound of retching. One of the *Bratva* loses his head entirely, shooting blindly into the smoke.

Yenin's men stampede out the doors on all sides, coughing and stumbling. It's child's play to capture them. I was looking for Rodion, but instead I spot the unmistakable blond head of Adrian Yenin. His pale face is flushed, his eyes bloodshot and streaming. He tries to fight me anyway until Mikolaj kicks his legs out from under him, seizing a handful of hair and jerking his head back so he can hold a knife to his throat.

"Get in the fucking car," Miko hisses.

In terms of hostages, this is a better prize than Rodion, whom I would have killed on sight.

I call Yenin on Vale's phone.

It rings several times before he picks up.

"I assume I'm not receiving a call from a corpse," he says.

"Not yet," I reply. "I have your son."

There's silence on the other end of the line while Yenin considers this.

"I suppose you want me to turn myself over," he says lazily.

"No," I snap. "I think I know you better than that by now. I just want to meet. Face-to-face."

More silence. Then Yenin says, "You know the Midewin Prairie?"

"Yes," I say.

"Come there in two hours. It's private, quiet—wide open, with no cover, so we can both have a certain level of…trust. You bring your men. I'll bring mine. We'll have a conversation. Or, if you're determined…something less civil."

He hangs up the phone without even asking after the state of his son.

I look at Adrian trussed up in the back seat.

"I don't think he cares about getting you back alive," I say.

Adrian stares at me furiously, unable to speak because of the gag in his mouth.

His eyes are very like Yelena's. It makes me feel guilty to have them fixed on me, so I turn back around again.

Mikolaj is watching me, still wearing the gas mask because the tear gas has permeated Adrian's clothing and is still leeching out in the car. It's burning my eyes.

He's checking to see if I'm stupid enough to believe Yenin.

I was before. But as idiotic as I might have been, at least I'm a fast learner.

"Funny that he wanted to meet in two hours," I say. "All the way out there."

"Yes." Mikolaj grunts. "Sounds a fuck of a lot like a distraction."

I pick up my own phone and call Greta. She answers almost immediately, sounding slightly hectic. I don't bother to ask what the problem is.

"Get Yelena," I tell her. "And get out of the house. Go to the safe house in—"

She interrupts me. "Yelena isn't here. She escaped the cell. She's gone."

I cast a swift glance back at Adrian, then press the phone closer against my ear.

"How did that happen?"

"There was a sticker on the—Never mind," she says. "It doesn't matter how it happened. It was ridiculous to lock her up in the first place! Now she's—"

I don't have time to listen to Greta's scolding.

"Never mind that," I snap. "Get out of the house now. Don't stop to pack. Just leave. You promise me, Greta?"

"Yes," she says, sounding slightly scared.

"Go to the safe house, and stay there until I call you again."

"You ought to go there yourself!" Greta cries.

"I will," I tell her. "To pick you up later. After this is done."

She makes an irritated sound that shows exactly what she thinks of that promise.

I hang up the phone.

Miko is still watching me. "I take it we're not going to the prairie."

"No," I say. "Yenin wants to destroy my family, root to leaf. He wants to shame us and decimate us. And most of all, he wants to hurt us. We've lived in that house for a hundred years. More than our businesses or our holdings, he wants to destroy our home."

"Are you sure?" Miko says.

I shrug. "No. But if we want to draw him out...that might be the perfect bait."

CHAPTER 30
YELENA

I HAVE NO IDEA HOW TO FIND MY BROTHER. AND NO IDEA HOW TO find Sebastian.

But there's one person I can locate quite easily: Aida Gallo.

I suppose I should call her *Aida Griffin* now.

From what Sebastian told me, she rarely leaves her husband's side.

And Callum Griffin spends most of his time downtown in his alderman's office.

So that's where I go, driving Enzo Gallo's BMW. I park it a few blocks away from city hall, not wanting Aida to have the nasty shock of seeing her father's car parked out front.

Sebastian told me Aida works part time in Callum's office, ostensibly as his assistant but actually brokering some of his most crucial deals via her connections with the other influential Italian families.

I'm expecting to meet her inside, probably dressed in chic business wear like she had on at the charity auction. So I barely pay any attention to a woman pushing a fancy stroller up to the steps of city hall. I almost plow right into her in my hurry.

"Oh! Sorry!" I say.

The woman looks me up and down with a puzzled expression. "Is that my shirt?"

"Oh my god, Aida!"

"In the flesh," she says. "I wondered where you went...Sebastian was being strangely evasive on the topic."

"That's because he locked me up under the garage."

"Hm. Kinky," Aida says.

It's hard to read her expression. A range of emotions seems to flit across those gray eyes, like storm clouds fleeing before the wind. She certainly doesn't have the same boundless mirth I witnessed at the date auction. There's no hint of a smile on her lips.

"Aida..." I say. "I'm so, so sorry about your father."

Her chin trembles, but she shakes her expression clear again with one ruthless toss of her head. "It wasn't your fault."

"It... What?"

"I saw you the night of the auction. Unless you're Meryl Streep... I'm pretty sure you're head over heels for my brother."

My mouth is hanging open. Everything I've heard about Aida is that she's pure fire. The last thing I expected from her is forgiveness.

"I'm a Mafia daughter, too," she says. "I know how little power you have in your own life...until you rip it out of a man's hands."

The baby in the stroller gives a loud and angry squawk.

I peer in at him, startled by his shock of black curls and his furious expression. His gray eyes are every bit as fierce as Aida's—startling in comparison to his smooth chubby face.

"He looks just like you," I say in wonder.

"I think he's got a worse temper, if that's possible." Aida laughs. "Poor Cal."

"What's his name?"

"Miles."

As I look down on the baby, I feel the strangest rush of emotion. I never particularly wanted a child. I felt like I'd barely lived my own life yet. But the thought of having a baby like this, with soft dark curls like Sebastian's, and maybe his autumn-brown eyes, too...

I didn't know you could want something so suddenly and so hard.

"Aida," I say in a rush. "Sebastian left this morning. I'm pretty sure he's on some kind of revenge rampage. I don't know where he is...but I'm worried."

Aida frowns, for a moment looking just as ferocious as her baby. "From my last conversation with Sebastian, I was under the impression he was going to chill the fuck out so Nero could recover and we could bury my father... Then we'd reevaluate."

I shake my head helplessly. "I don't think that's what he's doing."

Aida pulls her phone out of her purse and hits a number—presumably Sebastian's. She waits, the phone ringing several times. Then, right when she's about to hang up, someone answers.

"It's not a great time right now, Aida."

I go limp with relief. I can barely hear the words since Aida doesn't have the call on speaker, but I'd recognize Seb's voice anywhere. He's alive, and he sounds in relatively good condition.

"Oh, it isn't?" Aida says sharply. "Is that because you're trying to launch a full-scale war on your own?"

A pause, then Sebastian says, "I'm handling it. And I'm not on my own—Miko's with me."

"Why didn't you call *me?*"

Seb sighs. "You're about to be the First Lady of the city. This was my mistake. I'm the one who's going to clean it up."

My stomach lurches. Was the agreement with my father the mistake? Or was it just...me?

"Where are you?" Aida demands.

"I'm at the house," Sebastian says. "But don't come here, Aida. If you want to help, go take care of Nero. He's having another surgery tonight; you could give Camille a break..."

"Seb, I'm not—"

"I've gotta go," he interrupts. And he ends the call.

"God damn it," Aida mutters, shoving her phone back in her bag.

"He's at the house?" I say, making sure I heard right.

"Yeah." Aida nods.

"That's where I'm going, then." I turn around to leave.

"Wait," Aida says. "Let's get Cal, too."

I feel tense and anxious, wanting to get back to Sebastian as quickly as possible, but I see the utility in having Callum Griffin with us as well. Even though he's set his sights on the mayorship, he's still the scion of the Irish Mafia. He's no pencil-pushing politician. He's a force to be reckoned with.

As we scale the steps to city hall, I lift the front of the stroller so Aida can bring Miles up without going all the way around to the wheelchair ramp.

Several people nod or wave to Aida, obviously recognizing her. I mostly get side-eyes because while she's dressed in a chic pantsuit, I'm still wearing the tattered Converse, pajama pants, and a ripped Van Halen T-shirt. To make matters worse, my shoulder is bleeding again, and it's soaking through the bandage, spotting the front of the shirt.

"You know, those shoes saved my life once," Aida says cryptically. "Or at least one of them did…"

"They must be lucky, then," I say. "I had a close scrape myself today."

"Lucky," Aida says. "But not your size."

I'm limping along, my toes crushed together and jammed against the front of the shoe. "I'm a size ten," I admit.

"Eight and a half," Aida says.

We've reached Callum's office. I hold the door for Aida so she can push the stroller through. The receptionist jumps up, saying, "Good afternoon, Mrs. Griffin! The alderman just got back; he's right in there…"

She trails off, catching sight of me. It's a testament to her training that she only makes a baffled face for a moment before inquiring, "Can I get a bottle of water for either of you?"

"Yes, please," I say eagerly.

In the aftermath of an adrenaline shock, you get intensely thirsty. My mouth feels dry as dust.

The secretary hurries off to get the water.

Meanwhile, Callum Griffin is already striding out of his office, having heard Aida's voice.

He's tall, dressed in an austere dark suit, his brown hair meticulously combed, and his cool-blue eyes take in the situation at a glance. He shows no surprise at the sight of me—just a quick, analyzing sweep of his eyes and then the rapid ticking of his brain as he puts the pieces together at lightning speed.

The only emotion he betrays is a flicker of pleasure at the sight of his wife and son. He bends to kiss Aida on the cheek, then looks down at Miles in the stroller, his jaw tight with pride.

"How has he been today?" he asks Aida.

"An angel, of course."

Callum snorts, not believing that for a second. "Well, he isn't screaming now, so that's something."

"He likes getting out of the house."

"Looks like someone else got out of the house, too," Callum says, cocking an eyebrow at my outfit. "Yelena Yenina, I assume. Recently escaped from your husband?"

"Sort of." I can feel my face flushing under his cool, direct stare. "I'm not trying to escape—actually, I want to go back. I think Sebastian needs our help..."

"*Our* help?" Callum says, his tone even more frosty.

"Seb is taking on the Russians," Aida says.

"Without much of a plan, sounds like."

Aida looks him in the eye, her body tense. "Cal," she says quietly. "They killed my father."

"I know that. And I would do anything—*anything*—to bring him back to you, Aida. But that isn't possible. Yenin wants a bloodbath. Sebastian seems determined to give it to him."

He pauses, looking down at his wife. Now I can see Callum

isn't as impassive as I thought. In fact, it's clear several impulses are fighting inside him, all at once: His anger at this situation. His desire to give his wife what she wants. And his fear of what will happen if he does.

"Look, Aida," he says, his voice surprisingly gentle. "Dante might be right. Revenge is for people who have only themselves to consider."

He casts a meaningful look at Miles, who seems oblivious to the tension in the room—he's finally stopped scowling and has fallen asleep in the stroller.

Aida bites her lip, torn between her loyalty to four different men: her husband and son on the one side, and her father and brother on the other.

For a moment I think she's going to agree with her husband. Then she shakes her head hard.

"We can't leave Seb alone in this. You owe him, Callum, you know you do. And so do I. The night that brought us together ruined his life. He's never blamed me. He's never complained. And besides that, Cal, Alexei Yenin is a fucking psychopath—no offense, Yelena. He is coming after all of us. If we're going to join World War II, let's do it now and not after Pearl Harbor."

Callum frowns. "Don't use the History Channel against me, Aida."

"CAL!"

"All right, all right!" He holds up his hands. "We'll help him. But we have to take Miles to my parents' house—"

"Obviously."

"And you're wearing a vest. And we're bringing men along with us."

"Reasonable," Aida says, trying to hide the fact he agreed more quickly than she expected. She has the look of someone who had about eight more arguments ready to go if her first one failed.

The secretary comes hustling back into the room, carrying several different bottles of water.

"Sorry!" she pants. "We only had sparkling left in the fridge, so I ran down the hall to get some Evian as well…"

"Thanks," I say, grabbing a bottle out of her overladen arms. "I'll take it to go."

CHAPTER 31
SEBASTIAN

I'M STANDING IN THE MUSIC ROOM. SINCE MY MOTHER DIED, THIS has been the shrine in our house. The chapel, the most sacred space. But as I learned at the Russian Orthodox church, sacred spaces don't mean much.

The last time I came in here was with Yelena.

Now I have her brother tied to a chair in the center of the room.

A few days ago, he officiated my wedding. He put the ring on my finger, planning to put a bullet in my head only a few minutes later.

Life is endlessly surprising. For all of us.

I haven't bothered to gag Adrian. I don't care if he wants to talk. It won't change anything.

He's been stubbornly silent, watching me with those violet-colored eyes that are so disturbingly like his sister's.

As the light fades in the room, his skin looks pale and bleached as if he's already dead. He's as still as a corpse. Only his eyes move as he follows my progress back and forth across the room.

The two-hour window in which I was supposed to meet his father on the prairie has almost passed. Yenin hasn't called or texted Vale's phone. I don't expect him to. I don't believe for a second that he's driving out of the city right now. In fact, I think that any moment Mikolaj will call to tell me that Yenin's armored car is heading down my street.

I'm not really thinking about Yenin, though.

It's Yelena who's on my mind.

Where did she go when she left my house? Why did she run? Did she think I was going to hurt her?

She gave herself to me last night, fully and completely. I think it was as cathartic for her as it was for me.

But maybe she changed her mind this morning.

Or maybe she thought I did.

I should have talked to her before I left.

The problem is this impossible dilemma that neither she nor I have been able to successfully navigate. The survival of each of our families depends on destroying the people the other loves. No amount of conversation can change that. And the more time I spend next to Yelena, the more I can't bear to do what has to be done.

I wish I ran away with her the day I met her.

In a game of winners and losers, the only happy ending is not to play at all.

I'm looking out the window, at the sky flushed with the last tinges of sunset. No stars yet.

Maybe Adrian knows where Yelena went. He won't tell me if he does.

His voice startles me, speaking after so many hours of silence.

"You underestimate my father."

I look over at him, considering this statement. "I don't think so."

"He's brilliant," Adrian says. "And relentless. He's a force of nature. Anyone who's tried to stand before him has been swept away."

"Is that why you betrayed Yelena for him?" I ask Adrian coldly.

His face flushes, his arms straining against the rope holding his wrists bound behind him. "Yelena turned her back on us. She proved herself to be exactly what my father always said she was—a woman, with a woman's weakness."

"You and your father have a man's arrogance."

"The endgame will tell if it was arrogance or accuracy."

His use of the word *endgame* jolts me. "You play chess?"

"Of course I do," he says, lifting his chin in a manner that reminds me painfully of Yelena. "All the best masters are Russian."

A ridiculous statement—I could ask him, *What about Jose Raul Capablanca or Magnus Carlsen?* But that's an argument we would have if we sat across from each other in this room as brothers-in-law. Not as bitter enemies.

In another life, we could have been friends. Yelena told me Adrian is an athlete, too—that he did boxing, fencing, and gymnastics in school, that he likes to run and swim. She told me of his humor and his kindness to her.

I don't see any of that in his face now—just hatred and the burning desire to finish the task he failed to complete in the Russian Orthodox cathedral.

"This house is a shithole," Adrian says. "And your father was half-senile. We did you a favor killing him."

He's trying to make me lose my temper. Maybe because he doesn't want to be used as bait against his father. Maybe he thinks I'm stupid enough to untie him so I can beat the shit out of him better.

What he doesn't realize is that all my wild emotions burned away. I'm finally taking my father's advice—the last piece he gave me.

Play the endgame like a machine.

I'm a fucking android now. Nothing will stray me from my course. Rodion dies. Yenin dies. Adrian dies. There will be no loose ends this time. No forgiveness. No enemies left alive to seek their revenge on me and my family.

The room is almost fully dark now. Adrian looks unnerved that I didn't even respond to his taunt.

"I wonder if you'll feel sorrow when I kill your father in front of you," I say. "I did when you shot Papa in the face. My father was a good man, and he loved me. I don't think you can say the same. You might be surprised by the relief that washes over you. If you're alive to see it happen at all."

Adrian looks frightened, and that makes him look young.

A seed of sympathy tries to sprout inside me. I crush it at once.

My phone buzzes in my pocket with a text message from Mikolaj:

They're coming.

I go back to the window so I can see the three black SUVs creeping down Meyer Avenue with Yenin's armored car in the center of the group.

My mother's music room is one of the only rooms in the house that faces the street, unobscured by the massive oak and elm trees crowding the house.

I stand in front of the colored-glass window that runs from floor to ceiling, almost the exact same height as my six-foot-seven frame.

Now it's me who takes out Vale's phone and dials.

After a moment, Yenin answers. He doesn't actually speak—just picks up the call, listening silently.

"I must have a terrible memory," I say, "because I thought we were meeting in Midewin."

Two of the SUVs are pulling up to the curb. I watch Yenin's men jump out, dressed in dark clothing, their faces covered by Halloween masks. I see a Michael Myers, a Slenderman, a Jigsaw, and a scarecrow. In their hands, they clutch dark cylindrical objects that I recognize too well. I sigh, knowing what's coming next.

"I wouldn't do that," I say to Yenin.

With that, I flip on the lamp next to the window, illuminating the room in which I stand. I can't see Yenin inside his car, but I know the light will draw his eye up to my window. He'll see me standing there.

With three swift strides, I grab the back of Adrian's chair and drag him over in front of the window. Now it's Yenin's son who is silhouetted in front of the glass, while I stand to the side of the window frame, shielded from any gunfire.

"I've got your son," I tell him. "Your daughter, too." That part is a lie, but I doubt Yenin knows that. Wherever Yelena might have gone, it's not back to her father. "Will you sacrifice them both to get your revenge?"

"I'm only sixty," Yenin says, with chilling calm. "I can make more."

Responding to his unseen signal, his men rush my house. I don't see Rodion's massive frame among them, but he must be here, maybe in Yenin's armored car. There's no way Yenin would come to the last dance without his top lieutenant.

I stay next to the window, watching.

Just as I hoped…just as I assumed…Yenin has stepped out of his armored car. He can't help himself. He has to watch the culmination of his efforts. Not through glass—out in the open. Unprotected.

There are at least a dozen soldiers, masked and armed. They break down the front door and throw their incendiary grenades inside. I hear a deafening boom, and the entire house shakes on its ancient frame.

I'm wearing a Kevlar vest, but that's not going to do much good against grenades or the collapse of the entire structure. I start sprinting toward the back of the house.

"*Wait!*" Adrian screams after me.

I don't even look back at him. As the next grenade detonates, I hear Adrian's chair topple behind me.

I run to the back staircase. Instead of going down, I'm going up—all the way to the rooftop. I spent the last few hours in my family home in my mother's sanctuary. Now I'm going to my father's.

I sprint across the deck, beneath the pergola laden with grapes so heavily ripe that they've almost turned to wine on the vines. I see my father's favorite chair next to the little table where we always set up his chessboard. His worn woolen blanket still sits neatly folded on the seat cushion.

Already, smoke billows up from the windows below. The house

creaks and groans as the ancient wood succumbs to the immense heat of the fire.

Gunfire breaks out on all sides beneath me. Mikolaj and his men are attacking Yenin's soldiers, closing in from two directions, aided by Bosco Bianchi, Antonio Marino, Stefano, Zio, and Tappo.

We're slightly outnumbered, so I've got to get down there. This battle has to be swift and decisive, before the cops arrive. Yenin isn't slipping away from me this time.

Reaching the corner of the patio, I scrabble across onto the branches of the ancient oak tree that grows right next to the house. I've lived here all my life—I know a dozen different places where I can climb down unseen.

I wait in one of the lower branches, peering down, until I see a man in a Pennywise mask. He's got his AK up on his shoulder, aiming at one of Miko's men. I drop on top of him, hearing his muffled scream of pain through the rubber mask as his leg breaks beneath him.

I pull my Glock and shoot him twice in the chest. He stops moaning.

My family's house is going up in flames like a tinderbox. Everything is burning: The pictures of my great-grandparents in their dusty frames. The posters on my bedroom walls. My mother's piano.

I never could have let this happen if my father were still alive—it would have killed him. But like Yenin, I'm willing to lose something I love to get my revenge. I sacrificed a piece that had great value to me to lure him out of his car.

And now I can see him, standing on the opposite side of the street, his arms crossed over his broad chest, his lank gray hair loose around his shoulders, his craggy face illuminated by firelight.

Distantly, I hear the wail of sirens. I have minutes to kill him. Only minutes.

As I jog toward him, something explodes inside the house. I'm thrown sideways by the force of the blast, bits of leaded glass cutting the right side of my face and body. The heat from the inferno is so intense that the fighting is driven outward toward the street. Looking up, I see Mikolaj shoot Jigsaw in the face, then pull a knife from his belt so he can slash Slenderman once, twice, three times across the belly, chest, and throat.

Mikolaj moves with shocking speed and grace. He's like a dancer himself—a cruel and lethal analog of his wife. In less than a second, he's seized Michael Meyers by the hair and cut his throat as well.

It's almost like having Nero with me. Nero always prefers knives over guns.

But I don't have time to appreciate any of this. I'm fixated on one thing only: the grizzled form of my enemy across the street, glowing in the reflected flame light like the devil himself.

I shove myself up off the grass, and I run toward him, the Glock still clutched in my hand.

Yenin has kept two of his biggest guards at his side. Both are wearing masks, but neither has quite the size to be Rodion. I'm disconcerted, wondering where the fuck his lieutenant has gone. I can't imagine Yenin would dispatch him for anything trivial.

I can't help worrying about Yelena. If Rodion had a choice of where to go, it would be to find and drag home the object of his fixation. If he found Yelena…if he even fucking touched her…

Yenin's guards see me coming. They already have their weapons drawn. The one on the left has the quicker reflexes of the two—but not quick enough. Before he can even aim at me, I've shot him in the neck and chest. His friend is slightly more successful. He shoots me in center mass before I can hit him between the eyes. Too bad for him that my vest is stronger than his bullet.

The impact fucking hurts, though, and it throws me off-balance. This turns out to be a good thing because it means Yenin's shot goes wide, grazing my bicep instead of my head.

Not wanting to risk another shot, I plow into him, tackling him like a football player. I let go of my Glock so I can grab his gun hand in both of mine, slamming his wrist repeatedly against the cement until his Colt skitters away beneath his armored car.

If at any point I actually did underestimate Yenin, it would be right now, in this moment. He's a sixty-year-old man, four inches shorter than I am. I should be able to pound him into the pavement.

But he has the kind of strength and strategy that can only be honed by a lifetime of combat. He attacks me with the rabidity of an animal and the precision of a sniper. He slams the heel of his hand up into my nose, then elbows me in the throat. Then he goes for his real target: my knee. He brings his foot smashing down on my formerly shattered kneecap, right in its most vulnerable place.

It's like I've time traveled back to the lakeside pier three years ago. My kneecap breaks apart once more in a supernova of pain that wipes all signals through my nerves. I can't move or even breathe. All I can do is scream.

Yenin tries to roll away from me, his blue eyes gleaming with triumph. He's getting to his feet, whether to grab his gun or to kick me in the face, I have no idea. My pain-addled brain decides he's trying to run away, and whatever else happens, I'm not letting that happen. With every bit of strength I have left in me, I grab him around the knees and jerk his legs out from under him, sending him crashing down to the pavement once more. Then I launch myself on top of him, ignoring the shrieking agony as the pieces of my kneecap grind together.

This isn't a fight anymore. It's a fucking brawl. We're punching and clawing and headbutting each other, fighting with a viciousness that makes me want to bite and tear, to rip off his fingers and his eyelids, to destroy any part of him I can reach. I find those hateful blue eyes, and I dig my thumbs in, trying to blind him.

This man took my father's hand in friendship, and then he blew Papa's jaw off, so I couldn't even identify his face. He stole the last years of my father's life—our last chess games together, Papa's last opportunities to hold his grandchildren. Yenin will never have the chance to feel those pleasures himself. He doesn't get to gloat. He doesn't get to win. I'll eradicate him off the face of this earth so he won't feel another moment's satisfaction ever again.

Yenin is strong, but I'm stronger. He's cruel, but I'm a fucking sadist. He's dying at the hands of the monster he made.

Our hands are locked around each other's throats, and he's squeezing with all his might. I choke him back twice as hard until I hear the bones in his neck snapping. My fingers dig into his flesh until the blood runs, and still I keep squeezing till the only light in his eyes is the sparks of my house burning down.

Only then do I let go.

And still I'm not done.

I cross the road, heedless of the bullets flying all around me. I'm limping along, leaning heavily on my good leg, dragging my screaming knee after me.

Mikolaj's men are still fighting the last of Yenin's soldiers. The fire is raging, and the sirens are drawing closer. With a crunch of tires on broken glass, I hear another car pull up. Someone shouts my name.

I keep walking.

I see nothing but fire. I feel nothing but rage.

This isn't over yet—not until Rodion and Adrian are dead.

I'm searching for the hulking figure of the silent giant. Or the white-blond head of Yelena's brother.

I almost step on Adrian.

He's lying in muddy trampled grass on the front lawn. His hair isn't blond at all anymore because most of it has been burned away. The whole right side of his face and body is charred. I can see the smoking remnants of the rope around his left wrist and a piece of the broken chair to which he was tied.

He looks up at me, one eye swollen shut, the other clear and tinged that particular shade of violet.

"Please…" he croaks.

I look around the ground. There's a discarded Kalashnikov a dozen yards away. I pick it up, limping back toward my enemy once more.

I point the barrel right between his eyes, my finger curled around the trigger.

"SEBASTIAN!" someone screams.

Not someone.

Yelena.

I'd recognize her voice anywhere.

I'm frozen in place. Every impulse of my brain is screaming at me to kill Adrian, to do it now. He would shoot me, given the chance again. He'd shoot anyone I love. He might even shoot Yelena.

But as soon as Yelena gets close to me, my brain isn't in charge. My body takes over. It turns toward her, without thought or choice, like a flower turning to the sun.

She looks filthy, frantic, scratched, and beaten up. She's smoke stained, in torn and bloody clothing. And yet she's so beautiful, I can hardly stand it.

Her lovely eyes are fixed on my face, filled with tears and pleading with me.

"Please, Sebastian," she begs. "Please don't kill him…I'm begging you. Please don't."

The gun is still pointed at her brother.

I swore to myself that I wouldn't stop. I swore I'd be a machine.

But my heart is throbbing, straining against my chest in automatic impulse the closer Yelena gets to me.

"Please," she whispers.

I flex my fingers to see if I still have control of my hand.

I do. I could shoot Adrian if I wanted to.

But I don't want to anymore. The sight of Yelena has washed away the remnants of my pain. She came back. And not for Adrian—I can see that in her face. She's here for me.

I drop the rifle on the ground.

With a sob, Yelena flings herself on me, almost knocking me over. I grunt with pain.

"Are you okay?" Yelena sobs.

"Yes," I say. "Are you?"

"Yes."

She hugs me hard, with that same ferocity I saw the very first day I met her. She hugs me like a Valkyrie. Like she'd kill anything that tried to come between us.

Then, when she releases me, she drops by her brother and cries, "Adrian!"

Her brother looks up at her, his teeth gritted in pain.

"The ambulance is coming," Yelena cries. "Hold on…"

"This…this…" Adrian grunts.

"What?" Yelena says. "What are you saying?"

"Your fault…" Adrian hisses. He's not looking up at his sister with love or even relief that she's still alive. He's looking at her with pure hatred.

I see that look, and I want to snatch up the rifle and kill him here and now. I don't want him in an ambulance or a hospital bed. I don't want him recovering in his body while his mind still seethes with rage at Yelena.

Yelena casts a swift look up at me, like she knows what I'm thinking. Her lips press together, and she gives one quick shake of her head.

She won't do it. She doesn't want me to do it either.

I don't like that at all. It makes me worried and afraid.

But my love for Yelena is stronger than my worry.

Someone grabs me by the shoulder and pulls me around.

"Seb!" Aida shouts. Her face is likewise smoke streaked, and she's clutching a gun in her free hand. Callum is right beside her, covering her in case anyone tries to attack her from behind. The yard is littered with dead Russians and at least two of Mikolaj's men. I see a facedown figure that looks like Bosco Bianchi.

But the gunfire has died out. The sirens are wailing close by, and I don't think there's anyone left to fight.

"Let's go!" Aida cries.

"Where's Mikolaj?" I ask.

"He already left with his men."

"We better do the same, right the fuck now," Callum says. "Or no amount of bribes are going to get us out of this shitstorm."

Leaning heavily on Yelena, I hobble as best I can back to Callum's car. Yelena and I get in the back, while Callum takes the driver's seat and Aida sits shotgun.

As Callum speeds away down the street, Aida casts one devastated look back at our burning house. The rearview mirror is full of the flashing lights from squad cars, fire trucks, and ambulances.

I assume they'll find Adrian in time—but I hope they don't.

CHAPTER 32
YELENA

I HUDDLE AGAINST SEBASTIAN IN THE BACK OF THE CAR. HIS HEAVY warm arm around my shoulders is the only thing keeping me sane right now.

I can't get the sight of my brother out of my mind—his handsome face burned so badly all down the right side, and even worse than that, the hatred in his eyes when he looked up at me. I never, never, never would have thought he and I would find ourselves on opposite sides of a battle. But that was my father's last act—to wedge between us as he always tried to do when he was alive.

I saw his dead body lying in the street.

Unlike with Adrian, seeing my father bloody and battered raised no sympathy at all. I didn't feel the relief I expected either. Instead, it felt like closing a book. The end of him, at last.

I press my face against Sebastian's shoulder. He smells of smoke and blood. Beneath that, I find the scent of his skin.

He strokes my hair gently, not caring how dirty or tangled it's become.

"Where are you going?" he says to Callum as the car makes a turn.

"The hospital," Cal says. "Nero should be out of surgery soon. And it looks like you two might need a doctor as well…"

"I'm fine," Sebastian says stubbornly. I really doubt that's the case. He had to lean on me heavily just to get to the car. His knee is injured again, I think.

Callum drives us over to Midtown Medical. He pauses, confused, when he sees the entire road is cordoned off. "What's going on here?"

"Something on that side of the street..." Aida peers out the passenger side window. "I can't see what it is..."

"Someone fell off the roof of that apartment complex," I tell them. They all turn to stare at me.

"Who fell off?" Callum demands.

"Rodion," I say, mostly to Seb.

"Ro—How do you...?" He looks at me in confusion, and then I see both understanding and horror sweep over his face. "Yelena," he says. "Were you up there?"

I nod, suddenly finding myself unable to speak.

"But how...? Why did you...?"

I see him look back and forth from the apartment complex to the hospital, right across from each other. The color bleaches out of his face.

"Oh my god," he says.

My heart is racing as those moments on the roof rush back to me all too vividly. The feeling of Rodion's hand around my throat, and my feet dangling in the air as he carried me over to the ledge...

Callum and Aida can't put the pieces together quite as well.

"Who's Rodion?" Aida asks.

"He's Yenin's top lieutenant," Sebastian explains. "He was here to kill Nero, wasn't he?"

"Yes," I say quietly.

"And you stopped him?" Aida says.

"You saved Nero's life," Sebastian says, looking at me in amazement.

"I meant to follow Adrian," I admit to Seb. "That's why I left this morning. I hoped to find my brother before..." I have to swallow back a sob. "Before anything could happen to him. I hoped I could convince him to leave. To abandon our father."

Sebastian's mouth is open. I can see he understands the decision

I made, here on this street, between my brother and his. This time I chose Sebastian's family instead of my own. I did what I could to make up for my mistakes. But it was Adrian who paid the price.

Sebastian throws his arms around me and hugs me hard. A little too hard, quite honestly, because my shoulder is still burning where Rodion hit it, opening the stitches again. But I don't care—I'd rather feel the pain if it comes along with the warmth of his arms.

"Thank you," Sebastian says in my ear.

"How did you do it?" Aida asks curiously. "Did you knock him over the ledge? Did you shoot him?"

Seeing my wince, Sebastian says, "Leave her alone if she doesn't want to talk about it."

I still feel like I owe Aida a hell of a lot for forgiving me so easily.

"I shot him," I say. "But it was close. It was almost me who went over the edge."

Fear flashes across Sebastian's face. He holds me tighter than ever, as if the fight on the roof is something he can still protect me from now and not something finished and in the past.

"I can't fucking believe that," he says. "I mean, I guess I can. I've seen you when you're mad. But, Jesus Christ, Yelena, he's a fucking ogre…"

"It wasn't my favorite afternoon," I murmur against his neck.

As we enter the hospital, the nurse seems highly suspicious that we're just there as visitors, considering the state of us all. Even Callum and Aida look disheveled and dirty, despite the fact we arrived when the fighting was almost over.

Reluctantly, the nurse gives us our badges and lets us go up to the top floor. Two of Sebastian's men are guarding the elevator and the hallway. The taller one tells Seb, "He's out of surgery. He's in the room with Camille."

We all hurry down the hall, trying to be quiet in case Nero is still asleep.

But when we peek in the door, he's sitting up in bed, pale and thin but surprisingly alert.

"Why do you all look worse than I do?" he says.

"Yenin's dead," Seb says by way of explanation. "He burned the house down."

"*Our* house?" Nero says.

"Yeah." Seb nods. "Sorry. I kind of let him."

"Well…fuck."

Nero sounds stunned and disbelieving, which I can understand since that house was in their family for a hundred years. It is baffling that something that stood so long could be destroyed in a matter of hours.

"Did you at least move my cars?" Nero asks.

"No." Seb winces.

Nero glowers at him, and I see that his temper is still alive and well, however weak his body might be.

Camille squeezes Nero's thigh through the bedding. "It's all right," she says. "Your favorites are at our shop."

"Some people died, too," Callum reminds him.

Nero shrugs, not caring nearly as much about that. "People are more common than a 1930 Indian Scout Motorcycle." But after a moment, his curiosity gets the better of him. "Who's dead?"

"Bosco Bianchi, for one," Seb says.

"*Pfft.*" Nero snorts. "He's barely worth a gasket."

I'm lurking in the doorway, embarrassed and thinking I shouldn't be here. I doubt Nero wants to see me, or Camille either.

Before I can think of an excuse to sneak out, Nero fixes me with his sharp gray eyes and says, "Don't be so twitchy—if your dad's dead, then we can all relax."

"I'm really sorry—" I begin, but he waves me off.

"Ah, save it. Your wedding did suck ass, though, just so you know. I'm glad I only got you the two-slice toaster and not the four."

Aida snorts, and I see that this is Nero's idea of a joke. Or perhaps his idea of forgiveness. Either way, I'll take it.

Camille looks utterly exhausted from all her hours at the

hospital, but she's smiling while she rests her chin on her palm, leaning against Nero's bed. She's obviously thrilled to have him fully awake and talking like this—like what I assume is his usual self.

"We can't stay long," Cal says. "We left Miles at my parents' house."

"If we don't get back soon, Imogen will probably have bought him twenty more outfits and tried to cut his hair," Aida says.

"It is a little crazy," Cal says.

"He's a *baby*." Aida rolls her eyes. "Just be glad he's not bald as an egg like you were till you were three years old."

"It grew in eventually." Cal rubs his head self-consciously.

"Anyway, goodbye all," Aida says, giving us a little wave. "Glad you're alive, big brother."

"Me, too," Nero says. He looks at Camille as he answers, not at Aida.

"We'd better go, too," Seb says.

We head back down to the elevator, letting Callum and Aida go on ahead of us because Sebastian and I are both stiff and slow. On the way out, Seb bribes a PA to take a look at my shoulder. For five hundred dollars, the guy puts a couple of more stitches in the wound, then slips me an extra dose of antibiotics and a couple of sample packets of painkillers.

Whatever he gave me, it takes effect almost immediately. I feel warm and relaxed, and the aching of my shoulder dies down to a gentle twinge. Seb swallows a couple himself so he won't have to lean on me so heavily to walk.

By the time we've hobbled a few blocks down from the hospital so we can catch an Uber where the road isn't blocked off any longer, all the lights in the buildings look bright and twinkly. A breeze is blowing in from the lake, making the air smell clean and fresh.

Sebastian has his arm around me.

"Should we take a car back to our apartment?" he asks.

I hadn't even thought about where we would go. We can't go

back to Sebastian's family home, obviously. There's no way in hell I'd go to my father's house. So it makes sense that we'd go where we were meant to go directly after our wedding: the beautiful loft Seb and I picked out together, when nothing awful had happened yet, when our future seemed bright and full of promise.

I want to go there now, more than anything.

I want to recover that feeling that everything will be all right. That Sebastian and I can build a life together, the two of us, and shape it to be whatever we want.

He's watching my face closely.

He's not just asking where we should sleep tonight. He's asking if we can try again—if we can try to bring that dream to reality, to put the train back on the tracks.

I tell him, "There's nowhere else I'd rather be."

Sebastian stops on the sidewalk. He grabs me and he kisses me.

I can taste the smoke on his lips. It's not unpleasant.

Fire doesn't always mean death and destruction. Sometimes it clears away the old and rotten brush so new things can grow.

We take the Uber back to our apartment building.

It seems like forever since we picked this place out together and sent over the few furnishings we had time to purchase.

When we open the door, it smells clean and new inside, not like Sebastian or me. It's antiseptic and anonymous—no hint of his soap or cologne or of my favorite brand of coffee beans.

I barely recognize the gleaming modern kitchen and the wide-open living room with no couch, only the beautiful piano Enzo gave me as his last gift.

It's not our home yet.

But it will be. It will be very soon.

Every hour we spend here will imprint a little more of our personalities on this space. We'll laugh and talk here, building memories and experiences.

"I should have carried you over the threshold," Seb says.

"No offense, my love, but you can hardly carry yourself at the moment."

"Don't worry, I've got plenty of energy left," he says with a half smile. "After all...technically we're still on our honeymoon."

That smile makes him look boyish again, and ridiculously handsome. He looks like the man who tried to save me from a kidnapper. The one who beat me at pool and was too much of a gentleman to take his prize.

Grabbing his hand, I pull him toward the bedroom.

Carefully, gently, we strip off each other's clothes. We shower together, taking turns scrubbing the blood and mud and smoke off each other's skin. It's hard to tell what's dirt and what's bruises. Each of us is cut and battered to a ridiculous degree, all over our bodies.

It doesn't matter, though. It's all evidence of what we went through to be together. In a strange way, it makes me happy. Because if none of that could kill us, if none of that could tear us apart, then nothing can.

When we're completely clean and still slightly damp, we roll onto the bed, onto crisp new sheets that have never yet been slept on.

Sebastian lies on his stomach between my legs. He licks my pussy with long slow strokes. His mouth feels incredibly warm, and his lips and tongue are soft since he just shaved his face in the shower.

I lie back against the pillow, feeling like I'm floating and drifting along, like I'm half in this world and half out of it.

The other day I needed rough sex. I craved it; I couldn't get enough of it. And today I need this gentleness, this care.

Sebastian always knows what I need. He already seems to know my body better than I do. He touches me better than I could touch myself, sending surge after surge of pleasure up through my belly and down through my legs.

The more he touches me, the more sensitive I become. My pussy is throbbing. I can feel every millimeter of skin, every nerve ending igniting in response to his tongue.

The sensation rises to such a fever pitch that I hardly realize it when I start to come. I sink into an orgasm that is deep, and sensual, and seems to go on forever.

Sebastian keeps lapping away at my clit, not speeding up or slowing down, just dragging out the climax as long as possible.

When it's finally over, he climbs on top of me and thrusts inside me, his cock already hard from the arousal of eating me out.

I'm so swollen and sensitive that the thrusts are wildly intense, even though he's being careful. After a few minutes, I can tell that our position is putting too much pressure on his knee, so I climb on top of him instead, letting him take his turn lying back against the pillows while I ride him.

The moonlight is streaming in through the thin curtains, highlighting every line and curve of Sebastian's face. His eyes look more gold than brown, intent and serious as he looks up at me.

I slowly roll my hips, taking long strokes up and down on his cock. He reaches up to caress my breasts, then sits up on the pillow so he can take one in his mouth and suckle it while I ride him.

I think he might be obsessed with my tits because he's constantly touching or sucking on them while we fuck. I'm becoming addicted in turn. Every time he does it, they're more and more sensitive, and that sensation is becoming linked to how good his cock feels inside me.

Like any good athlete, Sebastian is ridiculously coordinated. He can suck my tits and fuck me and finger my ass all at the same time. Having so many erogenous zones stimulated simultaneously is—simply put—fucking phenomenal.

It makes my whole body thrum with pleasure. It makes me greedy and drunk with lust. I can already feel another orgasm building. I try to slow my pace so I can ride him longer—it all feels so good that I don't even want to come, I just want to keep doing exactly what we're doing.

But there's no holding it back.

I throw my head back, and I cry out, my pussy clenched tightly around his cock, clenching and squeezing every inch of his shaft.

Sebastian grabs my hips hard, his fingers digging into my ass cheeks. He thrusts up into me, his cock erupting. Greedily, I keep riding, wanting all his cum inside me, every drop. I love how his orgasm triggers mine and mine triggers his. For each of us, there's nothing more erotic than making the other person come.

When we're finished, we lie side by side on the bed, our long legs tangled together, and my face pressed against his neck. Every breath I take fills my lungs with his scent.

Today was the worst day of my life in some ways. In others, it was the best.

Because I'm finally home with my husband. We're sleeping in our own bed for the very first time.

I hope we'll have thousands more nights like this, until we're gray and old. I hope to spend my last night on earth wrapped in his arms.

As I'm drifting off, Sebastian says, "It's you and me now, Yelena. Thank you for saving my brother today. But I want you to know... your safety is more important to me than anyone's. I love you more than anyone. I'll love you and protect you and adore you all our lives. I'll never stop."

"I'll never break your trust," I tell him. "I won't keep anything from you. You're everything to me, Sebastian. I'll show you that, every minute of every day."

"I know you will," he says, kissing me softly where my face meets my ear.

I lift my chin so he can kiss my lips as well.

CHAPTER 33
SEBASTIAN

I WAKE UP NEXT TO MY WIFE, IN OUR NEW BED, IN OUR NEW APART-ment.

Even after everything we've lost, I can't help but be happy at what I've gained.

Yelena is a gift. Just like the night on the pier when my knee was smashed, the night I met Yelena was a turning point. A singular event that altered the course of my life.

I'm starting to think nights like that are a good thing.

Maybe there is such a thing as fate after all.

Because what I thought I wanted for myself could never have made me as happy as this.

I slip out of bed to get fresh coffee and croissants from the little bakery on the ground floor of our building. By the time I get back, Yelena is just stretching and stirring in bed, her silvery-blond hair wavy from falling asleep when it was still wet.

She opens her eyes and says, "Don't sneak away—it makes me nervous."

I hand her a cup of coffee, saying, "There's nothing to be nervous about anymore."

Yelena takes a sip of her drink, her face serious. "That's never really true for us, is it?"

I suppose she's right. In our world, there's always another

enemy. Always another threat. Yenin is gone. But who will take his place?

"Do you want to leave?" I ask her. "Go to Paris like Dante? Or Barcelona, or Tokyo?"

Yelena considers this, taking a bite of her croissant and chewing slowly. At last, she swallows and says, "I'm just starting to like Chicago. Besides, Sebastian...we are who we are. You never wanted the crown, but it came to you. I never wanted to be a *Bratva*'s daughter, but I killed Rodion, and I'd kill again if I had to. I want choice in my life...but I'm not afraid of the darker side of myself. I hated it when I thought I was split into two halves—good like my mother and evil like my father. Now I think...they're both just me. And they always have been."

I thought something similar. I thought I was a good man until a switch flipped inside me and the monster was unleashed.

Now I wonder if Yelena is right, if she and I are simply a shade of gray. I wonder if we could be comfortable in a straight-edge life, law-abiding and upstanding, never making use of that other part of ourselves.

"I have to go see Mikolaj today," I tell her. "Do you want to come with me?"

Yelena says, "I want to come everywhere with you."

After we shower and dress, we drive up to the mansion on the north side of the city.

Yelena looks at the overgrown gardens and the Gothic house with great interest. "What a strange place. So dark and so far away from anything else. It's beautiful, though..."

I say, "I think Miko and Nessa like to be alone."

When I knock on the door, it's the housekeeper who answers instead of Nessa. She's a pretty girl with dark hair and a Polish accent much like Mikolaj's.

"Come inside," she says politely. "Would you like a drink?"

"Just water, please," I say.

She brings us each a glass while we wait in the same formal sitting room as last time. I can tell Yelena wishes she could get up to examine all the books and paintings and the ornaments along the mantel of the large and empty fireplace. But she doesn't want to seem rude, so she drinks her water, letting her eyes do the roaming.

After a few minutes, Nessa and Mikolaj come in together, arm in arm. Nessa looks pale and quieter than usual. She seems tired but pleased, like she accomplished something difficult. She's dressed in a loose dress instead of her usual dance wear.

Mikolaj, by contrast, looks happier than I've ever seen him. He's buzzing with energy.

"We meet as victors," he says. "I hope that doesn't offend you, Yelena—I am sorry for your loss."

"Thank you," Yelena says quietly. "My father was no loss. It's only my brother I regret."

"He is alive, though, isn't he?" Mikolaj says.

"Yes," Yelena says without offering more information.

We called the hospital repeatedly to inquire about Adrian. He is indeed alive but refusing all visitors.

"I hope our partnership will continue," Mikolaj says to me. "It's my understanding that you will be taking over as don in Chicago."

"That's not decided yet," I say. "Dante doesn't want it, but Nero is next oldest."

"Callum Griffin told me Nero isn't interested in leadership, only in control of the investment arm of the business."

My stomach gives an uncomfortable squeeze. "That might be right," I admit.

Mikolaj looks me up and down with his ice-blue eyes. "I know a boss when I see one. Let's not wait on the formalities to proceed in our partnership. There are many things I want to accomplish in the upcoming months."

"Like what?" I say, curious despite myself.

"It's not the what," Mikolaj says, smiling fully now. "It's the why."

He casts a glance over at Nessa sitting next to him on the couch with her bare feet tucked under her, her cheeks flushing pink beneath her light dusting of freckles.

"Miko…" she says warningly.

"Sebastian is an old friend, isn't he?" he says. "We can tell him."

"You just want to tell anyone you can." She laughs. Turning to Yelena and me, she says, "We're having a baby."

"You are? Congratulations!" I glance automatically to Nessa's belly. Sure enough, I see a slight swelling on her otherwise slim frame. "When are you due?"

"February," Nessa says. "It's still early. We probably shouldn't be telling anyone yet."

She gives Miko a stern look, but Nessa's version of a stern look is much too warm and adoring to actually chastise her husband.

I doubt Mikolaj could be brought back to earth either way. He's clearly beyond excited that Nessa is carrying his child.

I'm happy for them both. But I feel something else, too—something I don't want to admit. I glance over at Yelena. She has a strange expression on her face, like she just thought of something that puzzled her. Quickly, she shakes it off, saying, "That's so wonderful! You must be thrilled."

We stay for another half hour or so, Mikolaj and I talking business, Yelena and Nessa sometimes joining in and sometimes having their own conversation on other matters.

Miko is brimming with energy and ambition. Fate is smiling on him.

His optimism is contagious. I was already inclined to feel like the king of the world with Yelena right beside me—buoyed up by Miko, I'm soon matching him in enthusiasm. We make plans that would have seemed impossible a month ago. Plans that are half dream and half mad but maybe achievable all the same.

As we leave at last, I shake Miko's hand. "Thank you for standing by me."

Looking me in the eye, he says, "Nessa always spoke highly of you. I think this will be the beginning of a long friendship."

Nessa gives Yelena a hug. Yelena looks startled at first but then hugs her back, smiling a little.

"I want to come see your new place," Nessa says.

"Come anytime," Yelena replies warmly.

Climbing into the car, she says with a look of wonder, "I've never invited anyone over before. I never could at my father's house."

"You can invite anyone you want now," I say. "Except we don't have any furniture."

On the way home, we stop at the hospital where Adrian is being treated for his burns. I try to argue with the nurse that Yelena is Adrian's only family, but she turns us away without debate.

"He was very clear. He won't see anyone."

Yelena looks up at me as we turn around to leave, her eyes cloudy and troubled. "Do you really think he hates me?"

"I…" I want to say no, but I can't lie to her. I saw his face when he hissed at her, *This is your fault.* "I don't think he's in his right mind at the moment," I tell her.

The problem is, I don't know if that's temporary or not. Without seeing him, there's no way to tell.

When we get home, Yelena lies down for a long nap. She looks as tired as Nessa, exhausted from the events of the day before.

CHAPTER 34
YELENA

THE WEEKS THAT FOLLOW ARE SOMETHING OF A BLUR.

The death of my father and the bloody battle outside the Gallo house whip up a shitstorm of epic proportions with the Chicago PD. The police were already investigating the massacre at the cathedral—it doesn't take much detective work to link the botched wedding, the bodies on the Gallos' lawn, and the charred remnants of their house.

Sebastian and I are forced to sit through endless consultations with the Gallos' legal counsel and then endless more police interviews. Meanwhile, Sebastian is paying a king's ransom in bribes, plus relying on every bit of collective political pressure the Griffins and the Gallos can muster to make the whole thing go away.

It probably wouldn't work if there weren't an almost total lack of witnesses.

The Gallos have lived in Old Town for generations. Enzo Gallo was an institution. No one wants to testify against his son.

The official story is that my father killed Enzo at the cathedral, then came to the Gallo house to burn it down. He was killed by Bosco Bianchi, who was shot in turn by one of my father's men.

Vincenzo Bianchi is perfectly willing to go along with this, for a price. Sebastian gives him my father's sports betting operation, though he keeps his half of the money that Mikolaj wired to his account.

The rest of the *Bratva*'s operations are handed over to the Polish Mafia. Mikolaj is full of plans for expansion, determined to give his unborn child a life worthy of, as he puts it, "the most beautiful baby in the world."

I've tried to visit or call my brother a hundred times. He won't allow it. I think of the pain he must be suffering and how angry he must be at what's happened to him, and I want to cry. Adrian wasn't vain, exactly, but he was extremely proud of his looks and his success with women. He would consider disfigurement a fate worse than death.

I don't know what to do about it. And honestly, I haven't been able to focus on it as I usually would.

First I was exhausted. Then I was sick. And then I confirmed the thought that came into my head the morning we visited Mikolaj and Nessa.

When Nessa announced her pregnancy, I had a strange realization. I remembered I hadn't had a period in well over a month.

Sebastian and I hadn't exactly been careful about protection. Most of the times we had sex, it was spontaneous and in public places, sneaking around before we were married. Not the most convenient circumstances for a condom. Then there was our hookup down in the basement cell, when caution was the last thing on our minds...

So I suppose I shouldn't have been surprised. I guess I just thought it took a lot more "trying" to make a thing like that happen.

I took the test not really believing it would be positive.

The double pink line popped up immediately, bright and clear.

I dropped the test in the sink, stunned into clumsiness.

I have no idea how Sebastian will react. Part of me is afraid he'll be angry—we already fell in love and got married so fast. It seems like I should have been a little more cautious with this next and most permanent step.

One thing I know for certain is that I won't be hiding this from him, not for a single day. I promised never to do that again.

So I wait in our empty living room, sitting on the piano bench because we don't yet have a couch. I try playing to distract myself, but my hands are too tense and jittery.

I sit up straight when I hear his key in the lock. Everything I planned to say seems to have flown out of my head in an instant.

Sebastian pushes open the door, at first pleased to see me waiting there, then concerned when he reads the nervousness on my face. "What's wrong?"

"Nothing," I say. "Or, I mean, I don't know if it's wrong…it could be good…"

"What?" he says, half smiling and half concerned. "Are you okay?"

"I'm…pregnant, actually."

He stares at me for a moment, frozen with shock.

Then he sweeps me up in his arms and spins me around, something only a man his height could do.

"Are you serious?" he says over and over. "Are you sure?"

"Yes." I laugh. "I'm very sure."

"This is the best news you could give me," he cries, his face lit up past anything I've seen before. "The best thing that could possibly happen."

"Really?"

"*Yes!* God, I can't believe it. I'm so excited!"

He gets down on his knees right there in our living room, pressing his ear against my belly.

I laugh. "You're not going to hear anything except my stomach growling. It's only the size of a pea right now."

"When do we go to the doctor? I want to see him!"

"You don't know that it's a him!"

"I don't care what it is. I want both. It could be both—aren't twins hereditary?"

"God, I hope not. One will be crazy enough."

I feel a twinge of sadness, imagining having twins if Adrian isn't

there to see it. He would have thought that was the best joke—another little blond twosome running around, wrestling and teasing each other...

I shake my head hard to get rid of that thought. I don't think I'm having twins. I'd know if I were. When I press my hand against my belly, I only picture one baby in there.

Besides, my child won't be blond anyway. The Gallos are dark even for Italians, and Sebastian is brownest of all. I knew from the moment I saw Miles Griffin that any baby I had would look like Seb. And that's exactly how I want it.

Sebastian's happiness washes away my worry. I want this baby just as desperately as he does. Seven months seems far too long before our baby will come—just a month after Nessa's. They won't be cousins by blood, but they'll be cousins-in-law, or second cousins, or whatever's the English term. I'm glad Nessa and I are swiftly becoming friends so I'll have someone to share this experience with.

Aida is over the moon when I tell her.

"That's fantastic!" she shrieks. "I didn't think Miles was going to have any cousins around on my side. I was so annoyed with Dante moving Serena away before we even got to know her. Ours will only be a year or two apart in school—that's barely anything!"

She looks me up and down appraisingly.

"You're not showing at all yet," she says. "You're lucky to be so tall. I looked enormous by the end. And don't let anyone trick you into giving birth naturally—it's fucking awful! Take all the drugs!"

The only thing inconvenienced by the pregnancy is Sebastian's and my planned honeymoon to Europe. I'm too nauseated to want to hike around the Alps.

It doesn't matter. Our loft already feels like a vacation—like the most beautiful and peaceful escape. I'm so happy exactly where I am that I don't want to go anywhere else.

Sebastian and I spend all our time furnishing, decorating, and cleaning it so we can throw a party for Nero when he finally gets out of the hospital.

To be funny, Sebastian orders him a cake shaped like a race car—the kind you'd usually get a kid for his fifth birthday.

After weeks of hospital food, Nero looks at the cake like it's the most beautiful thing he's ever seen.

"I love it," he says sincerely. "I want to eat the whole damned thing."

"It's all yours," Seb says. "It's the least we could do."

"Damn right." Nero digs into the cake with his fork without even cutting off a slice.

"Don't worry," Greta says. "I brought cannoli for the rest of us."

She starts passing around the little pastries expertly filled with just the right amount of ricotta and dusted with powdered sugar. They look like they came from a fancy bakery, but I know Greta well enough by now that I would never expect anything less than homemade from her.

Camille is sitting next to her father, who is medium height, balding, with dark hair and eyes and a kind face. I remember Sebastian saying he was a mechanic, responsible for teaching Camille her wizardry with cars.

He looks at the cannoli with great interest, then takes a bite.

"My god," he says, "I've never tasted anything better."

Greta flushes with pleasure. "They're my specialty," she says modestly.

"Have you ever thought of opening a bakery?" Camille's father says. "Or a café?"

"Oh, no. I mean, I guess I thought of it once or twice, but not seriously..."

"You should! It would be a crime to keep these just for ourselves..."

Greta laughs and flaps her hand at him in embarrassment, but I notice she sits down right next to him to eat her own cannoli. They spend the rest of the night chatting and laughing together.

We're all healing, slowly.

Sebastian has to go back to surgery himself to get his knee fixed. He jokes that he and Nero can carpool to physiotherapy together. Nero lost his gallbladder and a piece of his liver but should recover in full, other than six distinct and dramatic scars on various areas of his body.

Even Adrian goes home eventually, back to the mansion my father rented on Astor Street.

I hear about that through our cousin Grisha Lukin. He calls me shortly before Christmas, saying, "They sent Adrian home."

"Have you seen him?" I ask, my heart fluttering against my ribs. I feel another little motion in response, down below my belly button—the baby kicking, as he always seems to do when I feel any strong emotion.

He is a boy after all. Sebastian was right—the twenty-week scan proved it.

"No," Grisha says, and I can almost hear him shaking his head over the phone. "He won't see anyone. He's shut up in his house with just his nurse there with him."

"What nurse?"

"He hired the one from the hospital, I guess. Mikhail told me—some pretty blond girl. She worked on the burn unit, and now she's taking care of Adrian full-time. Mikhail says he thinks there's something going on between them."

"Romantically?" I say, in surprise.

"I dunno. That's just what Mikhail told me. But you know he's a fucking turnip."

Strangely, the thought gives me comfort. I don't want Adrian to be alone. If he has at least one person there who cares about him, that's so much better than no one.

"Who is she?" I ask Grisha.

"Fuck if I know. It's all just gossip. I only called you 'cause I always liked you best. My little Elsa."

Now I know he's grinning on the other end of the line. Usually,

I'd tell him to fuck off, but somehow the nickname doesn't bother me as much anymore.

"Thanks, Grisha," I say.

"Come on," he coaxes me. "Sing just one line for me…"

That's too far.

"No fucking way," I say, and I hang up on him.

I sit there for a while, watching thick, puffy snowflakes drift down outside my window.

I can see the lights of our tree reflected on the glass. Sebastian and I picked it out together and decorated it. Then we made popcorn and watched a movie, cuddled on the couch that was finally delivered last week.

Such simple pleasures, and yet I wouldn't trade them for anything in the world. That's what life is made up of—tiny moments of happiness, like lights on a string. Put them all together, and there's nothing more brilliant.

Digging through our stationery drawer, I find a blank Christmas card with a picture of a deer on the front, standing in a birch forest beneath a starry sky.

My brother changed his number, and I know he won't let me in if I go to his house. But he might open a card.

I sit down again, and I write.

Dear Adrian,

I heard you're home now. I hope you're doing well. Grisha told me you have a girl taking care of you, and I hope that's true, too.

You were always good at taking care of me when I was sick. I had to do the same for you after—I don't think there was ever a cold or flu that only one of us caught.

I miss you. I'm so sorry for what happened. I want you to know, I don't hold anything against you, and neither does Sebastian. All that's over now.

I hope you'll call me sometime.
You know I'll always love you.

XOXO
Fasol

I close the card and slip it into its colored envelope. Then I seal it and write the address.

I don't really expect Adrian to respond.

Sometimes you have to reach out. Even when you know you're only reaching into empty air.

EPILOGUE
YELENA

EIGHTEEN YEARS LATER

WHEN I GET HOME FROM THE GROCERY STORE, THERE'S A LETTER lying on the table in the hall.

That's where Seb and I keep all our mail—or at least the mail the other person will want to see. Fliers and ads go in the trash. Actual correspondence is placed here.

Of course, we don't get much of that these days. It's almost always a birthday or thank-you card, sometimes a formal invitation to a party or a charity event.

That's what I'm expecting when I pick up the heavy envelope with its expensive slate-gray stationary. It's only when I turn it over that I see the seal.

It's an old-fashioned crown set inside the arch of twin olive branches. The image has been pressed into melted wax, deep crimson, the color of dried blood.

It startles me so badly that I almost drop the envelope right back on the table. But I force myself to break the seal by sliding my thumbnail beneath the flap, lifting it open, and pulling out the two sheets of paper within.

The letter is handwritten in neat cursive.

Leo Gallo,

I am writing to inform you that you have been accepted to Kingmakers Academy. You have furthermore been granted automatic admission to the Heirs division, as is your right as the undisputed heir of the Gallo empire.

School will commence on the first of September. You are expected to report to the Grand Villa in Dubrovnik, no later than August thirtieth. From there, you will be taken to our secure campus.

As you are probably aware, admission to our campus is singular and irrevocable. If you decide to leave for any reason, you will not be permitted to return.

For that reason, please be sure to bring all items you will require for the duration of the school year.

Enclosed is a list of our rules and regulations. Sign and return your acknowledgment of the contract, including your willingness to abide by our arbitration and punishment system. Your parents' signatures and imprints are likewise required.

We look forward to meeting you. You will be joining an elite institution with a long and storied history. Perhaps someday your name will be inscribed on the wall of Dominus Scelestos. For now, please convey my regards to your parents.

Sincerely,
Luther Hugo

Necessitas Non Habet Legem—Necessity Has No Law

Enclosed with the letter is the mentioned list of rules and regulations. These are likewise handwritten in ornate but highly legible script.

1.   *Violence against fellow students is not permitted. All violence shall be answered in kind: Blow for blow. Injury for injury. And death for death.*

2.   *Students are not to leave the island for any reason during the school year.*

3.   *Students cannot transfer between divisions. Once you have been assigned a division, you must...*

I throw down the letter, not wanting to read any more.

Thank god Leo is at school and probably hasn't seen it yet.

I storm into Seb's office, shoving open his door without knocking. He looks up from his computer, pleased to see me and not particularly bothered by how aggressively I arrived.

It's very inconvenient how attractive my husband has stayed all these years. It makes it hard to rage at him when the sight of him still fills me with butterflies every single time.

There's a little gray in his hair now, and he wears black-rimmed reading glasses, but those things only give him an air of intelligence and gravitas to replace his former boyishness. He's still as tall and fit as ever, with a handsome lean face and those intent brown eyes beneath brows as straight and dark as ever.

"There you are," he says, smiling at me.

"Why is there an acceptance letter from Kingmakers in the hall?" I demand.

"I assume because Leo has been accepted," Seb says calmly.

"Why did he apply in the first place?" I cry. "Why does he even know it exists?"

Seb takes off his glasses and folds them, standing from his desk. He comes around next to me, towering over me as only he can do.

He doesn't do it to intimidate me. He wants to comfort me. But there's no smoothing this over.

"He's not going," I say.

Sebastian sighs. He doesn't want to argue with me. He never does. But he also never lies to me. It's a promise we've kept to each other, all these years—to tell the truth, always. Even when it's hard. Even when it hurts.

"He turns eighteen next week," Sebastian says. "It's not our choice, Yelena."

I turn my face up to his so he can see the anguish in my eyes. "It's not safe. That place is stuffed with the children of the worst criminals from every corner of the globe..."

"Yes," Sebastian agrees. "But that doesn't mean it's not safe. It's the only place he *will* be safe, Yelena. The only place with sanctuary."

What he's saying is true, though I don't want to admit it. If Leo went to a normal school, he could be attacked or killed by any one of our enemies. Only at Kingmakers is there a sacrosanct rule against attacking any of the students for the duration of their program.

But rule or no rule...Leo will be attending classes with the people who hate us most—or at least one very specific person.

"Dean is going, too..." I whisper.

Sebastian sighs. "I know."

Dean is Adrian's son. Only six months younger than Leo. They'll be in the same year at Kingmakers. The same division, too. Both Heirs.

I say, "I can only imagine what Adrian has told him."

I never reconciled with my brother. He never let me. He's hated me for eighteen years. He's hated Sebastian more. His son will loathe and despise Leo, I'm sure of it. I can't imagine how they could live side by side without killing each other.

Adrian moved back to Moscow shortly after his son was born. It's the only reason the resentment between us has persisted as a low-level Cold War and not an all-out battle.

"Anna will be attending," Sebastian says.

Anna is Mikolaj and Nessa's daughter and Leo's best friend. They've been inseparable since they were toddlers. I wonder if that's why Leo wanted to go to Kingmakers in the first place—to stay close to her.

"I'm surprised Nessa's okay with that. Wasn't Anna admitted to Juilliard?"

"She chose Kingmakers," Sebastian says simply.

The implication is clear. Nessa and Mikolaj allowed Anna to make her own choice—we should do the same.

"It's so far…" I moan. "And they're not allowed to come home…"

"They can visit in the summer," Seb assures me. "Just not the school year."

The anxiety I'm feeling is unbearable. Leo is our only child. He's the center of our world. If anything happened to him…

"He'll be fine," Sebastian says, reading my mind. He pulls me against his chest so I can feel the strength of his arms wrapped around me and the steady beating of his heart. "You know how smart he is. And how talented."

"Too smart for his own good," I say.

I feel Sebastian's chest shake as he laughs quietly. "Yes, he is," he says. "But at the end of the day…when have we ever been able to stop him from doing what he wants?"

"Never," I say sadly.

"He's a fighter like you. Brilliant like you. If I wanted an ordinary son with an ordinary life"—Sebastian grins—"I would have married one of those other girls who wanted me."

I snort, shaking my head at him. "Remembering your glory days?"

He kisses me softly on the lips. "There was only one glory day. The day I met you."

I came in here determined not to be comforted. And yet I am comforted, against my will. I can't feel anything but peace when Sebastian holds me.

"I wish life were always easy," I say.

Sebastian kisses me again.

"If it were, then it wouldn't be *our* life."

READ ON FOR A SNEAK PEEK OF AN ALL-NEW STANDALONE

CHAPTER 1
RAMSES HOWELL

TODAY'S MY FAVORITE DAY OF THE YEAR, AND IT'S ALREADY RUINED because Anthony Keller just walked in with the most stunning woman I've ever seen on his arm.

The Belmont Stakes are one of the only things that get me excited anymore. Last night it rained just enough for the grass to smell like a rainforest and the dirt to turn over like velvet. I'm in the presidential suite, best seats in the house, the finish line right under my nose.

And here comes Keller, strolling in with the one and only thing that could make me give a shit what he's doing next door.

My head turns. The way a racehorse looks running—how the muscles flex and flow under the coat—that's how her body looks inside her dress. It's a modest dress otherwise, up to the neck, long sleeves. Only her curves make it outrageous.

Her face isn't what I expected. Beautiful, yes, but the word that pops into my head is *serious*. She's focused, unsmiling, until she catches me looking. Then her mouth quirks with something I can't read. Amusement? Disdain?

She steps into Keller's suite.

I'm left with a cold drink and the heat of being caught like an amateur. I know how to glance at a pretty girl and then turn away to examine the image in my mind. It was that goddamned body in motion that kept me staring for so long.

"Every dog has his day." Briggs takes a pull of his beer, watching Keller whoop it up next door with disgust. "I fucking hate seeing that mutt happy, though."

Some people, Briggs hates just because I hate them. Some, he has his own reasons. Keller's both.

He was your classic balding tech nerd with a start-up. Now he's got hair plugs and a personal trainer, and he's strutting around like King Shit 'cause his company goes public tomorrow.

I want to ask Briggs about the girl, but that's admitting out loud Keller did something good. Right now, I wouldn't say I liked the color of his socks.

Instead, I tell Briggs, "Next year I want both suites, and I want them connected."

Briggs makes that grunting nod that means he's filing away some task I've asked him to do. He doesn't write it down, but he always gets it done. No questions, no excuses—Briggs delivers.

That's why he's my right hand, and I mean that about as literally as it gets. He does all the work I'd do if I had an extra hand. I trust him to act as me, for me. He's the only person I trust like that. If Briggs were to die or retire, there wouldn't be another hand. I'd just have everybody else who works for me.

"Here comes Bosch," Briggs mutters.

John Bosch is sitting in my box, but I've heard he's got his eye on Keller's company. I want to know if a deal is struck.

I want to know everything that happens at Belmont Park today, when the air's thick with money. Everybody has chips on the table, amped on the adrenaline of knowing someone's going home a winner. Alcohol and loose lips…whether they leave thrilled or disappointed, they're less in control, and that's an opportunity for me.

I'm in the main suite, a full spread on the table, every single beer made in Germany laid out on ice. All these busy little bees should be buzzing around me, information flowing in…

Instead, my own traders are sneaking next door.

"Where the fuck did Pennywise just go?" Briggs says.

He answers his own question by watching Penn duck through the doorway into Keller's suite.

"Ah." Briggs says that syllable like he already knows exactly what's going on.

I finally crack. "Who's the girl?"

Briggs grins. "Blake Abbot."

"Who's Blake Abbot?"

"Probably the highest-paid escort in Manhattan."

My face relaxes a little. It takes the sting out of Keller bringing a girl that hot, knowing he had to pay for her. Now I'm curious instead. "What's a night with her cost?"

Briggs grins. "There is no night with her. You have to get on her roster. It's like a country club membership—with only three members."

A hooker with a business model. I kind of fucking love it.

"Can't be that exclusive if she let Keller in."

Briggs shrugs. "Vickers tried to get a seat. Offered fifty K—didn't even get a phone call."

I snort. "Is her pussy gold plated?"

Briggs picks up a prawn the size of his fist, dunks it in cocktail sauce, takes an enormous bite, and talks while still chewing. "Fuck if I know. She makes 'em sign an NDA. But Lukas Larsen says she'll change your fucking life. Look at Keller—a year ago he could barely get a deal done. Now he's the man of the hour."

"Keller ain't shit," I say with more venom than I intended.

He offered us a stake in VizTech. We turned it down after looking at his books. A week later somebody filed a complaint against us with the SEC. Took Briggs about an hour to confirm it was that spiteful little weasel.

I've got no problem with a man who swings a hatchet at my face. Business is war. But if you stab me in the back, I better never find out your hand was on the knife.

"Who else is she seeing?"

"Zak Simmons." Briggs had the answer at the ready. He's my fixer and my attack dog, but his number one job is keeping his eye on everyone who matters.

"Larsen's having a great year. Simmons even better."

"Yeah. Well, that's what they say—date her and you run hot."

I bet they do. Finance guys are superstitious as fuck. Our whole job is numbers, but there's nothing more subject to hysteria than the stock market.

"Desmond Lowe used to see her, too—said the sex was insane, wouldn't shut up about it." Briggs smirks. "'Till she cut him loose."

Lowe's an arrogant piece of shit. The idea of him getting dumped by an escort makes me smile. "I like her already."

"Well, don't." Briggs frowns.

"Why not?"

"Because I know how competitive you get."

I give him a sideways look. "Not over some girl."

"Right." Briggs snorts. "Just everything else."

I crane my neck, trying to peek into Keller's box. I spy a tantalizing slice of the girl's back, her shoulder, and the edge of her ear.

I don't believe in "running hot." But I am intrigued by the idea of country club sex.

Eyes on the curve of that hip, I say, "I have the best of everything else…why not that?"

"Fuck no." Briggs shakes his head.

"Why not?"

"Because what if it's really that good? And it never feels that good again? Nah, pass. I'll stick with sloppy, drunken, last-call sex—the kind I can get anytime I want."

Yeah. That definitely settles it.

I cross the room to grab a Reissdorf I won't be drinking. From here I can see unobstructed into the junior suite.

Keller really does look different—his head up, his shoulders back, tanned and almost stylish. But it's Blake Abbot who's the magnet in the room. The most important people have clustered around her. She's talking to Freidman, who runs the sixth-largest hedge fund in the city. I don't think I've seen that cold-coffee-drinking vulture so much as crack a smile. Now he's got all his dentures on display, his bony shoulders shaking with laughter.

If she's not careful, she'll give a coronary to a future client.

I'm revolted at my own thought.

The idea of Freidman's wrinkled old claws touching that lush body makes me want to puke.

Besides, that's dismissive. Freidman isn't hanging on her every word because he wants to fuck her—she genuinely made him laugh.

I want to know what she said.

I head into the hallway, passing the door to the junior suite. There are no discernable words from the babble of conversation within—just the smell of too many men, threaded with a hint of perfume. My feet lurch like I missed a step.

I watch the way she stands, how she positions her body, rests a fingertip against her jaw. The slow smile, the eye contact. She's good at what she does, really fucking good.

She's not the only woman in the room—Miriam Castro, head trader at Bridgewater, moves through the crowd like an assassin. What *really* impresses me is how Blake chats her up just as easily.

Blake is so natural that I almost miss the moment where she slips. Keller interrupts her conversation with Castro, placing his hand possessively on the small of Blake's back and whispering something in her ear. Her upper lip curls, a flash of irritation she hides with a smile.

She's alluring. I don't want to be allured; I'm actively annoyed. Yet I find myself wanting to abandon my own suite to squeeze in next to Keller.

BRUTAL BIRTHRIGHT

Callum & Aida

Miko & Nessa

Nero & Camille

Dante & Simone

Raylan & Riona

Sebastian & Yelena

ABOUT THE AUTHOR

Sophie Lark writes intelligent and powerful characters who are allowed to be flawed. She lives in the mountain west with her husband and three children.

The Love Lark Letter: geni.us/lark-letter
The Love Lark Reader Group: geni.us/love-larks
Website: sophielark.com
Instagram: @Sophie_Lark_Author
TikTok: @sophielarkauthor
Exclusive Content: patreon.com/sophielark
Complete Works: geni.us/lark-amazon
Book Playlists: geni.us/lark-spotify